RISE OF THE ELVES

THE FESTIVE AND THE FURIOUS

BOOK 3

HEIDE GOODY

IAIN GRANT

1

GALLAGHER

The woman at the garage handed over Gallagher's keys. "Okay, so we've done the full service. That exhaust has been replaced. Hard to get hold of now. Brake pads changed also. That problem you described..."

"Yeah?" said Gallagher, rubbing the shaving itch from his tattooed neck.

"You say that once it stops, you can't start it again?"

"Not until it's cooled down."

The woman stuck out her bottom lip and shook her head. "The mechanics tried to replicate it. Started the car, stopped it. Started it. No problem."

"But it only happens after it's been running for a while."

"He left it running for half an hour. Couldn't replicate the problem." She looked at him. "Maybe it's something about you."

He frowned. "Like bad karma?"

"I don't mean bad luck. I meant something you're doing," she said. "Anyway, here's the list of work and the total owed."

Gallagher looked at the cost of his car repairs and groaned inwardly. Why did he even bother? There was no number that could have been a good number. When all your credit cards were at their limit, the concept of money lost all its meaning.

He put a bank card in the machine and typed his PIN. The woman took the printed receipt and stapled it to his sheet of repairs.

"And that's that," she said. "Have a Merry Christmas."

He grunted at that.

"Not a Christmas fan?" she said, and her face softened. "It can be a hard time of year, can't it?"

"Oh, you have no idea," he said.

"All the kids wanting presents while the bills keep rolling in," she said, nodding as though this was a universal problem.

"Oh, no kids," he said. "If I had kids, at least I'd have someone to blame it on."

"I'm not sure that's what kids are for. But it can be a lonely time of year, too."

He pulled a face. This was true, but it was not the root cause of his woes. He had friends. He certainly had Luka – who was somehow a work colleague, surrogate uncle, best buddy, and a whispering shoulder devil who enabled the worst side of Gallagher's personality all rolled into one. And, yes, Gallagher was definitely lacking that special someone. He would never put it directly into words, but he *yearned* for a special someone who would look at him – a scrawny miserable tattooed streak of poor life choices and uncontrolled debt – clutch him to her bosom and tell him it would all be all right. He yearned for that, but that was not what nagged at his every waking hour right now.

He gave the woman a bright smile. "Do you want to know what it really is?" he said. "Christmas?"

She looked past him. There was no one else waiting behind him in the dingy reception of the repair shop. "Sure."

"I work at a garden centre on the outskirts of town. I'm a plantsman. Looking after the plants, lugging things around, making sure we don't run out of supplies of compost. That sort of thing. It should be a simple life."

"Sounds it."

"Except Christmas is coming up and things get kind of chaotic. Big Christmas grotto, Christmas trees. Elves everywhere. Aisle after aisle of decorations. But all containable. Me and my mate, Luka – he's the big lunk waiting outside; you've probably seen him..."

"The papa bear with the Father Christmas beard?"

"Ha! I won't tell him you said that."

"He's not a fan of Christmas either."

"I don't even know if they have Christmas where he came from. Anyway, we just keep ourselves to ourselves, except Luka said we could make a little money transporting a bit of weed for this local drug dealer."

"Should you be telling me this?" she asked.

"Are you a fed? You wearing a wire? I think we're fine. Anyway, that went wrong – like twelve stoned reindeer and all the weed vanishing kind of wrong. We were up to our necks in it, thought we'd sorted it out but then along comes her boss, this miserable Scandinavian troll called Snømann."

"Snowman?"

"Snømann. Marti Snømann. He made out like we still owed him big style and he's forced us to find space to store these big crates of his."

"More drugs?"

"I dunno. Could be. Or guns. Or worse."

"What's worse than guns?"

"Point is," he said, "we're totally under the cosh with this guy and there's no way out. He's started dating one of the women at our place, Sophie, like he's gonna be hanging round for ever. Every day we have to find more space at Hedgelord to store these—"

"Wait, wait, wait," said the woman, holding up her hand. "You work at the Hedgelord garden centre." There was a faint smile at the corner of her mouth.

"Yeah," said Gallagher.

"Isn't that the place where the Santa—?"

"Yeah, yeah. He was killed in a runaway trailer accident the other week."

"No. The other thing. Didn't your Santa make a porno and post it online? Shagging Rudolph or something."

Gallagher nodded. "Er, yeah. That too. Different Santa. One dead, one made a porno movie. And he didn't post it online. Our own Christmas sales manager, Charlotte, did that."

The woman pulled back, confused. "Why would she do that?"

"Not entirely sure. Something to do with a trip she took

to Europe with her opposite number at Bloomers garden centre. Jack. Kind of a whirlwind affair which turned sour and then— Look, Charlotte has an explosive temper at times, despite claiming to be a Christian woman. I think the Santa video was meant to be some sort of revenge when he dumped her, or she thought he'd dumped her. Anyway, that backfired, didn't it? At least that's one thing that's not currently biting me personally in the arse."

The woman was nodding slowly. "All this at a garden centre?"

"Yep."

"Aren't you just meant to be about selling shrubs and wheelbarrows and things?"

"You'd think, wouldn't you?"

She took a deep breath. "I think you've got bad karma."

He blinked. "That's what I said."

She rooted around beneath the counter and came out with a business card. It was black and purple with ghostly yellow writing on it. "My cousin Vileda does psychic therapy and fortune telling."

"Oh?"

"If you've got karma problems or a curse hanging over you then she can shift it."

"Shift it? Like bang and the curse is gone?"

She shrugged. "Dunno. I don't believe in that crap personally but, you know, if you do..."

Gallagher took it in the spirit in which it was offered. "Thanks," he said.

"Might struggle to fit you in now," she said. "I mean it's only eight days until Christmas."

"Sure. Sure. Thanks though." He waggled the card at her and went outside.

Luka Sibersky was waiting by the short wall opposite, hands stuffed into the pockets of his big overalls. "You took your time," he said.

"Chatting to the lady," said Gallagher. "And if you got your own car fixed, you wouldn't need to wait around on me."

Luka gave a big, very European sort of shrug. Gallagher unlocked the door of his little hatchback and they both got in.

"Best step on it or someone will notice we're late for work," said Gallagher, noting the time.

Luka blew out his lips. "Is not a problem. Tom is not the boss of us."

"I mean he is, technically."

"Yes, but you know," said Luka. "And Charlotte... Have you noticed she's been acting a bit odd lately?"

"More than usual?"

"In fact, we should hurry back or we'll miss the show."

2

CHARLOTTE

Charlotte Mitchell leaned into the grille. "Forgive me father for I have sinned. It has been a long time since my last confession."

There was a light cough from the other side of the grille.

"Uh, yeah," said Charlotte. "I guess it's my first time – not actually a Catholic – but better late than never, eh? I wanted to clear my conscience before Christmas."

She paused, but there was no comment on this.

"I have quite a few things to confess. There's all the times I lost my temper. Actually I can't list those or we'd be here all day, so maybe we can just do them as a job lot. I've lied to a lot of people to try and get my job done, but in my defence it's pretty tricky being an events manager at Christmas. All of the lies I told were to protect Hedgelord. Well, quite a few of them anyway. No – the big one is that I betrayed someone I really cared about in a fit of temper..."

Had she just admitted out loud that she really cared about Jack Hartigan?

"Go on," said the deep, paternal voice behind the grille.

"Jack Hartigan, the events manager at Bloomers. I thought I hated him, but we spent some, erm, unexpectedly intense time together. One thing led to another and we became close."

"Describe close," said the voice. "Tell me all about it."

"What? No! Let's just call it intimate. Anyway, there was a horrible misunderstanding where I thought he'd dumped me for his ex, so I released a Santa porn sex tape to discredit Bloomers. It turned out I was wrong. I was wrong about everything. He wasn't seeing his ex, and the tape didn't just discredit Bloomers, it discredited Hedgelord too. I betrayed Jack for no good reason and now he hates me."

"I see," said the voice. "Now can we go back to the 'intimate' thing? You need to tell me more about that."

"For fuck's sake, Daffyd!" yelled Charlotte. "You had one job! All you had to do was stay in character for ten minutes!"

Daffyd moved the grille, which had come from the barbecue display and been propped up between them on a picnic table wedged inside a summerhouse in the Hedgelord plant area. "I was just showing an interest in some of the detail," he said, dropping the deep priestly voice for his usual slightly nasally whine.

"No, you were being a pervy twat is what you were doing," said Charlotte to Hedgelord's head elf. He'd removed his pointy hat and put on a dog collar for the part, but he still quivered with the intense energy he brought to his grotto work. "Why on earth would you be interested in my sex life? I assume you're..."

The bald man raised his eyes at her, daring her to say it. "I'm what?" Had Daffyd even thrown in a slightly camp tone to dare her further?

"An ... an elf," she said.

Daffyd shrugged. "That I am. I'm interested in everyone's sex life. Don't flatter yourself. So, did you get what you wanted from that exercise?"

"No!" said Charlotte. "Not at all. I want someone to forgive me. Jack won't forgive me, St Stephen's church won't even let me through the door after the incident with the pigeon and the candlestick, and quite honestly I can't even forgive myself. I thought this might work."

"I thought it was going rather well."

"Your peculiar appetites got the better of you."

"Blame yourself for making me pretend an Anglican vicar would run a confession box," sniffed Daffyd. "What's your next step then?"

"I have no idea," said Charlotte. She scuffed the ground with her toe.

"You could try apologising to Jack directly, maybe?" said Daffyd.

"I tried that. He won't listen. It was a really awful thing that I did."

"You just need to remind him of what he's missing. For example, I bet the sex was really something. Run through it for me and we'll come up with an angle that will grab his attention."

Charlotte turned to Daffyd. "What on earth is wrong with you? Did you sell fucking tickets to this or something?"

Daffyd's expression altered by a millimetre and Charlotte gaped. "You did? You actually did? Who the fuck is listening in here?"

Gallagher and Luka, the two team members who looked after the plant area, shuffled forwards from a position hidden at the side of the summerhouse. Gallagher had the decency to look embarrassed, while Luka simply looked like someone who was resigned to not getting his money's worth.

Charlotte shook her head. "Really?"

Gillespie and Anika, who worked as elves in the grotto, emerged from the other side.

"You two as well? You work for me! I expected better, I really did."

"I would never miss an opportunity to understand what motivates my colleagues," said Anika without missing a beat. "That's good solid advice from the company handbook."

Charlotte had to hand it to her. Anika Chowdhry, still only a teenager, was the fastest-thinking person at Hedgelord (and possibly the only one who'd read the company handbook Charlotte had written). She'd managed to keep the entire events department running while Charlotte had been tracking down the Santa porn with Jack Hartigan. Only last week.

"Gallagher and Luka, I've half a mind to report you to Tom."

Tom was their boss, but it was well known he had no control over his plants-men, so it was something of a hollow threat. Charlotte knew it, Gallagher and Luka knew it, and

Tom knew it too, even though he wasn't here. He wasn't, was he?

"Is there anyone else round the side of this shed?" she said. Nobody else emerged. "Get back to work, all of you!" she snapped. Then her expression softened as she contemplated where she was. "But if anyone has any bright ideas about assuaging guilt or building bridges, then please share them with me."

Everyone left, apart from Daffyd, who twirled in his robes and dog collar, snapping selfies. He did a coquettish pose, looking over his shoulder, and pouted at the camera. Charlotte shook her head and stomped back towards the building.

3

GALLAGHER

Gallagher and Luka made their way back to their own shed. They considered all of the Hedgelord display sheds to be theirs to a greater or lesser degree, but really, Gallagher thought, they were like the rooms of a stately home. The tea shed was part of the inner sanctum, through which the public wouldn't be permitted to traipse. Of course, there was also the secret, hidden shed where they had stashed a whole load of sinister crates for Marti Snømann, the terrifying gangster.

"Well that was a fucking let down," said Luka. "Daffyd promised scandal and spice. He better give me my fiver back."

"You'll be lucky," said Gallagher. "I felt sorry for Charlotte, didn't you?"

Luka shrugged. "She is management. She can dry her tears with her massive piles of cash if she is sad." He pretended to wipe his face with tumbling bank notes.

"Harsh," said Gallagher. He put the kettle on, and while it was boiling made a quick check on the secret shed in which they had stored crate after crate of God knows what. There was a poster (emblazoned with a huge Asian hornet) that covered the secret door leading to it. He smoothed it back into place after checking. "All fine in there. No leaks and all the crates look fine," he reported to Luka.

"Is good," grunted Luka.

"Snømann though. It looks as though he's sticking around," said Gallagher. "If he's Sophie's new boyfriend he might be round here all the time. I don't like it."

Sophie had turned up at the staff Christmas party last week with Snømann on her arm. It had put Gallagher right off his sausage on a stick.

"We just keep our heads down and he will go soon," said Luka. "Will be fine."

Gallagher knew that Luka was lying to make him feel better. He made the tea and handed Luka his mug. "Soon be Christmas anyway."

As soon as the words were out of his mouth he felt himself sag. Normal people would be heading to the bosom of their families and spending Christmas day in a cocoon of warmth. Gallagher would be spending his Christmas day in his poky flat with a turkey breast dinner for one, *if* he summoned up the energy to go and buy one.

Luka must have caught the look. "Fucking Christmas is overrated."

"What are you doing for Christmas anyway? I don't think you've said."

There was a lot that Luka hadn't said. He lived his life as

if information was a valuable resource and he was determined to hoard it all for himself. Gallagher still had no idea which country Luka came from, just the understanding that it was somewhere in Eastern Europe. Or possibly Central Europe. Southern Europe was an outside possibility.

"Me? I have options," said Luka. "I am currently undecided."

Gallagher rolled his eyes. Classic Luka.

"Yeah, same. I've got the option of whether to have cornflakes for breakfast, or bring out the big guns and have Coco Pops."

"Coco Pops are for kiddies. Could definitely work for you."

ANIKA CHOWDRY SPENT the morning in the grotto being an elf with Sophie as Mrs Claus. Sophie normally worked in the café, but her head had been turned by the prospect of dressing up and loudly entertaining children, so for a few weeks she had split her time between the two roles.

Anika thought Sophie was perfect for Mrs Claus. Her face was mature, but had a doll-like quality to it. The kids loved her. She'd also accessorised her outfit with a number of gaudy Christmas badges, including a gaudy Christmas tree brooch made from bubbles of coloured plastic.

There was a different vibe in the grotto during the last few days before Christmas. These were the prime slots, and they'd mostly been booked up since the summer. The parents who brought their children to these slots were organised in a way that was slightly scary. They arrived in matching jumpers, with fresh haircuts and bright smiles for the camera. Most had even pre-booked which photo packages they wanted, so the hurly-burly and confusion which had reigned earlier in the month was completely absent. The families that came through all seemed to know how to make reindeer food, and once complete, the packets were put neatly away in handbags with minimal mess.

"I'm slightly nostalgic for the chaos of two weeks ago," Anika said to Sophie between groups.

"Are you really?" asked Sophie, her eyes wide.

"No. That was a joke. Seriously though, it's so much easier these past few days."

"They even know which songs they want to sing," said Sophie.

"Yes!" said Anika. "And they're not all weird pop songs we don't know the words to. Feels like we're winning."

"Mrs Claus always feels like she's winning," said Sophie with a wink.

Daffyd rushed through the door, on his way to check each room of the grotto. "Need any more supplies?"

"No," said Anika, "but I do have a question."

Daffyd paused and pulled a face. "No you can't have a refund for this morning's confession show. It was sold in good faith and the experience was—"

"No, not that," said Anika. "It was about the elf uniform. I wondered if I could get one of those belts like Sophie's wearing? It would be good to have the dungarees a bit less baggy at the front."

"Not part of the Hedgelord uniform package I'm afraid," said Daffyd, squinting at Sophie's belt.

"This? It was a present from my Marti," said Sophie with a girly giggle.

Sophie had turned up with a steely-eyed silver fox of a date at the Christmas party the previous week. Anika and Karen off the tills had spent considerable time and effort trying to get the sixty-something singleton back into the dating scene, and almost immediately, Sophie had landed herself a middle-aged Scandinavian hunk.

Sophie gripped her new belt. "You can have it if you like, Anika."

"Oh no! I can't take your gift," said Anika.

Daffyd moved in closer, peering at the belt in a way that alarmed Sophie, judging by her expression. "Hmm. Well, if I'm not mistaken that's a Hermes. It has the big 'H' on the buckle. See?"

"Oh – I thought that was 'H' for Hedgelord," said Anika.

"Noo, that is a super expensive designer belt," said Daffyd. He reached out a hand to touch it, but Sophie batted it away.

"I'm sure Marti won't mind if you take it, Anika," she said. "I've got lots of other belts."

"Enough belt talk!" said Daffyd, holding his hand up imperiously as he cocked his head. "I hear the next group coming through. Action stations!"

4

CHARLOTTE

Charlotte spent a few hours running through her events calendar. Partly in a continuing effort to punish herself (she was not above a little metaphorical self-flagellation), but she also wanted something to occupy her mind and crowd out the various demons that squatted in there.

There were a number of festive events on in the town in the final lead up to Christmas. There was the traditional children's nativity play on Christmas Eve afternoon at St Stephen's church. Another that caught her eye was also at St Stephen's and due to take place on the nineteenth, in two days' time. It was part fundraiser, part celebration. In every other year, the Rotary club's Santa sleigh would park up by the church after it had toured the local area for a couple of weeks, and there would be carols and collections. This year was a little different – because the sleigh had been destroyed in an unfortunate pile-up that had also killed Hedgelord's Santa. Santa Raymond had been feted as a hero though, because he'd been the one to save two children who were directly in the path of the runaway sleigh.

A Rotary Club without a Santa sleigh might be an opportunity for Hedgelord to put some of its recent bad publicity behind it and help out the local community. Could she get Luka and Gallagher to knock up a replacement sleigh with wood panels and other materials in the garden area? Could she even convince Luka (who had a white beard, if not a particularly bushy one) to take on a Santa role for the local charities. This thing had legs!

She looked through her phone and found the number for Glen Lightfoot of the Rotary Club. She called him at once.

"Hello?"

"Glen! It's Charlotte Mitchell at Hedgelord. How are things?"

"Oh. Oh, hello. Charlotte." There was an immediate reticence in the middle-aged guy's voice. She didn't need to question what that meant. In the minds of all the people in the know, Hedgelord and Charlotte Mitchell were currently synonymous with last week's horrific pornographic Santa business. Dead Santas, porno Santas. Hedgelord had really cornered the market in bad-for-business Father Christmases this year.

"Things are great, Glen," she persevered in her most enthusiastic voice. "Look, it's the Santa Sleigh charity thing in the town on the nineteenth, and it just occurred to me that you don't have a sleigh. I wondered if we could help."

"*Well, isn't that just sweet of you,*" he said. "*And thoughtful too. No, don't worry. We've already sorted out a fresh sleigh.*"

"Oh. Oh, okay. That's good."

"*That lovely man, Mr Hartigan at Bloomer's, stepped in to say they would provide a sleigh. It's a wonderful thing. Bright red. Polished lacquer finish. All scrolled and twiddly. You know, a sleigh off a carousel ride. A work of art if you I do say so myself.*"

"Oh, I see. Bloomers, huh?"

"*Yes.*"

"Well, that's just lovely."

"*Isn't it?*"

"Okay. Well, I must go. This tree won't decorate itself!"

He laughed. She forced a laugh. The call ended.

Charlotte stared at nothing. She'd tried to throw herself into her work to avoid thinking about the man she'd lost, only to discover he was back in the old business of beating Hedgelord in the festive stakes.

Normally she would be burning with annoyance that she'd been pipped to the post by Jack Hartigan again. Now, her feelings were a bit more complex. She still burned for Hedgelord to be the pre-eminent festive season garden centre, while at the same time she felt a small and confusing pang of pleasure for him, that he'd scored that win.

"Fuck my life," she grumbled as she slammed her laptop shut.

"You want to watch that," said Tom Eccles.

Tom, the sales manager, shared an office space with her as they were essentially Hedgelord's management team, reporting directly to Cameron Clasp, the owner. "You break a connection to the motherboard and it's game over."

"Game over?" said Charlotte. "Game over for the laptop?"

He nodded and Charlotte rolled her eyes.

"Your concern for the office hardware is noted," she said. She tried to send him a telepathic message that his lack of concern for his colleague was also noted. He failed to notice and went back to his own work.

"Fucking laptop," murmured Charlotte, actively wishing it harm now. She stared at it, knowing that a slightly less mature Charlotte would by now have taken it outside and slammed it against something hard and unyielding until that bastarding motherboard wished it had never been assembled.

She visualised it, pleased at the idea.

Charlotte, who recognised the anger issues she sometimes battled with, had often taken out her frustrations on physical objects. She had built up a habit of taking a baseball bat to any smashable items that had been moved to the recycling area for disposal. Any chipped terracotta pots destined for the bin would undoubtedly get pulverised by Charlotte when she was working through her emotional issues.

Destroying her laptop would not be much different. Would she use the wall of the garden centre building, or get more creative in the decorative stoneware section? She thought of the fat-cheeked cherub statues, instantly knowing they would be perfect for motherboard killing. She walked herself through the scene, mentally slamming the laptop against the head of a cherub until something broke. She wasn't all that bothered whether it was the statue or the laptop.

"Hi?" came a voice.

Charlotte opened her eyes, not even certain when she had closed them. It was Anika.

"Are you all right?" she asked.

"Of course," said Charlotte.

"Only it sounded like you were growling. I wondered whether you might need a first aider? Sophie would know if it's a symptom of someone having a stroke."

"Not a stroke. I was doing it on purpose. Now, how can I help you?"

Anika took a seat and smiled. "Well it's more like I wanted to help you. You said earlier that you wanted ideas to assuage guilt and build bridges? I thought I might have some ideas for you."

Charlotte frowned. She'd been startled and vulnerable after realising Daffyd had set her up with an audience. Who knew what she'd said in the moment? She shoved her embarrassment aside and considered the idea. Anika was smart, maybe she'd come up with something. "Go on, tell me what you've got."

"So. The situation, as I understand it, is you and Jack did that whole enemies-to-lovers thing while you were on the road. You got mad when you thought he was back with his ex and did the dirty on him. Now he won't even speak to you, and you're feeling bad at what you did. You're hurting that he won't let you in."

Charlotte reeled at the casually accurate summary of her heartache. She nodded.

Anika became animated. "Right! So, this is just like one of those movies where the two main leads *know* they should be together but their stupid, stubborn pride keeps them apart. What normally does the trick is some sort of massive gesture. You need to make him realise how truly sorry you are."

Charlotte realised that while Anika was smart, her life experience was still that of a very young person. "Yeah, but that's in movies, not real life. Where do I find a massive gesture in real life? Do I need to emigrate to Australia so he has to rush to the airport? Should I become a nun?"

Not for the first time, Charlotte wondered what being a nun was like. It would be orderly and soothing, which sounded heavenly, but then she imagined the crashing disappointment of being kicked out of a convent when her temper got the better of her. It wasn't a pleasing picture.

"No, you can have a big gesture without making enormous life changes," said Anika. "Like flowers. Except flowers are not for everyone, especially if they work in a garden centre."

"No, he can probably get access to flowers," said Charlotte. "Did you have any thoughts on what that gesture might be?"

"You will probably have a better idea of what he enjoys," said Anika, "but from what I heard, he finds you impressive, so—"

"Wait! I don't understand."

"What?"

"Impressive. That. Where did you hear that?"

Anika flushed deeply and chewed a lip as she hunted for the right words. "Just, you know. Around."

"You were listening in on that phone call," said Charlotte flatly.

That had been back in Stockholm, last week. It had been an insane week. Charlotte and Jack had chased a bloody elf with an SD card of Santa porn across half of Europe. It had been exhausting and exhilarating, and the excitement of it all had woven some magic over the two of them. They had gone from work rivals to lovers in a matter of days. While Charlotte and Jack had been so wrapped up in finally getting naked together, there had been some kind of mishap with Jack's phone and it had relayed the sounds of their lovemaking to Maremba and Marcus, owners of Bloomers. They'd been convinced they were overhearing Charlotte torturing Jack, so they had patched it through for Cameron to hear. And apparently Anika as well.

Thinking back, it all seemed so very ... unlikely. And yet it had happened, there was no denying that.

The key thing right now ... the horrifying thing right now ... was the realisation that Anika had heard Charlotte's attempts at sexy talk.

"Cameron wanted me to help," said Anika. She looked mortified. "I'm sorry,"

Charlotte waved a hand. "It's fine. I have no dignity left anyway. Let's move on from your overhearing my most intimate moments. Continue."

"Impressive. So, you need to play on that – nothing half-hearted or passive. You need to really go for it in a big way."

Charlotte raised her eyebrows. Anika might be on to something. She nodded.

"So I made a list." Anika handed her a piece of paper.

- *write a song and either record or perform it live for Jack*
- *write a poem and either record or perform it live for Jack*
- *do that thing like in Love Actually where you write a heartfelt message on pieces of card*
- *turn up as a strippergram or private dancer round at his house (not at work)*
- *be delivered in a massive cake or gift box and jump out wearing sexy undies*

CHARLOTTE PUT it on the desk and studied it. "That's quite a list."

"I could come up with others if you wanted to give me a steer in a particular direction," said Anika.

"No, no, it's good. I can see some are more geared towards apologising than others. This one. Strippergram?"

"Yeah," said Anika. "I actually had to look that one up. I didn't know there were such things. Did you know there were these things call telegrams back in the day? I didn't."

"Right. So, like, if I jump out of a cake in sexy undies, that's a proper jump scare. Would I get my words out before he gives me my marching orders?"

"It's possible it could go the other way," said Anika with heavy emphasis and some eyebrow waggling.

"You mean sex? Hmm." It was a surprisingly delicious thought and she enjoyed it for a long moment, then she sighed. "No. I need to make sure I express myself first."

Anika was now looking over Charlotte's shoulder. "Yeah, so that means the private dancer option's no good either."

"Performing a song or a poem," said Charlotte, tapping the list with her finger. "It's nice, but it's that word *performance*. I don't want this to come over as pantomime. It needs to be sincere."

"Yep, yep. We're left with the pieces of card thing," said Anika. "Do you remember how that went?"

"Yeah, I can picture it now. Andrew Lincoln holds up cards for Keira Knightley while her actual husband sits in the other room." Charlotte frowned. "If I remember right, that was kind of creepy though, right?"

Anika shrugged. "Dunno. I mean, yeah, in that case the guy was doing it to the teen bride of another guy."

"Teen bride?" said Charlotte.

"Yeah. Kiera Knightley was only seventeen or something in that film. The guy with the cards was at least thirty."

"Ugh."

Anika shrugged again. "It's an old movie. I assumed social attitudes to underage brides were different in those days."

Those days? Charlotte did not see herself as old in any way. She considered herself to be barely more than a 'young adult', yet Anika had somehow managed to generation-gap her.

"And the husband's supposed to be his best friend if I remember rightly?"

"Ignore that part," said Anika. "It's more about the general idea. You can say whatever's in your heart. It's more vulnerable than pantomime. I think it will strike the right tone."

"Yeah," said Charlotte. "Yeah, you're right." She leaned back in her chair and contemplated the idea.

5

GALLAGHER

Gallagher and Luka were lighter on work this close to Christmas Day. Most of the people who wanted to buy Christmas trees had already bought them, so their day was mostly spent moving seasonal things to the front entrance so all those desperate and last minute shoppers could make a swift purchase.

"We could do two-for-one on door wreaths," said Gallagher, pushing a cart towards the tree baling machine where Luka was smoking a joint. "There's loads left."

"Nobody wants two door wreaths," said Luka.

"Yeah, but people love free stuff."

"Fine," shrugged Luka.

"Should I ask Tom?" Gallagher asked.

Luka stared at him and they both burst out laughing.

"Fine. I'll get Karen to update the till system and sort us a new sign," said Gallagher.

Luka stiffened and stared down the path behind Gallagher. Gallagher turned and saw Marti Snømann walking towards them.

Snømann was the walking embodiment of all Gallagher's current worries and fears. A ruthless criminal, a gangster of some sort, he had the two unfortunate plantsmen in his terrifying Nordic grip.

"Gentlemen." He spoke with an accent, but it was precise and formal, as if he'd learned English from those old films where everyone spoke with a plum in their mouth.

"Morning," said Gallagher. Luka gave a nod.

"You are well?" asked Snømann.

Gallagher glanced at Luka. This was new. It felt even more sinister than previous conversations when Snømann had simply threatened them with physical violence.

"Um, yeah. Never better," said Gallagher. "And yourself?"

Gallagher didn't know what to do with his face, so he tried arranging it into a politely curious expression. He tilted his head and smiled, knowing immediately that it was too much.

"I am also well," said Snømann. "Might we go and sit in your shed for a moment? I would like to talk with the two of you."

Obediently, Gallagher and Luka trooped to the tea shed, exchanging confused glances as they went.

"The crates are undisturbed I trust?" asked Snømann, indicating the concealed entrance to the secret shed with a wave as they sat down.

Gallagher nodded. He sat down, then jumped up again. "Er, Tea?"

"Yes. Please."

Luka's eyes indicated he wasn't a fan of this, but his mouth bent into a brittle smile.

"So, you might be wondering why it is that I am here," said Snømann once he was cradling a mug in his huge hand. "I have some interesting news for you."

"Oh, goody," said Gallagher weakly. He couldn't imagine any news was good news.

Snømann smiled. "I have become what you might call an investor in Hedgelord."

"Oh?" Gallagher had no idea how he was supposed to receive this news. It wasn't in the top fifty things he might have expected to come out of Snømann's mouth.

"What does that mean?" asked Luka.

"You know this word, 'investor'?" said Snømann.

"What is difference between 'investor' and 'what you might call an investor'?" Luka waggled his upper body to underscore the air quotes.

Snømann pointed a finger at Luka and smiled. "I like that you ask perceptive questions like that, Luka."

"Thank you."

"I have invested in this wonderful garden centre. It is as simple as that."

"As in a deal with Cameron?" said Luka.

Cameron Clasp, owner of Hedgelord, was a man whose wealth, naivety, and thoughtless man-child persona meant he barely understood anything that went on in his own business. And yet, although Cameron was capable of wild and random business decisions, Gallagher struggled to picture Cameron thrashing out any kind of business deal with this chilling crime boss.

"A deal. As you say," said Snømann.

"So Cameron knows? Like Tom and Charlotte know?"

"Always with the good questions." Snømann chuckled to himself. "I like this. I will value your thoughts on a great many things, I can already tell."

Gallagher smiled along, waiting for Snømann to answer Luka's question, but nothing was forthcoming.

"It is likely you will see some changes in how Hedgelord conducts its business," continued Snømann. "I really hope you can engage with them. You are very much on the list of people I can see at the heart of things, helping me to shape our future."

Luka still wore the inscrutable expression that was his stock in trade, but it was less guarded. He was apparently interested.

"What, er, changes do you think we'll see?" asked Gallagher.

"Ah, it's early days. Early days. I will get back to you with some thoughts very soon, though. I hope you will like them and support me in implementing change."

"Yeah, sure. You can rely on us," said Gallagher.

Luka glanced at him. Gallagher knew he was being a suck-up but didn't care. He wondered why, if Snømann was exerting new influence, Tom Eccles had never said anything that even remotely hinted the two plantsmen might be at the heart of things. He knew everyone's first response would be to suggest that wasn't Tom's style, but it was just an excuse. Did he value them at all, really?

Tom had definitely never invited Gallagher and Luka to implement change. All he'd ever wanted them to do was move bags of stones around. Snømann might be bloody terrifying, but oddly, Gallagher liked the idea of being invited to help implement change.

6

ANIKA

Anika got Operation Heartfelt Message up and running over lunchtime. She had asked Karen off the tills and Sophie to meet her and Charlotte in the garden centre's Pagoda Café to put ideas into action.

Despite the quantities of plants sold and the sheer numbers of families flowing through the Santa grottos at this time of year, Anika suspected the Pagoda Café was Hedgelord's main source of income. From the moment the store opened, even on quieter weekdays, the café was bursting with customers, often retirees, keen for a cuppa, a cake, or a selection from the café's range of hot dinners. A garden centre café was catnip to the grey-haired masses of the surrounding area.

Nonetheless, Anika had managed to find a table for the four women. Karen, Sophie and Anika covered the full age spectrum of Hedgelord employees, had very different roles within the shop, and entirely different personal lives. Still, over the past few weeks the three of them had formed a united band of women, ready to help each other solve life's problems or, failing that, just bitch about them.

The three of them would quite often sit and put the world to rights, but this time they had a particular task in mind: getting Charlotte and Jack Hartigan back together again.

"Thanks for coming," Anika addressed the group over a mug of hot chocolate. "I asked Charlotte to join us because we are going to help her apologise to Jack Hartigan in the most stylish and impactful way imaginable. Are you in?"

"Of course!" said Sophie, clutching her hands to the gaudy Christmas tree brooch on her chest and smiling dreamily. "Making love happen, what could be better than that?"

"Thank you," said Charlotte. "Er, lovely brooch by the way."

"Thank you."

"Hold on a second..." said Karen to Charlotte.

"Yes?"

"...I'd like to point out only a few weeks ago you were telling me that Jack Hartigan was your worst nightmare."

"Well, he was," said Charlotte.

"In fact, you drove me over to Bloomers garden centre on a secret mission to beat them – beat Jack – in a Christmas decorations competition."

"Er ... yes."

"And when I said I reckoned you secretly had the hots for him you told me off for behaving like it was the playground."

Charlotte huffed. "Fuck. Fine. Well I was wrong and you were sort of right."

"Sort of?" said Karen.

Charlotte squirmed uncomfortably.

"If I might," Anika interrupted, "I think Charlotte is uncomfortable in labelling her emotions with regards to Jack."

"That," said Charlotte. "Though I'm no happier having a teenager tell me what I do or don't think."

"But she does have the hots for Jack, right?" said Karen.

Charlotte gave the most minimal of nods.

Karen pumped a fist into the air. "I knew it! Come on bitches, let's make this happen."

"Ooh, yes," cooed Sophie.

"Can we have a group name that stands for something, like Let's Get Charlotte Laid? No, that doesn't even make a word. How about—"

"Karen," said Sophie, putting a hand on hers. "I think Anika wants us to get on and do something."

"Yes. Sorry."

"I brought supplies because we are going to help Charlotte deliver a heartfelt message to Jack, using handwritten signs," said Anika. "Like in *Love Actually*." She put squares of cardboard and marker pens on the table.

"Oh what fun!" said Sophie. "I like that film. I like the bit where the young schoolboy runs through the airport to tell the girl he likes her."

Karen grunted. "You'd probably get shot if you tried that these days."

"So," said Anika, trying to get them all to focus, "what I

thought we'd do is the three of us work out how best to write these messages, while Charlotte composes them. Then we can get them all written and ready."

Charlotte nodded, took a piece of cardboard, and started to jot some notes.

"Are we working out who's got the neatest writing?" asked Sophie.

"Yeah, let's do that," said Anika. "Everyone write down ... erm, what...? A line off the menu."

A laminated menu stood on the table and Sophie spent a long time choosing. "We're out of the Beef Pie so I can't use that."

"Sophie, it's just a writing sample. Use Beef Pie if you want to, love," said Karen.

All three of them wrote their menu choices, then pushed them into the centre of the table.

"These are all too small," said Anika. "Let's have another go – making the text big and eye-catching."

"Shall I use the special writing I do when I make signs for in-store?" asked Karen.

"I thought they came off a printer," said Anika.

"Mostly they do, but sometimes I hand write them if it's a rush job. I do outline letters like the fruit and veg guy on the market."

"Show us!" said Sophie. "I want to try!"

Karen picked up her pen with a flourish. "I will write 'hotpot'. Watch and learn. So a 'p' is easy. I visualise the outside of the letter and draw that, then I come back and add the little hole in the middle of the top part. Next up is 'i', also easy. It's a rectangle, but we give it a little flare on the lower part, to match the 'p'. Now the 'e' is a bit more tricky to visualise, but once you've done a few it will come easily. See?"

In no time at all, Karen had written TRY THE BEEFY HOTPOT WITH DELICIOUS GRAVY.

Anika was impressed.

"That's dead good, that is," said Sophie. "Could you do us one of those 'Don't forget to leave a review' we could put up somewhere.

"No problem," said Karen and set to work.

All of them had a go at the lettering which Karen demonstrated.

"What do you think?" asked Sophie, holding hers up for everyone to see.

She had written PIE AND CHIP'S in the stylised lettering.

"Looks lovely, Sophie, but why did you put an apostrophe in there?" asked Anika.

"Because it's a plural," said Sophie.

"What? No! That's not how you use apostrophes," Anika said. She wanted to scribble it out with her own marker pen, but she managed to restrain herself.

"It was back in my day," said Sophie. "I expect standards have slipped in schools nowadays."

Anika looked to Karen and Charlotte for support, but both were busy writing. She shook her head and resolved to keep a careful eye on what Sophie wrote. Rogue apostrophes could not be permitted. "Charlotte, have you come up with what you want to say to Jack?" she asked.

Charlotte looked up. "Maybe? See what you think. I will read it out."

They all sat to attention.

Charlotte held up her card and read. "'Please don't shut the door. I have something important to say.'" She looked up at them. "I need to make sure I get to say my piece before he slams the door in my face."

They all nodded, and she continued. "'I want to address my behaviour first of all. I made a huge mistake and there's not a day goes by when I don't regret what I did. I am sorry. You are important to me and I wish you would give me another chance. We could be happy together. Yes, I did actually use the word *happy*!'"

There was a long pause, then Sophie said "Aww!"

"I think the tone is just right," said Anika. "Shall we split up the text and make the cards? You could pop round and do this later if you want?"

"Brilliant!" said Charlotte.

"Why don't we help?" said Karen. "One of us can pass Charlotte the cards, one of us can play some romantic music through a speaker, and the other can blow your hair with a fan so it looks amazing."

"Yeah, sure," said Charlotte slowly. "I need all the help I can get."

7

GALLAGHER

As the day wore on and the early winter sunset rapidly approached, Gallagher and Luka were entertaining themselves by taking statue selfies.

It was a game that had been born many months ago, when Daffyd was tasked with pepping up the social media feeds. He'd gone round all members of staff, asking them to take creative pictures of themselves with items for sale in the garden centre. Gallagher and Luka had started competing with each other in a bid to mimic the statuettes in the garden displays

Luka had a head start because he had a plump face and a beard, so he had the gnome market cornered. There were pictures of him fishing, posing and even sitting on a big fake mushroom.

Gallagher had discovered that his skinny body was better suited to mimicking the female nymphs and goddesses. If he threw a blanket around himself, picked up a big amphora-style pot and stared dreamily into space, he could master a lot of classical statues.

There had been a delivery earlier in the week, full of fresh inspiration, and Luka had been burning to work with a gorilla statue that had turned up. It wasn't clear why anyone might want a gorilla statue for their garden, but there it was.

"Right, I need you to sit up straight, but then lean your head forward with a really intense stare," said Gallagher, who was directing the shoot.

Luka sat on an upturned pot next to the gorilla.

"Now bring your right arm up, like you're going to rest your chin on your fist, but then put it a bit to the side. I think you might be chewing a corn-on-the-cob."

Luka grunted and twisted to look at the gorilla. "Is fucking banana!"

"Eh? No way. That's never a banana," said Gallagher.

Luka opened his mouth to argue.

"Fine. It can be a banana," said Gallagher.

He snapped a picture of Luka and the gorilla. He showed it to Luka and they both chuckled.

"I'll send it to Tom," said Gallagher.

"Who are those guys?" asked Luka, looking over Gallagher's shoulder.

"Huh?" Gallagher looked up from his phone and saw where Luka was pointing. Over in the recycling area there were four tall blond men wearing black boiler suits. "I don't know. Never seen them before."

"Not staff though, are they?"

As they watched, the four men removed the jumble of cardboard boxes which had been thrown willy-nilly into the cardboard recycling skip by Luka and Gallagher. In a small production line, they broke down each box, flattened it onto a pile, then made a series of bales of folded cardboard, tying them with string so they could be stacked neatly. In a few short minutes they had emptied the skip and reduced the overflowing mess into a tidy pile taking up less than a quarter of the space.

"What the fuck?" said Luka.

The four blond guys placed the bales back into the skip, making it look almost empty.

"Are they doing our fucking job?" said Luka.

Gallagher cupped his hands to his mouth. "Hey! Guys!"

One of them looked their way. His big jaw split in a wide smile.

"What are you doing?" Gallagher shouted.

"It's no problem," the men replied with a wave.

The men then jogged away. And they did it a weirdly synchronised style, as if they were part of a dance troupe.

"Did Tom hire these people?" Luka asked. His mouth was agape and his face stricken with horror.

Tom Eccles had often pleaded with Gallagher and Luka to be more efficient with the recycling of cardboard, but they mostly ignored him and flung boxes in as they pleased.

"Fucked if I know, mate," said Gallagher. "That was weird."

"Well, we'd best bloody ask him."

They walked into the rear of the garden centre shop, through the pet area, past the gas-fired barbecues, and to the management offices by the stairs climbing to Cameron

Clasp's managerial office, the only room on the building's first floor of.

Gallagher gripped Luka's arm before the big guy could knock. "Wait. What are we asking?"

"It's very simple," said Luka. "We are saying, 'Hey, you, did you hire some extra guys to do our jobs?'"

Gallagher did not loosen his grip. "Okay ... and if he says 'Yes, I did, and they're doing a much better job than you', what then?"

"Ah," said Luka heavily.

"Suddenly it's adios Luka and Gallagher, and you and me are down the job centre trying to get minimum wage jobs cleaning the toilets in the leisure centre."

Luka pulled a tight expression. "Good point. We must play it cool."

"Casual questioning," Gallagher agreed. He let go of Luka's arm. Luka knocked and entered.

The office was surprisingly busy. Tom Eccles sat at his desk in one corner, while a group of women gathered around Charlotte's desk in another corner. Karen, Sophie and young Anika were crowded round a computer screen while snippets of songs played out.

"Not that one. Too slow to get going," said Karen.

"Oh, I like that one," said Sophie.

"Technically, a break-up song," said Anika. "Not what we're looking for."

As they went through the music options, Sophie was sorting a pile of large white cards with writing on. One read *I WANT TO ADDRESS MY BEHAVIOUR FIRST OF ALL*. Gallagher wondered if they were prompt cards for a press conference or something. Maybe the boss man, Cameron, had committed one social blunder too many and had to give a televised apology before resigning. Gallagher didn't think his behaviour was that unreasonable.

"Gents," said Tom, drawing back Gallagher's attention. "Did you get lost?"

"Huh?" said Luka.

Tom gestured generally. "I don't think I've ever seen you come to the office voluntarily and under your own steam. In fact, I'm not sure I've ever seen you away from your potting shed kingdom. Perhaps you heard we had mince pies in the office?" He shook a tray of mince pies that were on the end of his desk.

"Sweet!" said Gallagher, stepping forward to take one.

Tom didn't stop him. Gallagher peeled back the tiny foil tray and bit into the super sugary pastry.

"You are here for a reason though?" said Tom.

"We had a question," said Luka.

"Is it 'Do I still want the pallets of compost moving from outside the landscaping office?' Yes, I do."

"No. Is..." Luka took a deep breath before plunging in. "Have you hired new staff?"

Tom blinked. "Me?"

"You see, we saw these guys," said Gallagher, dropping a few crumbs as he spoke.

"What guys?"

"Four dudes," said Luka. "Big guys, blond hair."

"Er, okay," said Tom.

"They were doing stuff around the recycling skips."

"Stuff?"

Neither of the plantsmen wanted to say the four men were doing Luka and Gallagher's job *and* doing a better job of it than they would have.

"You don't know them?" said Gallagher. "They were all dressed alike. In boiler suits."

"In boiler suits, yes," said Luka. "Like Blue Man Group, you know? The music guys with the blue faces."

"Did they have blue faces?" said Tom.

"No. Just the boiler suits."

"But they were all blond, if that helps," said Gallagher.

"Yes," said Luka. "Blond Man Group."

Tom gave them a helpless and frankly indifferent look. He glanced over to Charlotte. "Charlotte, do you know if we've hired a troupe of blond musicians recently?"

"Not musicians," said Luka. "Workers."

Charlotte didn't even pay attention. Anika pointed at the screen the women were looking at. "That's absolutely the tune you should use!"

"Really?"

"A hundred percent."

Tom took being ignored for an answer and looked back to the plantsmen. "Doesn't look like we hired Blond Man Group. Maybe you imagined them. Maybe they were Christmas fairies."

"Damn big fairies," muttered Luka.

Charlotte and the girls were on the move. Sophie gathered up the big bits of card.

"I'm going to go find some electric fans," said Karen.

"Really?" said Charlotte.

"You need that wind in your hair sexy look," Karen assured her.

Charlotte looked to Tom. "Tom, I'm getting off early. We've got, er, a project to sort out."

Tom shrugged. He clearly didn't care.

As the women all left as one, Tom looked from Luka to Gallagher. "Is there anything else, gents?"

"You didn't hire Blond Man Group?" confirmed Luka.

"Never even seen the guys," said Tom.

Gallagher shoved the remainder of the mince pie in his mouth. "Good enough for me," he mumbled.

8

CHARLOTTE

As evening fell, the outskirts of town filled with rush hour traffic. Charlotte navigated out of the Hedgelord car park, over the double roundabouts by the big supermarket, and round to the apartments on the riverside near the town centre.

There were Christmas lights up throughout the town, centred around the Christmas tree and nativity on the pedestrianised area near St Stephen's Church. Charlotte simply focused on controlled breathing as she drove. She felt as she imagined a marathon runner would do as they waited for the signal to go. She was all prepared for her apology to Jack, but could she see it through? She liked to think of herself as a brave person, but that was mostly angry-brave. If anyone needed to be rescued from an alligator then Charlotte reckoned she'd get a long way on pure white-hot fury. This required a different kind of bravery, one where she needed to make herself vulnerable.

She parked her car on Riverbank Way, just up from Jack's house, and turned to face Anika, Sophie and Karen. "We all know what we're doing, yes?"

"I've got the tunes," said Anika, holding up a Bluetooth speaker and her phone.

"I shook down my kids' rooms for all the portable fans they have," said Karen. She reached into her bag. "Seven! Can you believe they had seven battery powered fans between them? I reckon that's enough to fluff up your hair."

Charlotte wasn't certain if the fan thing was necessary, but she recognised these women were really there to support her, and she was grateful.

"I've got the cards," said Sophie. "I will pass them to you, so that you can maintain eye contact."

"Yep. Very important, that eye contact," said Karen.

"Are we sure he's in?" said Sophie.

Anika pointed. "That's his car. He's home."

"Okay," said Charlotte and took one more cleansing breath.

They walked along until they came to Jack's front door.

"There are lights on. I think we're in business," whispered Anika.

Charlotte rang the bell, Karen crouched down at the side of the door and Anika pressed play. The selected music was the Cher classic *If I Could Turn Back Time*. Arguably it lacked subtlety, but she was all out of half-measures.

A short while later, the door opened. Jack Hartigan stood there.

Jack Hartigan. To say her feelings about Jack were complicated was a towering understatement. Rewind no more than three weeks and Charlotte would have looked at that face and seen a pair of beady, shiny eyes, a mouth just waiting to break into a cocksure grin, and the perfect hair of a man who spent too much time on his morning routine. Charlotte Mitchell had, for want of a more passionate word, *despised* Jack Hartigan. He was her opposite number – she at Hedgelord, him at Bloomers. But whereas she had been trying to bring some Christmas cheer to a soulless town in need of comfort – to make the garden centre the heart of a real local community – he had been treating his garden centre as a money-making machine and the customers as little more than victims to be processed.

And then something had happened. To an outsider, that something might have looked like a madcap and poorly thought-out chase across Europe. From Hull to Rotterdam to Stockholm to Lapland, no less. But along the way, something deeper had happened. Charlotte had seen a new Jack Hartigan, a Jack Hartigan who was vulnerable, thoughtful, caring, fun— Fuck! They'd had *so* much fun! And she'd seen that, if anything, *she* was the broken one, the petty one, the shallow one. He wasn't the dark version of her – he was the counterpoint to all the darkness in her. Being with him shielded her from all the cracks in her own shambolic persona. It was a cliché, but he actually made her a better person.

Also, the sex had been good. It had been really good. She wouldn't say she was hungry for more, or that she felt herself getting moist for him because that was a ridiculous and laughable cliché. However, she was definitely getting regular memos from between her legs, gently but persistently querying when there might be another opportunity to slide down onto Jack's cock.

She'd hated Jack. She'd had Jack. She'd fallen in – if not love then something – with Jack. And then in a fit of stupid misunderstanding, she'd spurned him. She'd lost Jack.

And that was why she was here.

Jack stood on the doorstep. He was wearing a pair of snowman socks. On his face there was a momentary flicker of something that might have been pleasure at seeing her, but Charlotte guessed that was probably wishful thinking. His expression turned into a scowl.

"What do you want?" he asked. His eyes flicked to the three women gathered around her in the shadows. "And why are there so many of you? Is this your gang?"

Sophie handed Charlotte the first card.

Jack looked at it. "'Please don't shut the door. I have something important to say'. Oh really, Charlotte? Is this what we're doing?"

Sophie handed her another.

"'Try the beefy hotpot with delicious gravy'. Er, what?"

"Fuck," said Charlotte, panicking.

"Oh no! Sorry!" Sophie flicked through the cards. "It's here somewhere."

"Fuck's sake, Charlotte." Jack looked down at Karen. "What are you actually doing with all of those fans?"

"Use your eyes!" Karen snapped. "She looks like Beyonce!" She wafted some of the fans a little closer to Charlotte's face.

Charlotte was fairly certain not a single hair on her head had moved the whole time. She gave Jack a small shrug and an apologetic smile. If only he could laugh about this with her, it would be so nice, but he still looked annoyed.

"Found it!" said Sophie, passing a card to Charlotte. She held it up.

"'There's not a day goes by when I don't regret what I did. I am sorry'." He shook his head.

Sophie passed another card over.

"'You are important to me and I wish you would give me another chance'. No, not happening Charlotte."

Another card.

"'We could be happy together'. Interesting idea Charlotte. I don't know that I really associate you with the word 'happy'. 'Yes, I did actually use the word "happy"'. Oh, I see what you did there. Clever. Anything else?"

Charlotte grabbed for the next card.

"'Please leave a review on Google or TripAdvisor'?" Jack pulled a grim and embarrassed expression. "It's still a 'no' from me. Now take your circus back to the garden centre, will you?"

Jack closed the door and Charlotte was left holding her cards while Cher continued to sing, and the others looked on with something like pity. Charlotte wanted to smash something. If she'd been on her own she would have been stomping down the street at that moment, looking for something on which to take out her temper. But she had company, so she simply stood there, feeling the weight of their stares.

"Well I thought that went pretty well," said Sophie. "He got the joke about you being happy, didn't he?"

9

ANIKA

Anika sat in the back seat of Charlotte's car with Karen. Sophie was in the front passenger seat.

"I'm a bit worried about Charlotte not saying anything since he slammed the door on her," she whispered to Karen.

"She's processing. I think Charlotte has a rich internal life. She probably needs to go and break some stuff," said Karen.

"I can hear you both, you know," said Charlotte.

"Oh right. *Do* you want to go and break something?" asked Karen.

There was a long pause. "Did you have something in mind?" asked Charlotte.

"Oh *God*, yeah. A massive box of crap my in-laws have given us that I don't want in the house. We can get a rounders bat, or a spade or whatever, and *blam!*"

"Blam," repeated Charlotte. "I mean, blam does sound quite good."

"It kind of does," said Anika. "Is that an open invite, Karen?"

"It sure is. You coming too, Soph?"

"Oh you know me, I'm game for anything," said Sophie.

"Good. And while we're there, you can dish on how it's going with your new man."

"Marti?" said Sophie.

"Yeah. Unless you've already moved onto another one."

Sophie laughed.

"New lease of life, this one," said Karen, elbowing Sophie. "She's working through all the men on the Saga Holidays mailing list."

"Cheeky!" said Sophie. "I'm not that old."

"What's Saga?" said Anika.

"They sell holidays and stuff for old people," said Karen.

"How old?"

"Over fifty-five, isn't it?" said Charlotte.

"And how old are you?" Karen asked Sophie.

Sophie cleared her throat softly. "Over fifty-five."

Charlotte drove to Karen's and the four of them went inside.

"The kids are stopping over with their grandparents," said Karen. "They're a pair of arses, but they've been trying to behave themselves of late. The house is ours so we can do what we want. And by that, I mean I am definitely opening some wine."

"Ooh, lovely," said Sophie.

"Let me grab some glasses on my way to finding the box of crap."

Sophie poured wine as Karen struggled into the lounge with a giant cardboard box, a rounders bat balanced on top.

"Here we go, the party has arrived. We can go out on the patio to do this properly if you want."

They all crowded outside, each clutching a glass of wine.

"Charlotte, you have earned the right to go first," said Karen solemnly, handing her the bat. "Here is your weapon. If you'd care to select some tat from the box, I will explain its provenance and why we definitely should pound it into dust."

Charlotte nodded and reached into the box. "What the fuck is this?"

Anika thought it looked as if a teapot and a handbag had made an ugly beige baby.

Karen took it and held it high for them all to see. "This is folk art from Peru. It is made from a dried gourd and, believe it or not, it's a handbag." She knocked it with her knuckles and it sounded dull and hollow. "You will notice there is nothing at all practical or attractive about it, which is no doubt why it was given to me by Marcus and Maremba last birthday."

Karen was divorced, her ex-husband off elsewhere. However, her ex's parents, her ex-in-laws, were still local to the area. By Karen's account Marcus and Maremba (who also happened to own Bloomers garden centre) had some very specific ideas about parenting and relationships. Anika considered herself to be a caring and right-minded person – 'woke' and proud of it – but Marcus and Maremba seemed to take progressive and liberal attitudes to whole new levels. If Anika understood correctly, the grandchildren might even now be filling out mindfulness journals, or exploring their thoughts on global inequality through the medium of clay.

Marcus and Maremba sounded very much the sort of people to give Karen a Peruvian gourd handbag.

"They bought the bag to support Peruvian artisans," Karen continued, "but were not in the least bit bothered whether I could fit my mobile phone in it. Please do the honours and destroy it, Charlotte."

"I bet it was expensive," said Sophie.

"Yep. I reckon so. But it's fine, those artisans got paid already," said Karen.

Charlotte laid it on the floor with care and stepped back, raising the rounders bat above her head. She held it there, as if in silent prayer for the ritual she was about to enact, then she brought it down in a savage arc, shouting as she did so. "Fuck! You fucking *fuck*!"

She didn't stop at the first blow, but kept pounding and swearing, slamming the bat onto the patio with such animalistic force that Anika felt herself taking an involuntary step backwards.

Eventually she stopped and coughed, embarrassed. "Erm, I'm sorry Karen. I think I broke your bat. And your patio."

"Mate, that is definitely no biggie. In fact, I think you've set the bar for this evening. If anyone indulges in some smashing and they don't chip lumps off the bat, then they are definitely not trying hard enough. Now, who's next? I've got a delightful earthenware mug I am fairly certain is decorated with lead paint. You'd literally be saving my life if you smashed it up."

"Ooh yes! I can help with that!" said Sophie.

"And for you, Anika, I have a pair of drinking glasses made from old wine bottles cut up and fused together. Their unique selling point seems to be that they are actually painful to drink from. It's like they were made by the wine police!"

They drank wine and smashed things on Karen's patio for longer than Anika would have imagined possible. Eventually it grew so late and them so drunk that they needed to stay overnight at Karen's. She found sleeping bags and blankets, and cooked fish fingers for them all to soak up some of the wine.

"You know what?" Charlotte said from her sleeping bag after they'd put the lights out. "I don't know how I pictured today ending, but I definitely wouldn't have predicted that I'd be smashing up weird ornaments and having a sleepover. It's been brilliant. Thanks, ladies."

10

CHARLOTTE

The following morning, moving quietly so she wouldn't trigger the hangover headache she knew was going to get her at some point, Charlotte drove home to change into fresh clothes for work. There was frost on the pavements and in the grass, a crisp wintry feel in the air.

It was forecast to be cold but dry for the charity evening in the town centre tonight. The kind of night when folks would stamp their feet and want a hot chocolate or a bag of roast chestnuts to keep their hands warm...

That was a thought. She wondered if there would be room for a Hedgelord-sponsored hot chestnut stall or something. She should phone Glen once she was in the office.

Thoughts of how Hedgelord could elbow its way into the evening festivities vanished the moment she saw there was a car on her driveway, and Jack Hartigan standing by her front door. She pulled up.

"Jack?"

He turned. He wore a long coat buttoned up, with a red scarf wrapped around his neck. "Charlotte. I rang the doorbell. I wondered if I'd missed you."

She said nothing. He was here. She had given him her message and now he was here. She didn't want to say anything in case it broke the magic spell.

"I needed to come and see you," he said.

Needed. He said needed. There was a tight and hopeful feeling inside Charlotte.

"You came to open your heart to me and I was a little ... short with you," he said.

She wanted to speak, to agree, to tell him it didn't matter, but she kept her mouth shut. She needed to hear what he had to say.

"I should be able to tell you exactly what I feel," he said.

"Yes," she breathed.

He took a step towards her. She couldn't help herself. She walked toward him. She probably stank of alcohol, but the pull was unstoppable. And then he held up his hands to slow her. She stopped.

"I've just come out of a long-term relationship," he said. "Kathryn and I had split up the very day before you and I went on that crazy chase across Europe."

She wanted to tell him that shouldn't matter. Good things could happen on the rebound.

"And we've known each other for years," he said. "We've

been rivals when we could have been friends. We could have been more than friends."

"We still could..." she tried, but those waving hands said otherwise.

"I thought we had something," he said and the smile on his face became tight and pained. "There's so much I like about you."

She couldn't resist. "Like what?"

He laughed then and it felt good to hear him laugh. "You're clever," he said. "You damn near run Hedgelord all by yourself. And you care. You love your work and that garden centre."

"It's not all about the garden centre."

"No. Not at all. You love everyone and everything in your own weird way. You actually want to make the world a better place. And you try. You really try. You're like Wiley Coyote."

"Getting squashed by boulders?"

"Metaphorically maybe. I mean that you never give up. Things go wrong, things blow up in your face and you pick yourself up, dust yourself off and try again. I don't think I've ever seen you give up at anything. The most bloody-minded woman I've ever met."

"And these are good qualities?"

"They really are," he said. "You are indestructible, even if you don't feel like it. And that makes you too serious, sure. It means you struggle to admit when you're wrong. I was seriously impressed by last night. You don't do that often."

She twisted her fingers together. If he could see that she was sorry and wrong and was willing to change then maybe, just maybe...

"But I can't trust you," he said bluntly.

Her heart sagged.

"You are so focussed, so blinkered, so flipping bloody angry half the time that you don't see when you've going to hurt people." He shook his head. "No, that's not right. You *do* see. You see and, in the moment, you don't care. And that hurts. I'm not ready for that kind of hurt."

"I can change," she said, hoping she didn't sound as whiny and pathetic to his ears as she did to her own.

"Really?" he said sceptically. "I don't think you can. And I don't think I want you to."

She frowned.

"You are a wonderful person, Charlotte Mitchell. I don't want to be the one to tell you how you should be. But I can't be with a person like you."

He sniffed, and when he exhaled, the air misted in front of him.

"I respect you enough that I wanted to tell you to your face." He met her eyes for the briefest of moments, then walked past her to his car, his face bowed.

She watched him drive away.

"Fuck," she said, but it didn't feel enough. "Cunting bastard fuck."

Across the road, one of her neighbours stood in her living room window, in her dressing gown, watching her.

Charlotte gave her a little friendly wave and with a few more "Fucks" went in to get showered and changed.

Her mood was foul but she resolved to go into work with a positive attitude. Something not helped by the hangover which had now properly woken up and was bashing about her brain like it was rearranging the furniture. She got into the office, managed a hello for Tom Eccles, and sat down to her work.

She checked the information about the charity evening. It was starting in the late afternoon, but that didn't mean she couldn't find a way of getting Hedgelord in on the act. A hot chocolate stall or chestnut stand might suit the bill.

She put a call through to Glen Lightfoot at the Rotary Club. The call was short and sweet. Glen was up for anything that would add an extra bit of fun and Christmas ambiance to the event.

She put the phone down. All she had to do now was find something to fulfil her offer.

It was only then that she wondered if she was going to go along herself. By rights she should not even be thinking about attending the event because she was banned from St Stephen's (a complex story involving a regrettable angry outburst and a dead pigeon), but she needed to check up on Hedgelord's representation, didn't she?

A small voice in the back of her head said surely there was some trusted employee she could send instead, but she quashed it. An even smaller voice acknowledged that she just wanted a glimpse of Jack Hartigan again. Damn it. She was addicted to the man. Was she simply torturing herself at this point? Probably. She could wear that ridiculous sheepskin hat she had at home – with its massive bobble and earflaps – if it was as cold as the forecast suggested. Nobody would ever recognise her underneath all of that floof.

"Good morning all!"

She looked up. Marti Snømann was in the office, an expensive dark suit over a white shirt.

"Ah, Mr Snømann. Hello."

He pointed to the door which opened onto the stairs up to Cameron Clasp's office. "I will be working from here today. Redirect any calls to me, yes?" Without another word, he went through the door and upstairs.

Charlotte looked to Tom. "Is Cameron even in?"

Tom frowned. "Dunno. I thought he was just playing a lot of golf recently. Working on his teeing off or something. Don't think so. Mr Snømann was working there yesterday."

"He works here now?"

Tom's frown deepened. "Dunno. Doesn't he own part of the company now?"

"Does he?"

"I'm sure he said something like that." Tom did a happy little shrug. "Things change. No one ever tells me."

11

GALLAGHER

The morning was cold, so Gallagher thought he'd go over to the Pagoda Café to see if he might scrounge a couple of hot sandwiches for him and Luka. Cliff Richard's *Mistletoe and Wine* was playing over the café speakers.

He approached the counter. "Sophie, I heard you all had a 'smashing' time last night!"

It seemed to take her several seconds to work out what he was on about and he'd begun to wonder if he'd misheard Anika's explanation.

"Oh!" she said suddenly. "Oh, yes! Gallagher, my love, I haven't had that much fun in a long time. Who knew it could be so very entertaining to break things. It feels a little bit naughty."

"We should all be a little bit naughty every once in a while," he grinned. "Like sharing the bacon love with your favourite plantsmen, maybe?"

"Oh I don't know," she said, glancing over her shoulder. "I'm afraid of taking liberties with these new workers in here. They seem a little bit intense."

"Eh? What new workers?"

She beckoned him round the counter and pointed through the door to the kitchen. "Look."

Gallagher saw there were more of the tall blond men in black boiler suits in the kitchen. "Blond Man Group," he whispered.

He couldn't be certain, but he didn't think they were the same people that he and Luka had seen the day before. They wore the same black boiler suits, with aprons and hair nets, as they bent over the sinks and the stoves, working industriously.

"Fucking hell, when did they turn up, Sophie?"

Sophie shrugged. "I think some of them were here yesterday. Maybe the day before. I can't be sure how many there are, because they are so alike. It's like they've come from an agency or something."

"Yeah, an agency, that's probably what it is," said Gallagher. It would explain the uniform. "Extra cover for the busy festive period." He blew out his cheeks. "They do seem very professional."

"They do."

"A bit too professional."

"I know what you mean," whispered Sophie. "They're mad keen on washing their hands."

Gallagher frowned. "Aren't you supposed to wash your hands a lot when you work in a kitchen?"

"Oh yes! Yes of course, we all do," said Sophie. "But, you

know, there's washing and there's *washing*. They're mad keen on it, that's all I'm saying."

Gallagher went back outside to find Luka. "No bacon sarnies for us, those weird guys in the black boiler suits are all over the kitchen like a rash."

"Blond Man Group?"

"That's what I said. Sophie thinks they've come from an agency."

"Pah. I never see people from agency behave like they in the fucking Bolshoi. Those guys are like escaped from a circus or something. Is all performance."

He mimicked the graceful elegance they'd witnessed by the cardboard skips, twirling and pirouetting as he went.

Gallagher laughed. "Oh yeah, another thing. If Sophie makes you a sandwich? Get her to wash her hands first."

ANIKA FOUND Charlotte in the office. "Morning!"

"You seem bright and cheery," said Charlotte. "I guess you're young enough not to do hangovers."

"There's a cure for hangovers and I have it here in this bag," said Anika, putting the greasy bag down on Charlotte's desk. Her mum would have insisted on a place mat, but Anika was pretty sure the desks were all plastic and would come to no harm.

"Are these pakora?" Charlotte asked, peering into the bag.

"Uh-huh."

"They look amazing."

"Good, because I went home and got mum to make these. I think it could form the basis of your next attempt on Jack."

"Oh, I'm not sure about that. Last night was a disaster."

"Not at all. It was merely the opening salvo."

"Oh, this is a war, is it?"

Anika shrugged and tapped the paper bag. "And this is the next offensive."

"I win him over with delicious, home-cooked Indian food?"

"Absolutely."

Charlotte sunk her teeth into the crispy pakora and sighed with pleasure. "Oh, that is so good."

"See!"

Charlotte sighed. "I'm not sure that doing more and more creative apologising is the way to go. There's a point where it becomes harassment, isn't there?"

"Maybe. But that point is definitely not pakoras," said Anika.

"Very true. Can I have another? I can feel it curing me."

"Yes of course. Didn't know if you wanted to share some with Tom and Cameron." She looked around the empty office.

"Tom's around somewhere," said Charlotte.

"Okay."

"I haven't seen Cameron for a couple of days, I don't think. Maybe gone golfing or something."

"Really?"

"Hey, I'm not about to chase him down. He's the boss," said Charlotte. "And Marti Snømann is working in his office." She pointed a finger up at the ceiling.

"Oh. I heard Cameron and he were working together."

Charlotte made a dubious noise. "It's like we've had a whole change in management."

Anika didn't know what to make of it but decided to look on the bright side.

"He seems nice. And Sophie likes him."

"Yes," said Charlotte, uncertain. "She does."

12

GALLAGHER

Gallagher and Luka had invented a game to play with the many remaining door wreaths. It was essentially hoop-la, where the hoops were wreaths and they could score points by throwing them onto an upturned flowerpot with a number chalked on the side.

"See this one? This is going to be a fifty!" said Gallagher, planting a kiss on his wreath before throwing it. It was unwise, because the holly scratched his lip, but he threw the wreath like the seasoned pro he was and it landed over the flowerpot. "Yes! Get in!"

"Is not flat on floor," said Luka. "You don't get points."

"Course it's flat! How's that not flat?"

They walked over and Luka stooped to point. "See here? This edge is not on ground."

"It's the fucking bow! It's as flat as a wreath can ever be when it's got a bow on the front!" Gallagher protested.

Luka shrugged. "You threw it wrong way up. Rookie error."

Gallagher growled in frustration, but then tried to turn it into a cough as Snømann appeared around the corner once again.

"Here we are again, gentlemen!" said Snømann. "Might I join you?"

Gallagher had an overwhelming urge to make him go away, but that would be very foolish. "Sure."

What right did he have to keep appearing like that? Investor or not – whatever that meant?! – it was just plain annoying. Cameron would never keep popping up like this. Cameron Clasp showed only a half-hearted interested in his own enterprise at the best of times. Gallagher couldn't even remember the last time he'd seen the man.

Snømann picked up a wreath and made a big show of aligning his eyes, his throwing arm, and his target. He bounced on bent legs then gracefully swung his arm, throwing the wreath in a perfect arc to land on top of Gallagher's.

"Shot!" said Gallagher involuntarily.

He was impressed, not least because Snømann's wreath had flattened his to the ground, quashing Luka's nonsense about it not lying properly. Shady character or not, this old man could throw.

"I come to you with a plea for help," said Snømann as he picked up another wreath and fiddled with it.

"Plea?" said Luka.

"To us?" said Gallagher.

The man might have been oddly nice to them of late but

the darkness, the sense of intimidation, were never very far away. Snømann tweaked out a piece of holly and tested the wreath for balance, as if he was fine-tuning it.

"What kind of help?" asked Luka, cautiously.

"It is of a delicate nature, but I'm sure I can rely upon your discretion."

Gallagher listened intently, and he could see that Luka was paying attention too. They nodded as one.

"As you know, I have been romantically pursuing your colleague, Sophie," said Snømann.

"Er, we do?" said Gallagher.

"Fine catch," said Luka.

Snømann permitted himself a small smile. "I find her to be a fascinating woman. She is the yin to my yang, I think."

"Oh aye?" said Gallagher. He had a feeling nobody had ever described Sophie in those terms before, and yet there was sincerity in Snømann's face. And, yeah, he was a fucking dangerous international criminal while Sophie was about as threatening as a basket of labrador puppies.

"I would like her to properly commit to be my partner," Snømann continued.

"Big step," said Luka.

"But I feel her slipping through my fingers."

"Riiiight," said Gallagher. "I mean, this might be a bit outside of our expertise. You do know we're both single, don't you?" Gallagher glanced up at Luka. He was fairly certain that Luka was single, but he'd put nothing past that sneaky old bastard.

"Currently single," Luka admitted.

Snømann spread his arms wide. "You are smart and

resourceful people. If you do not know an answer, you will know where to find it, I think?"

He had a point. Gallagher nodded. "Well yeah, that's true."

Snømann embraced the two of them in his wide arms. "Perfect! I knew I could rely on you."

"You need to tell us a bit more about what's going on, though," said Gallagher. "How exactly is she slipping through your fingers?"

Snømann looked thoughtful. "She is a woman who is not motivated by the usual displays of affection. I need to know how to get through to her."

"Usual displays of affection like…?" prompted Gallagher.

"Expensive gifts. She is always polite when she receives them, but I am not sure she sees the difference between a Tiffany bracelet and one made from old shoelaces."

Gallagher wasn't sure if he was supposed to laugh at that. Was it a joke? He settled for a guarded smile. "Sounds like Sophie."

"I will leave this with you," said Snømann. "You will action this before the end of the day though, yes?"

"What? Is that all we have to go on. Come on, mate."

Snømann fixed him with an imperious stare. "You have been given your instructions. It is important."

Gallagher swallowed. "Okay. Yep. We'll do that."

"Good. You know where my office is, yes?" he said.

"Your office?"

He pointed across the way, to Cameron's eagle's nest office space on the very top of the Hedgelord shop building.

"*Your* office?" said Gallagher.

"A king must have a place from which to survey his kingdom," he said and smiled before walking away.

Gallagher and Luka waited for a few minutes and then withdrew to the tea shed. They sat in silence for a few minutes.

"His office?" said Gallagher. "His empire?"

"We are tiny cogs in a big machine," said Luka. "It is always the way."

"And what do we know about wooing women?"

"It happens that I know plenty," said Luka, sitting back in his chair.

Gallagher sat, waiting for him to continue, but Luka appeared to be lost in a silent reverie.

"You gonna tell me or what? Wooing women, how can you make it happen?"

"Ah. Yes. There are multiple approaches. Is complex subject."

"Right." Gallagher could have worked that much out for himself. "Like what? Give me some examples."

"Really? Well, was time when there was this girl I liked. She was really beautiful, well out of my league. I found ugliest, most annoying men that I knew and paid them small amount to ask her out. When I came along it was like breath of fresh air." He gave a chef's kiss to illustrate the brilliance of his strategy.

"Yeah. Mate. That's not so much wooing though, is it?" said Gallagher. "Snømann's got Sophie in the bag, so to speak, but he needs to somehow up his game. Make himself irresistible."

"Ah, irresistible is easy. Just need correct cologne." Luka nodded sagely.

Gallagher wondered if his friend had come from a world where things were so very different that a man who simply smelled nice could conquer any woman. "You do know that this is the twenty first century? Most men have access to cologne."

"I am talking about *correct* cologne," said Luka in a slow, precise voice, as if he was addressing an idiot.

"And what is that?" asked Gallagher.

"Is called *Gruczoły Zwierzęce*," said Luka.

"Super catchy name," said Gallagher. "It's not a mainstream thing then? Don't think I've seen it in Boots."

Luka shook his head. "Is very tricky to find, but I will check my sources. I might have a friend who has some at home. If Snømann wears this cologne then there can only be success with women. Is impossible for them to ignore the pheromones and shit."

Gallagher really hoped it didn't actually contain shit, but then he wasn't going to be wearing it, so maybe it didn't matter. "You get some of that then. We got anything else?"

"No. Is the answer."

"We could always tackle it from the other side. You know, ask Karen and Anika to help us?"

"Maybe. We just need to be careful. If we involve other women and he wears cologne then it could get ugly."

"What, they will all be driven into a frenzy of sexual desire and start beating each other up to get access to the man who's wearing it?" laughed Gallagher.

"I have seen it happen," said Luka, deadpan.

13

ANIKA

Anika had been arranging the grotto rotas for a few weeks now, simply because she was really good at it, and nobody had told her to stop after she'd filled in for Charlotte during her absence. In a few short weeks she had gone from mere grotto elf to elf-manager. It might have been a small step, but she knew it would all look good when suitably re-worded on her CV. Her parents, still smarting from her declared intention of not going back to university after the Christmas break, were just as quick to praise Anika's achievements, and predictably exaggerate them to the wider family.

According to Mummy and Daddy Chowdhry, Anika was single-handedly managing a whole programme of essential yuletide entertainment, upon which the entire town was dependent. It was embarrassingly far from the truth, even though it did sometimes feel like it was the case.

"Hey, Gillespie!" she called, as she spotted her fellow elf walking through the main shop towards the grotto.

Gillespie had started elfing at the same time as Anika. Although where she had seized opportunities for greater responsibility with both hands, big guy Gillespie had been happy to keep on with the elf duties throughout the season.

"Hi Anika."

"Next couple of days I have you down as full time, yeah?" she said, consulting her phone.

"Ohh, I can't do this afternoon. I need to get away early to prepare for my new venture. It kicks off this evening."

"New venture? What's that? Sounds exciting."

"The roast chestnut stall in town. Santa Raymond used to run it but, you know, he..."

"Died."

"...Exactly. So I bought the chestnut stall. I know there's not much of the season left, but I want to get cracking."

"Congratulations, Gillespie. That's amazing."

"*And* I'm working for Hedgelord tonight. It's the event in town – you know: the Christmas stuff on the pedestrianised bit by the church. Charlotte just called to confirm. I'm not even sure she realised it was me she was talking to, to be honest."

Anika nodded. Charlotte was very distracted, it was true. "I'll change the rota, we can re-jig to cover you. I might pop along and see you later. I don't even know if I like chestnuts, but I'll give them a try."

"Makes two of us!" laughed Gillespie.

Anika fixed him with a stare. "What do you mean? How can you not know?"

Gillespie shrugged. "I'll find out soon enough, won't I?"

"You mean you've never yet fired the stall up? How do you know it will work as you expect it to?"

"How hard can it be?" Gillespie grinned. "Chestnuts, hot plate, yummy stuff in a bag..."

Anika left him with an amused shake of her head. Gillespie got a long way in life with his good looks and charm, she wasn't so sure it would roast any chestnuts for him, though.

"It is here," declared Luka, coming down the path towards Gallagher.

Gallagher had been kicking his heels for most of the day. There was only a finite amount of fun to be hand with the last of the wreaths and the trees no one was going to buy. He was so bored, he even contemplated shifting those bags of compost from outside the landscaping office. Luka's arrival had fortunately saved him from any actual work.

"What is here?"

Luka raised a carrier bag. "*Gruczoły Zwierzęce.*"

"The cologne? I thought it was hard to source."

Luka sniffed. "I have friend from the old country. He had private stash in attic. Said he bought it in nineteen seventy-six."

"Bit out of date then."

"Matured," Luka assured him. "Like a fine spirit. Come. Let's go get ourselves in Snømann's good books."

Gallagher followed him into the shop. The place was

bustling. People might not be buying so many decorations anymore, but it seemed many of them were still buying Christmas presents and seasonal specialities from the food hall.

Luka knocked as he entered the main office. Tom, Charlotte and Anika were there. To Gallagher's eyes, Charlotte looked a bit done in, hungover even. The remains of some greasy food in a paper bag confirmed that suspicion in his mind.

Luka gestured to the door to the upstairs office. "Is the boss in?"

Tom and Charlotte glanced at each other.

"Which boss?" said Tom. "You mean Cameron?"

"Snømann," said Luka. He jiggled his carrier bag. "I have important delivery."

"Snømann's the boss now?" said Anika.

"He's in," said Charlotte.

"Good, good," said Luka and went up. Gallagher smiled at the office staff and followed.

At the top of the stairs was an office with windows on all sides, overlooking Hedgelord and the surrounding area. It was a considerable domain. Car park, nursery plant area, a pair of storage warehouses, and the wide open paddock used for outdoor events. Over by the warehouses, an articulated lorry was being backed in, guided by what looked like a couple of guys from the Blond Men Group.

Christ, those guys seemed to be everywhere these days.

Marti Snømann stood by the window, looking out across the road, past the big supermarket and to where Bloomers garden centre stood in the middle distance. His fingers rested lightly on the windowsill as he gazed.

"Mr Snømann," said Luka.

"It is beautiful, isn't it?" said Snømann, without turning round.

Gallagher had no idea what he was referring to. He'd lived in the area for years. There was little round here he could point to and call beautiful.

"Yes?" said Luka.

Snømann glanced their way. "Business opportunities. Plans." He turned to the table at the centre of the room.

The table was covered with large, printed sheets. They looked like building plans, although there was also something of a complex engineering bent to some of the designs. A great vat and some tubes. They made no sense to Gallagher. The heading OPERATION YULETIDE SURPRISE on another piece of paper offered no clues.

"You want something?" Snømann said to the two men, as though properly seeing them for the first time.

"Brought something," said Luka. He reached into his carrier bag and came out with a small bottle. It looked to Gallagher like one that had previously held sauce or salad dressing. It now contained a murky amber liquid, up to about the halfway mark.

Luka held it out to Snømann. "Special cologne. I have sourced some *Gruczoły Zwierzęce* for you. Very rare, very hard to get. Women cannot resist the man who wears this."

Snømann opened the top and gave a tentative sniff. He recoiled with a cough. "Powerful. What does a person do with this?"

Luka fixed Snømann with an intense look. "I will tell you how to use, but is important that you take great care. In wrong hands this can be dangerous. Very powerful ingredients, and they will have strong effects. When you are certain you will be spending time with intended recipient, make small dab behind each ear. Like this." Luka demonstrated the gentlest tap on his lobes. "Keep lid shut at all other times."

Gallagher wondered how much of Luka's warning was showmanship. If this cologne had the sort of effect Luka described, it would definitely be more well known. All the same, he was curious about it. "Can I have a smell?"

Snømann held it out for Gallagher to sniff.

"Oh! Fuck me! I thought it was perfume." Gallagher took some deep breaths, gulping air into his lungs to dispel the assault they had just suffered. It had been more than a smell. Something like a concentrated blast from a blocked toilet combined with freshly-laid tar. There was also an undercurrent of something briny, like seaweed. He had no idea that a smell could be so overwhelming.

"Ah, you make the mistake that finished perfume is same as active ingredients," said Luka. "Not at all the case."

"Huh," said Gallagher. "Does this only work on women, by the way?"

"What do you mean?" asked Luka.

"Could a woman use it on a man? Or what about non-binary people?" Gallagher asked.

"I have not done fucking scientific study," growled Luka. "Is ancient and well proven folk recipe."

Gallagher opened his mouth to ask what it was made

from, but decided he didn't really want to know and closed it again.

"Thank you for the gift," said Snømann, raising the bottle in a small salute to Luka. "I will put it to the test."

14

ANIKA

Anika was in the office, absorbed in the task of re-organising the staff rota. Charlotte had gone to do the rounds of the Christmas displays; Tom was busy ignoring what she was doing.

Nobody had asked her to look at the rota, but then nobody had commented on the fact she was now doing it. She was certain that both Tom and head elf Daffyd had spotted what was happening, and were determined to ignore the fact, because neither of them wanted to do it.

Luka and Gallagher came downstairs from the office upstairs.

Anika really wanted to ask what this business with Snømann being in charge was all about, but she got the strong impression Tom had no idea.

Two minutes after Luka and Gallagher had left, there was a bellowing roar from upstairs office. Anika and Tom exchanged a look.

"Was that Mr Snømann?"

It was. Snømann burst through the door, hands to his head. "It burns! It burns!" he hollered.

"What's wrong? Do you need a first aider?" Anika asked.

"Yes! Yes, it burns!"

His hands hovered over the sides of his ears, not daring to touch them. They looked red and inflamed.

Anika ran to fetch Karen from the tills. Karen grabbed the first aid box and hurried to the office. Snømann was in a chair now, with Tom making ineffectual patting motions accompanied by tiny shushing sounds.

"Tell me what's the matter, love," said Karen.

"My ears are burning," yelled Snømann. "They feel as if they are on fire."

Karen snapped on some gloves and gently tilted his head so that she could examine the skin around his ears. Anika could see it was not only inflamed but blistered.

"Can you tell me what you think happened?" Karen asked.

"I put on cologne that Luka gave me. Just a dab."

Anika and Karen exchanged a look, while Tom screwed up his face in confusion.

"Right, we're going to bathe the skin a little bit," said Karen. "Anika, find me a clean bowl of lukewarm water will you, love? A couple of clean tea towels as well."

Anika ran to the kitchen and returned with the water. Karen had swabs of cotton wool ready to go. She covered Snømann's shoulders with the tea towels and gently swabbed the inflamed skin with wet cotton wool.

"I want to make sure I wash it off but don't spread it

around," she said. "Any idea what the cologne was? Maybe I can get a data sheet for it."

Snømann grunted that he didn't. "It was called … called something. Luka made it sound like a black market thing. It was supposed to make me irresistible to Sophie."

"Oh yes?" Karen kept swabbing. "Is that feeling any better?"

"Maybe a little."

"Good. Tom, don't you have an aloe vera gel on the shop floor? Maybe some of that would be useful here."

Tom left to find the gel.

"Now, talk to me," said Karen. "What was this cologne business all about? Surely Sophie already finds you attractive, or the two of you wouldn't be together?"

The big Nordic guy sighed. "It seems that it's not so simple. I find her a difficult woman to read. She plays things so cool."

Karen and Anika looked at each other. Was this the same Sophie they both knew?

"How do you mean?" asked Karen.

"I buy her a Louis Vuitton handbag and she puts sandwiches in it. Is she spurning my gift? She is not made happy by such things?"

Karen laughed. "Oh, well, that one's easy to explain I reckon. Sophie's not materialistic. I know she likes pretty things but I'm not so sure she wants *fancy* things, if you see what I mean. Don't you reckon, Anika?"

"Yeah, definitely," said Anika, pleased to be part of the conversation, but feeling out of her depth.

"Well what *does* she want?" Snømann asked.

"Without asking her—" Karen broke off from swabbing to look him in the eye "—You *have* asked her, haven't you?"

Snømann gave a tiny, non-committal shrug.

"Hm, well if I had to guess," said Karen, "I would imagine that she wants your time rather than your gifts."

"Ahh," said Snømann. "That might be where the problem lies."

"Oh? Why's that then?"

"I am so busy right now. A brand new business to set up. Did you know that I am now the owner of both Hedgelord and Bloomers?"

Karen looked as surprised as Anika felt. They looked at each other for a long moment while Snømann continued talking, his head tilted downwards.

"...The merging and redevelopment that I have in mind is an enormous project. Very demanding. I have been neglecting Sophie, I see this now. I cannot send one of my men in my stead if it's my time that she craves."

"Yes love, you're right," said Karen. "You need to carve out some special time for just the two of you."

"Oh, but right now it feels I can only offer an hour here, an hour there."

"That's all you need," said Karen.

Anika nodded in optimistic agreement.

"But what can you do with an hour? Certainly no romantic trip to Paris. Not even dinner at the Ritz."

Anika blew out her lips. "You don't need that. It's like ... it's like..." Her mind reached for the nearest thing. "...The charity event in town tonight. Christmas lights, a walk arm in arm, a bag of hot chestnuts."

"Hot chestnuts?" said Snømann, as though Anika had said the maddest thing imaginable.

"Yeah, sure," said Karen, throwing her weight behind Anika's suggestion. "Get some hot nuts in her. Make her feel special."

"Yeah, that," said Anika, with no idea if they were making things better or worse.

15

CHARLOTTE

After work, Charlotte had gone into town and spent an hour in the Flying Dutchman on Bester Street, needing some Dutch courage before walking over to St Stephen's to check on Hedgelord's contribution to the festivities. She wanted to see just how spectacular this new sleigh of Bloomers could possibly be.

A couple of glasses of wine warmed her core and took away some of her nerves. She avoided the temptation of a third one. She'd been caught out like that before.

She walked down the road with the general flow of locals in their hats and scarves, enjoying some of the late night shopping and the Christmas streetlights. There was music and general busyness coming from the pedestrianised bit on the curved road in front of St Stephen's. The church's nativity scene occupied a special glass-fronted shed in the centre of that space.

It was, Charlotte thought with something akin to

heartbreak, one of the most beautiful nativity scenes for miles around. There was a life-sized Mary, Joseph, wise men and shepherds gathered around the Christ figure in adoration, all wearing beautiful, hand-stitched clothes. Charlotte knew this because she'd done some of the gold trim on one of the wise men, back when she'd been a welcome part of this church community. St Stephen's had been at the end of a list of churches she had joined, alienated by her occasional angry outbursts and ultimately been forced to leave.

The vicar of St Stephen's, Ralph Robertson, still glared frostily at Charlotte every time he met her. Which was bloody rich, considering he was a man of the cloth and meant to be full of Christian forgiveness.

Well, there was nothing Charlotte could do about vicars with grudges, and there was nothing she could do about these charity festivities being here. This bit of pavement was one of the few parts of the town centre not taken up by a congested road, and it was also where the town's Christmas tree had been erected. It was a good specimen: at least three stories high and heavily laden with lantern-style coloured lights.

She would have to keep her fluffy hat pulled low over her ears, keep her head down, and check out the scene without anyone actually noticing that she, Charlotte Mitchell, social pariah and enemy of the church, was about.

"Hey Charlotte!" shouted a voice.

She whirled. A figure waved at her vigorously from by the chestnut stall.

She was surprised anyone had recognised her, and

equally surprised that she recognised the hot chestnut man. She hurried over.

"Gillespie! What are you doing here?" she hissed.

He gestured at the chestnuts cooking on his sizzling hot stove. "I'm the chestnut man."

She looked up and around at the stall. Yes, that seemed very much to be the case.

"You are the chestnut man," she concurred in surprise. "Did *I* book you?"

"You did. Look." He pointed at the A3 sheet pasted to the front of his wheeled stall. PROUDLY SPONSORED BY HEDGELORD GARDEN CENTRE. It was small and looked amateurish, but there it was.

"I see," she said. "*Why* are you the chestnut man?"

"Funny story! It's my chestnut stall now. How about that? I bought it, chestnuts and all."

"Well, how very enterprising of you. By the way, how come you recognised me with this huge hat on?"

"You have a very distinctive way of walking. Honestly, I spotted you a mile off."

"Distinctive how?" she asked.

"It's like you're a Terminator or something. Nobody else I know walks like that."

Charlotte gave a weak smile. "Terminator. Right."

"Listen, will you do me a favour? I'm supposed to be doing mulled wine as well as chestnuts, but I don't really know what it's supposed to taste like. Have a sup of that will you?" He thrust an insulated cup into her hand.

"Oh right, thanks." She tried the drink. "Mm, nice. That's

really nice." It really was. It had a sharp fruitiness that went straight to her insides.

Gillespie nodded and bent to his work. "Good. There was something about diluting it, but I probably don't need to do that."

"Oh." Charlotte realised the drink was actually quite strong. "Yeah, you probably do. Show me what you're putting in."

She came round and looked at the containers. She lifted the 'festive mulled wine base' cannister.

"Fuck me. Thirty-two percent?" she said, stunned. No wonder the stuff was warming!

There were boxes of orange juice by the side along with cartons of 'fruity spice mix'. "Okay, let's put some of these in."

She opened a box of orange juice and poured all its contents into the great cannister of gently heated wine. She gave it a stir with a big wooden spoon, then poured herself another cup.

"Maybe this is better," she said, sniffed it and drank.

"Yes?" said Gillespie.

She smacked her lips. "I think we're at fortified wine levels." She took a confirming sip. "Yes. Definitely a bit too strong."

She really didn't want or need more to drink. Charlotte was failing in her stated mission of staying relatively sober. She chalked it up to 'taking one for the team' and gave herself a mental pat on the back for ensuring that Hedgelord's offering was properly quality assessed.

She opened another box of orange juice to add to the

mix. Ten minutes later, after much testing, they declared it to be appropriately diluted.

Leaving Gillespie to his work, Charlotte pulled her hat more closely over her head and went to explore. She took great care not to walk as she normally would, but found it was not an easy task. She tried to force a different walk by sticking her feet out at an angle, but felt ridiculous. Besides, the mulled wine, in all its levels of concentration, had gone straight to her feet. And her head. The mulled wine had gone everywhere.

She spotted the new sleigh, emblazoned with vinyl banners, so that any photos couldn't fail to include the Bloomers branding. It was next to the nativity scene. She tried not to think about how she had helped to create the church nativity years before. The magnificent Christmas tree stood nearby, of a scale that could only exist in an outside setting, framing the scene beautifully. She recognised Joe from the Three Counties Echo newspaper, taking photos of kids by the sleigh.

"Fucking Bloomers," she muttered. There was no denying it was a nice sleigh, hitched up to the back of a small tractor. The previous one had been tiny and rickety, but this seemed much more substantial, with painted panels to give it the classic sleigh shape, and comfy bench seating inside. There was a sound system with a speaker on top of the sleigh, but this one was of a much higher quality than its predecessor. She could hear all the words of *I Wish it Could be Christmas Every Day.*

"Showoffs," she muttered.

She tapped on the sleigh's panels to see if she could tell

what they were made of, but was none the wiser. She wanted it to be poorly made. Ideally it would be illegal and someone would impound it for health and safety reasons. She sighed. Did she really want that? She didn't even know any more. She kicked a tyre for no good reason, confused by her own mixed feelings.

She heard voices and saw Reverend Ralph Robertson at the top of the steps of the church.

She automatically turned away and covered the side of her face with her hand. She couldn't have him spotting her. His anger at her was still something quite fearsome to behold.

She scuttled away to the side. As she neared the entrance to the church, she wondered if she might be able to sneak inside the church while she was wearing her huge hat, and Ralph was distracted greeting civic dignitaries. It had been so long since she'd been able to enjoy the warm glow she got from simply sitting quietly in a pew. She decided she might as well give it a go. She waited until Ralph had descended and was mingling with people on the pavement before trotting up the steps to the church.

Once through the door, the quality of the air changed. It was still and calm inside, with that gentle scent which came from candles, hymn books and Brasso. On the noticeboard by the door was a poster for the nativity play on Christmas Eve. A CHRISTMAS SPECTACULAR was the surprisingly bold subtitle under the heading.

She walked across the tiles, even remembering the feel of them as a couple of broken ones rocked underfoot. She made her way along a pew and sat down on the polished wood.

She focused on her view of the altar and smiled at the peace it brought her.

There was a pulse in her temple. The mulled wine was moving through her body like sluggish, spicy treacle. If she cut herself, her blood would smell festive.

She looked up at the altar, and the empty cross over it. This was the symbol of her God. The empty cross, Jesus gone, resurrected and ascended to Heaven. The victory of goodness and faith over death and suffering.

"How do you do it?" she said, putting her hands together.

She had come in here just for the peace and quiet, but now she felt an overwhelming need to pray, to speak to the one guy who had never let her down in her entire life.

"Jesus, why is life so hard? I try. I really do. All my motives are good. I've worked hard for this community and the people around me. I want to be a good person. I do. And I really don't want much..."

She paused. Was that true? It was always her anger that let her down. And why? Was it when things didn't go her way?

"Things never go to plan," she said to God, "everything I try to do. People get in the way. Dumb bad luck gets in the way. I had this thing with Jack Hartigan." She looked at the cross. "You know Jack. We got to know each other in ... in Europe. We had a thing in that hotel room in Stockholm. Well, you know that..."

Charlotte pressed her lips together. The fact that God was everywhere and saw everything was an integral part of her faith. She didn't have a problem with that. But the idea that He was literally there while she had straddled Jack in the

Grand Hôtel, Stockholm, riding him like a bucking bronco...
Now she had a weird picture in her mind of God standing in
the corner, silently watching, and munching on cinema
popcorn.

"Look, I know you're possibly cool with pre-marital sex,"
she said. "It's all about love. I'm all about love. I do nothing
but love people. But still shitty stuff happens to me. I lost
Jack and it hurts."

She glanced at the cross. "Okay, it's not up there with the
whipping and the crown of thorns and being nailed to a
cross. And you managed to rise above all that. 'Forgive them,
for they do not know what they are doing.' But people are
such twats, Lord. Me included." She sighed. "We're all a
bunch of twats. Eight billion twats." She sighed even deeper.
"I wish I was more like you, Lord."

She felt like she had expunged something from her
system. Or maybe the mulled wine had stopped coursing
through her brain.

Prayer hadn't fixed anything. Prayer wasn't really meant
to fix anything. She had spoken her fears and worries to God
and knew that he had listened. God might speak back to her
but, in her experience, it was never going to be a deep, wise
James Earl Jones voice speaking great truths in her mind.
God's message was already there for her to see. In the world
around her, in the words of the Bible, in her conscience.

She prayed to the Lord and he listened. God spoke to her
at all times and she just needed to recognise the truths she
already knew in her heart. She closed her eyes in silent
prayer for several minutes and finished with the Lord's
Prayer.

She felt a strong sense of peace with that final amen. God, it felt good.

As she opened her eyes, something at her feet caught her eye. She saw that some of the kneelers had been replaced. Even though they were pushed below the pews she recognised new ones. She was pleased that the small things were being cared for in her absence. She pulled out the nearest one and looked at the design on the upper surface.

She frowned.

She tried to make sense of it. There was a picture of a person with a lighted candlestick and above them a bird. Surely it wasn't really showing the killing of a pigeon with a candlestick? It was! It really was!

There could be only one person this was meant to depict, and that was her. The crime which had got her expelled from St Stephens was here on this kneeler, like a warning; even if it was a limited, cartoonish rendering that came from trying to create a picture on something the size of a shoebox. She wondered who might have executed this horror. Her mind automatically turned to Barbara Winger, a very competent sewer from the congregation who had also been quite a vocal supporter of Charlotte's expulsion from the church.

She glanced at the kneeler next to it.

"Oh, my fucking God!"

It was an image of the dead bird, misshapen beak bent down, its bloody chest smashed open, wings wide. It was the bird she had accidentally killed!

The congregation of this fucking church had actually done it. They'd commemorated her unintended sins in kneeler art.

"Well, fucking hell!" she growled.

She picked up the kneelers. She couldn't let this lie. Kneelers stayed in the church for decades. She thought of all the good things that she'd tried to do with her life, and how there was no lasting memorial to any of that. One mistake though – *one* little mistake – and it apparently was to be immortalised in tapestry for probably longer than she'd be around.

"Fuck that for a game of soldiers."

The kneelers were heavy. Were kneelers filled with sawdust or something? Not to worry, these things needed to go. She held them by the tiny leather handles sticking out from their sides and swung them in a low arc while she tried to contain her fury. Common sense said that she should just drop them quietly into a bin somewhere. The world would be rid of these dreadful artifacts and she could move on. Common sense knew nothing of the depth of Charlotte's anger. She was incandescent with rage.

"Fucking fuck *fuck!*"

The profanity count beeper on her smartwatch buzzed repeatedly at her outburst.

People that she'd known and loved had done this to her. They thought of themselves as good people; Christian people.

Jesus might be able to forgive them with His infinite patience and love, but Charlotte fucking Mitchell could only take so much shit from the so-called faithful.

"Fuckers!" she growled.

She increased the swing of the kneelers as she walked outside to the top of the steps.

It was at this point she realised the mulled wine hadn't exited her system at all. It had just gone quiet while she'd been sitting in the church. This sudden fury, this sudden movement, brought spicy drunkenness roaring back to her head and body.

She looked across at the cheerful crowd that had gathered. The beautiful low-lit nativity, the decorated tree, the new sleigh and the chestnut stall were arrayed in front of the church. Members of the Rotary Club wearing Santa hats circulated with collection tins so that the crowd could make last minute donations to this year's collection. Charlotte was suddenly incensed at the scene. She was the one who spent every day of her life striving for the good of the community. Her daily efforts at Hedgelord were to make it into a pleasant working environment and to make the garden centre the very heart of the community. She'd tried to do the same thing here at the church, before being rejected. Here, in front of her at this moment, were the smiling faces of that same ungrateful community. They had gathered together to celebrate the wrong garden centre and pay homage to a church which had insulted her in the form of painstaking needlecraft.

All it really needed now was Jack Hartigan to complete the unholy trinity. All the parts of her life which had rejected her. With a start she realised he was actually standing beside the new tractor sleigh. He was in conversation with Reverend Ralph, the two of them smiling widely. How dare Jack smile like that when she felt so very wretched?

"A fucking kneeler?" she roared, running down the steps. "Seriously? It's not exactly a Netflix mini-series is it? What's the actual point of commemorating a social pariah if the only people who ever see it are those with a dodgy knee who want to say their fucking prayers?"

Jack and Ralph turned towards her.

"Charlotte?" said Jack.

"What are you doing here?" demanded Ralph.

Her arms took over from her brain. She only got onboard with what was happening after she'd swung her arm right back and launched one of the heavy kneelers high into the air towards Ralph and Jack.

The kneeler missed Jack, but it smashed squarely into Ralph's forehead, knocking him straight over onto his back.

Charlotte needed to get away from the scene. No – more than that, she needed to storm out. How dare these cunts have a merry sodding Christmas while she writhed in anguish? She was going to leave here, quickly, and with fucking panache.

And there was one very obvious way to do that!

Once again she trusted her bodily actions to carry her through while her brain was still processing what was happening.

She ran to the tractor sleigh's driving seat. Glen Lightfoot of the Rotary Club had somehow magically intuited what she intended to do. He came towards her. She batted him aside with the second kneeler, burying it in his stomach. He curled round it. She stepped up to the tractor, climbed inside, and depressed the handily labelled green starter button.

The tractor spluttered into life and that gave her a momentary blast of surprise and clarity.

She was at the wheel of a tractor. Why? Because she needed to make a big, noisy getaway. Why? Because she had just clobbered a minister of the church with a church kneeler. Why? Cos the fuckers had pushed her too far!

And while Charlotte recognised that if she could have rewound as little as an hour then she would do everything differently, possibly starting with not helping Gillespie taste-test his super-strong mulled wine. But here she was! And she couldn't currently see a better way out of it.

She grabbed something that looked like a gear stick and shoved it. The tractor shunted forward a good few feet, then stuttered to a stop.

The door opened and Jack stepped up into the cab.

"Get the fuck out, Jack!" she spat.

"Whatever you're thinking about doing Charlotte, don't."

"Didn't you say this morning that we need some time apart? Get out of my tractor."

"What was that thing you just threw at Reverend Ralph?"

"A fucking kneeler! He got some of his parishioners to mock me via the medium of bastarding tapestry."

"I don't think so," said Jack. "Are you seriously saying they had some sort of meeting where they sat around giving out jobs to eager volunteers, and one of them was 'Make a kneeler to humiliate Charlotte'?"

"Yes! That is exactly what I am saying!"

"Nope. Didn't happen. Now, take the keys out and let's—"

"Ain't no keys in this motherfucker!" she snapped, only then spotting the keys below the starter button. She pressed the starter again.

"Someone's gonna get hurt," he said.

"Good!" she shouted back and shoved him.

He wobbled in the doorway but held on.

"You don't know how to drive this thing!" he said. "Please. Let's just get out and talk."

"You don't want to talk to me!"

In front of the tractor, Reverend Robertson had got to his feet. There was a trickle of blood under his nose. "Get out of there!" he said, pointing a wobbly hand.

If she wasn't going to listen to Jack then she definitely wasn't going to listen to a treacherous and vindictive priest.

Charlotte started the engine again. "Get out now, Jack, I'm leaving." She put the tractor into drive, but Jack reached over and yanked it back.

"There are people about. Families."

"It's a tractor! They can fucking run faster!"

Charlotte stamped on the accelerator. She realised the tractor was no longer in drive but in reverse as it shunted backwards, pushing the sleigh behind it. Jack launched himself across the cab in an attempt to stop her.

In the days since their catastrophic split, Charlotte had imagined having Jack's body pressed up hers again. She hadn't pictured it would be in cramped cab of a Massey Ferguson tractor.

She wanted to say something but the smashing noise from the rear ended all conversation. The tractor had shunted backwards into the huge Christmas tree in the square and there was nowhere left to go. The sleigh was compressed against the tree. Whatever those sleigh panels had been made from, Charlotte could see in the rearview mirror they were now buckled and broken. Above the shouts and screams around them was the sound of metal wires pinging.

"Shit shit shit," said Jack. He had rolled, pretty much laid in her lap, and was looking up.

Overhead, the high tree was wavering in an alarming manner.

"Out!" screamed Jack. "Out! The tree's coming down!"

Charlotte bodily pushed him out the door and lunged after him. She landed awkwardly and stumbled painfully across the ground.

Above her the Christmas tree swayed, but it was definitely coming down. Families fled. People ran. Reverend Robertson helped up Glen Lightfoot and they stumbled away.

The huge Christmas tree slammed into the roof of the tractor, squashing it flat. As the spreading branches swept over Charlotte and Jack, the truck pivoted over the tractor and came smashing down across the nativity shed. Wood splintered, glass smashed.

"Ooh, me chestnuts!" yelled Gillespie.

The very top of the tree had clipped Gillespie's set up, upending cooking chestnuts and the metal stove onto the ground. Pine branches and needles smouldered where the stove rested against them.

"Oh fuck," whispered Charlotte, pushing herself away from the tree.

"What did you do?" whispered Jack as he helped pull her up from the debris.

Charlotte looked at the crushed nativity shed. Was there

a possibility of the figurines in their fine hand-stitched garments still being in one piece?

"Oh, this is such a mess!" she said.

"You think?" roared Reverend Robertson from a safe distance. "You think?!"

"Maybe we can salvage some of it," said Jack hopefully.

Then the smouldering branches under the stove caught fire. That fire raced along the branches to the trunk. Sap bubbled, fizzed and spat.

Charlotte and Jack clutched each other and ran as the Christmas tree and nativity were consumed in a blooming fireball. Charlotte felt the heat of it on her back, wondering distantly if her big fluffy hat had caught light.

They ran to the sanctuary of the church steps and looked back. A massive orange fire filled the square, sun-burning the faces of the crowd who could not resist standing and watching. As soon as it had started, the blaze started to burn itself out.

"You said you could change," said Jack hollowly.

"Sometimes I can't help myself," she replied, numbly.

There was a camera flash as their picture was taken. "Can I quote you on that?" said Joe from the Three Counties Echo.

"Oh, fuck, no," whispered Charlotte.

And across the way from her, their faces aglow in the orange blaze, stood Snømann and Sophie, arm in arm. Sophie's eyes were wide with wonder, like she was watching a wondrous fireworks display. Snømann's gaze, directed straight at Charlotte, was far more severe.

16

CHARLOTTE

Charlotte had never been arrested before. This was a first.

The cell in the town police station was cold and – thank goodness – the custody officer had concluded that her big hat was not a possible aid in either escape or suicide attempt and let her keep it.

The police had bundled her and Jack away from the scene, into a car and down to the nick, where they were swiftly processed and put in separate cells.

Once there, Charlotte could only stew with thoughts of the monstrously stupid thing she'd done to the Christmas tree, nativity scene, and her own rock bottom reputation in this town. Those miserable thoughts were occasionally tempered by a flash of rage as she recalled it was the grossly offensive church kneelers (and a helping of undiluted mulled wine) which had led to the incident.

She might be feeling very guilty and sorry for herself, but

the anger was never far away. That bastard Reverend Ralph Robertson had surely been responsible. He might not have stitched the kneelers himself but he had surely encouraged their creation, or at least sanctioned them. Her church had rejected her and now – by God, she had got the message! – she would reject them back.

As she hugged herself on the narrow cell bed, Charlotte swore she would never set foot in St Stephen's church ever again and wouldn't utter a single word to Reverend Robertson until the day she died.

That oath barely lasted half an hour, for when the cell door opened, the sergeant led her out, upstairs, into an interview room where Reverend Robertson stood, a wad of cotton up one nostril to plug his bleeding nose. On the table were the two kneelers with the vile depiction of her pigeon-killing incident on them. One was smeared with dirt, or possibly fir tree ash.

Reverend Robertson's glare had not eased in the intervening hours. "I will be brief, Charlotte," he said in a vicious tone. "I think you are mentally ill."

"Er..."

"I say this not as an insult, but as the only assessment of your behaviour that makes sense. You have significant on-going issues and I hope you get all the treatment you need."

"Treatment?" She could feel her anger rising again. As she opened her mouth, Ralph stabbed a finger on the first kneeler.

"After the birth of Jesus, King Herod was consumed with rage at the possibility of a newborn king usurping his throne."

"Is this...?"

"And so they fled to Egypt, sacrificing two doves to God before the journey."

Charlotte blinked repeatedly as she tried to make sense of this. He was referring to the kneeler. She looked at it again.

"Oh no, they're definitely pigeons. Look at them!" said Charlotte, but she knew she was on the back foot.

"You are familiar with scripture, Charlotte," he said.

She flung her arm at the second kneeler. This was just one bird, alone, its chest cavity cut open. No Mary. No Joseph.

"And I suppose you're going to tell me this is a sacrificial dove too!" she scoffed. "I can totally see Barbara Winger's handiwork here!"

"Of course it's not a dove," he said. "It's a pelican."

She spluttered. "Really? For fuck's sake...!"

"'Lord Jesus, Good Pelican, clean me, the unclean, with your blood, one drop of which can heal the entire world of all its sins'."

"Good Pelican?"

"Thomas Aquinas," he said. "Referring to the myth of the pelican cutting open its own breast to feed its chicks on blood, a symbol of generosity and sacrifice."

She looked again. The beak did look long and crooked, and maybe it was more pelican than pigeon. "I thought I saw —" she began.

"You chose what you saw," he said, not one shred of generosity in his voice.

"I..."

"You see yourself as a victim and rage against the world,"

he said. "Everything you hate is within you, Charlotte." His one unblocked nostril flared angrily as he looked at her. "I think you deserve to be locked away for a long time."

"But—"

"For everyone's safety!" he snapped, then adjusted his vestments. "But I have been convinced otherwise by someone who has everyone's best interests at heart." He went to the door, knocked, and left.

The sergeant looked in on her. "You should consider yourself to be very very lucky, my lass," he said.

"Lucky?"

He stepped aside to let in another person. It was Marti Snømann.

He took off the winter gloves he was wearing and sat at the table. He gestured. "Sit."

She hesitated.

"Sit," he insisted.

She sat. He watched her a few seconds.

"I was told so many good things about you," he said. "When I bought Hedgelord, people said, 'That Charlotte Mitchell, she practically runs the place single-handedly.'"

Bought the place? she thought wildly. In a matter of days had he gone from stranger to investor to owner?

"I was lied to," he said. "You are a liability." He laced his fingers together on the table and leaned forward. "This evening, on the advice of a wise young women, I was in the town centre with my belle, Sophie."

"Yes, I—"

"A walk around the town. This country is busy and crowded with too many cars, but it has its charms. Your fine stone churches. Your Christmas lights. Such an evening should not be spoiled by two drunken fools, fighting over the wheel of a tractor and ramming Santa Claus's sleigh into a church. And the fire! Oof!" He shook his head sadly.

"Jack had no part in it, I swear!" she said.

He held up a hand for silence. "What is done is done. This outrage cannot stand." He raised his chin as though rising above the moral filth she represented. "There are reputations to uphold. However, I have made donations to the church of St Stephen and had a friendly chat with the police inspector, a pragmatic man, and you will be released without charge."

"What? Oh, wow. I mean, thank you."

"And your contract with Hedgelord has been terminated with immediate effect."

A lump appeared in her throat. "I'm fired."

He nodded. "With immediate effect. You are fired. You will not come to work tomorrow. Any personal effects will be brought to you."

"Please, no."

"It is done," he said simply.

The old anger flared up again. "I don't accept. I don't know that you're the boss. You turn up and say that Hedgelord is yours. I've not heard any such say-so from Cameron. It's bollocks, you hear me?"

He nodded patiently and removed his phone from his pocket. He swiped and opened a video. He held it up to show Charlotte.

It was Cameron Clasp. He was sitting on a leather sofa in what appeared to be an upmarket log cabin. In the corner of the screen was a white fur rug and the suggestion of an open fire. Cameron had a half-full glass of whisky in his hand. He was talking into camera.

"She did what? Christmas tree and Santa sleigh?" He spluttered. *"Bloody hellfire. No, that's absolutely right. She should be fired."* He stared straight into the camera. *"We have no choice. She's fired. Charlotte, you're fired. Sorry, old gal. You had a good innings."*

The video ended.

Such abrupt finality.

"Do you need to watch it again?" asked Snømann.

"No," she said numbly.

"Good." He stood and went into the corridor. "Sergeant Akhtar, we are done."

"And nice doing business with you too, sir," said the policeman jovially.

Their voices receded as they walked down the corridor together. Charlotte was left alone, effectively forgotten.

She'd been fired. Losing her church community had been bad enough, but this...? Hedgelord, the one place, the one community she had truly loved more than any other, had been taken from her.

17

GALLAGHER

On the twentieth of December, Gallagher and Luka enjoyed the first couple of hours of the day in the plant area. There were rarely any customers and they could ease themselves gently into the day with hot drinks, and maybe a breakfast sandwich. Today, a heavy frost had rimed the shed windows, providing a palette for them to practise some artwork.

"See this?" Gallagher said to Luka, pointing at his stick man creation. "This is you and Tom. Tom has just asked you to do something and you're laughing, yeah?"

"Why the fuck is Tom wearing a top hat?"

"So we know he's the boss. It was easier than trying to make it look like him."

Luka shook his head. "Is not very fucking obvious. Nobody wears a top hat. You would do it like this, look." Luka used another pane for a drawing. "You are like this, the skinny one here."

"To be fair, when you're drawing stick men, everyone's skinny."

"And when I want to draw someone normal, I give them an actual fucking body. This one is me, with beard, see?"

"It does actually look like you. Do another one!" said Gallagher. "Do Sophie!"

"Easy." Luka drew a woman and gave her huge wide eyes, with exaggerated eyelashes like a doll.

Gallagher laughed. "Bang on! Now Charlotte."

"Here, I will use accessories." Luka gave the woman an axe and posed her in a position where she wielded it above her head in an act of pure aggression.

A noise behind them made Gallagher whirl round. It was Snømann. Gallagher tried to shift position so that his body hid the caricature of Sophie that Luka had just drawn. It did not seem prudent to share it with her most ardent (and violent) admirer.

Only as Snømann got nearer did Gallagher see there was something different about him. His earlobes were an angry red colour, so bright that they practically glowed. They were slathered in glistening cream, no doubt meant to ease the irritation.

Gallagher put two and two together very quickly indeed. "Oh, shit," he gulped.

"Gentlemen," said Snømann. "Today you will help me. Come." He turned to walk back towards the garden centre building.

Gallagher and Luka (who must have realised those burned ears were his fault) both started to mumble about the things they definitely ought to be doing in the plant area.

Snømann whirled to face them again. "You are coming with me."

"Mr Snømann..." began Luka. "Sir..."

"I am a busy man, Luka. I had a late night in which I had to dispose of a much-valued employee. You do not find me in good humour and I do not have time to debate this with you."

They both fell silent and followed Snømann, eyeing each other as they went.

They walked through the retail space and back out into the car park. Snømann led them to a huge Volvo SUV that looked as if it had been modified in some subtle way Gallagher couldn't put his finger on.

"In you get," said Snømann, opening a door for them.

The open door gave some clues as to how the vehicle was different. The window glass had a strange greenish tint to it and was very thick. The entire door seemed chunkier than expected.

"Is this armoured?" Gallagher mouthed to Luka as they climbed into the back.

"Maybe?"

They pulled away with no further conversation, Snømann at the wheel.

"Nice ride," said Gallagher. He wasn't enjoying the weird, oppressive silence.

"Thank you. Now we will make our way to a place with a higher degree of privacy. You will see that it's necessary," said Snømann.

Gallagher made no reply. When Snømann's predecessor,

Sonia Patterson, had cornered them in a place with more privacy it had been to torture them by putting their heads in a cider press. Did Snømann plan to kill them or torture them? Had anyone even seen them leave Hedgelord?

He stared at Luka, trying to convey these concerns, but Luka now wore his trademark poker face.

Eventually, beyond the nowhere village of Clopton Howes, they turned off the road and drove along a track into an isolated field. They passed several more fields before coming to a stop. It was literally in the middle of nowhere: flat countryside punctuated only by low hedgerows in every direction. It was the perfect place for a murder because there was clearly no other person for miles around.

Snømann put the car into park and jumped down. "Come on!" he yelled, a cheery tone in his voice now.

Gallagher and Luka got out of the car to find Snømann busy at the tailgate of the vehicle.

"Here we are," he said, opening a massive metal case. There were guns arrayed inside, embedded in foam.

It was too much.

Gallagher threw himself on his knees. "Please don't shoot us!" he pleaded.

Snømann turned to look at him. The expression on his face was amused surprise. Gallagher surely wasn't the first victim to ask for mercy?

"We didn't mean to do it!" said Gallagher.

"Do it?" said Snømann.

Luka did not get down on his knees. He crossed his arms in front of his chest. "If I am to die, I will die on my feet."

He sounded all cool and stoic, but Gallagher could hear the trembling edge of his voice.

"Die?"

Luka gestured to his face. "*Gruczoły Zwierzęce*. It burned you. You are offended."

"Oh." Snømann put a hand to a burned ear. "An allergic reaction perhaps." He grinned. "And you thought I would shoot you for that? Ha!"

From his position on the floor, Gallagher squinted up. "So, you're not going to kill us?"

"No!" Snømann laughed. "It is true that this inflammation did not improve my mood, and my evening out with my beloved was ruined by a drunken Hedgelord employee who is now an ex-employee."

"So, when you said disposed of...?"

"Fired, Gallagher. She has been dismissed from her role. I was up late, smoothing matters over with the local constabulary. It has been a tense and difficult twenty-four hours and so—" he gestured to the boot and the weapons "—I thought I would reward two employees who, despite certain hiccups, have been nothing but hard working and compliant. Together we should blow off some steam." He gestured for Gallagher to get up. "I would like to invite you to try out these weapons for yourselves."

Gallagher and Luka stared at each other, then at the guns, before looking at Snømann.

"We're going to have a go at shooting?" asked Gallagher.

Snømann nodded.

Gallagher's world flipped round.

"Oh. Cool! What do we need to do?"

"Well," Snømann started to pull things from the boot. "We'll need some targets. Do the two of you want to erect this stand in the next field? Put some bottles on it. We can try paper targets too, but smashing stuff is always fun, yes? I will prepare the guns."

Gallagher and Luka carried the stand as instructed. They waited until they were a good few yards away before talking.

"I was so fucking sure he was going to shoot us," murmured Gallagher. "Weren't you?"

"No. I knew it was all fine," lied Luka.

Gallagher rolled his eyes. "This could be fun, though! How come he's doing this with us?"

"I wish I fucking knew. Let's just have some fun, eh?"

The stand looked very much like ones they used at Hedgelord. It was made from pressed steel and was a series of shelves arranged like a stepladder. They hefted the stand so that it sat level and was squared towards Snømann, then Gallagher pulled some empty bottles from the carrier bag that was hooked over his arm.

"Smashing glass in a field is definitely against the Countryside Code," he said as he placed them on the shelves.

"You don't want to do it?"

"Oh, I definitely want to do it," said Gallagher. "But I might pick up the glass afterwards. I don't want the fucking bunnies to cut themselves."

"You are friend to the bunnies," laughed Luka as they returned to the SUV. "Me, I would follow the trail of blood so I could find my Christmas dinner."

"Sure you would buddy, sure you would."

Gallagher took a shotgun from Snømann.

"Keep your finger well out of the way of the trigger for now and make sure to point the barrel down the range," instructed Snømann. "Keep the stock pressed hard against the shoulder, and squeeze the trigger gently. Not pull. Now stand like I show you." He stood square on to the target, legs braced.

Gallagher waddled his legs into position and bent his head to look through the sight. "Oh yeah, I can see a bottle. Shall I try and hit it?"

"Aim for a low one, before you get used to the recoil," said Snømann.

Gallagher pulled the trigger and was shocked at the hard thump he felt in his shoulder. "Fuck!" He moved the gun away so that he could rub the area.

"Barrel points down the range, always," snapped Snømann. "Not bad for a first go. I think you went a little high and to the right. You can counter for that."

Gallagher had a few more goes and managed to hit a bottle, much to his delight.

"Now it's time for you to have a go, Luka," said Snømann.

"Sure." Luka took the gun and the shells and loaded with much more ease than Gallagher had managed. He lifted the stock into his shoulder and squeezed off a shot, shattering one bottle, then another.

"Fucking hell mate, you done this before?" Gallagher asked.

Luka gave him a smug grin. "Many things I have done before."

"You two are doing well," said Snømann with a wide smile. "Let us put the shotguns to one side and I will fetch the AK47s. Gallagher, you will destroy the rest of your bottles with one of these."

"Fuck yeah!" breathed Gallagher. When he woke up this morning, he hadn't expected to spend time in the middle of an isolated field firing an assault rifle. This was a good day.

18

ANIKA

Anika went straight to the Pagoda Café as soon as she received Karen's urgent text.

Sophie joined them at their table, carrying prepared drinks. This was unusual. Normally they dawdled over the choosing of drinks, even though they tended to stick to the same choices.

Several men in black boiler suits hovered nearby. Anika glanced at Karen and Sophie who were ignoring the men, so she followed their lead.

"Did you hear about Charlotte?" Karen asked.

Anika shook her head. Karen put a Three Counties Echo down on the table.

"Ooh, Charlotte made the papers!" said Sophie.

Karen stabbed the paper with her finger. "Did you see the headline? 'Garden Centre rivals destroy Christmas'? She's been sacked?"

Anika stared. "Sacked? Like *sacked*?" She understood the

words, but the true meaning wouldn't quite go into her brain. She knew people got sacked from jobs, of course, but those were bad people. Charlotte wasn't a bad person.

"Yep. She cleared out this morning," said Karen. "Marcus and Maremba over at Bloomers have sacked Jack Hartigan, too. Well, I say Marcus and Maremba. That Snømann geezer says he owns both places now."

"My Marti is a very enterprising man," said Sophie.

"I don't get it," said Anika, waving at the pictures. "It looks just as if they're working together in this picture – but he wouldn't even speak to her when we went round there. How did this happen?"

Karen shrugged. "Whatever feelings those two have for each other are strong ones, I reckon. And complicated. It looks as if things got the better of them and they destroyed all this stuff as some sort of collateral damage." She swept a slow hand across the table to demonstrate the path of destruction caused by Charlotte and Jack.

"It was quite the spectacle," said Sophie.

"You were there?" said Anika.

Sophie pointed at one of the pictures on page three. "Look, that's me."

Anika peered closer.

"Excuse me," said a voice.

All three of them looked up. One of the blond-haired men in black boiler suits hovered over the table. "Can I offer you pastries or chocolates? With compliments from Mr Snømann to Sophie and her friends." He lowered a platter that was piled high with delicious snacks onto the table.

"Thank you, Sven," said Sophie, mildly irritated.

Anika examined the various offerings. Anika picked out a marzipan, apple and cinnamon swirl. Karen took an almond croissant.

The man withdrew. Sophie watched him go.

"Those new guys are everywhere," she tutted. "Always under your feet. 'Can I carry that for you, Sophie? Can I clean that for you, Sophie?' It can be too much." She looked back to the newspaper. "Charlotte's gone then? What a shame. Just before Christmas too. A terrible time for a person to lose their job."

"And she's been here for years," said Karen.

"Even though she was a bit odd, I really liked working for her," said Anika.

"Yeah," said Karen. "Someone will need to step up and take her place, won't they?"

Anika heard the tone in her voice. Karen and Sophie were indeed both looking at her.

"Oh, I don't know. It would be weird to try and take advantage of Charlotte's misfortune," said Anika, even though as she said the words, she could feel her brain itching to get to work on a to-do list. Did that make her a massive liar, or just conflicted?

"You could just help out a bit. Couldn't hurt," said Karen. "There's one job that *will* need doing, and I can't see anyone else doing it."

"Yeah? What's that?" asked Anika.

"A leaving collection for Charlotte."

"Do we have leaving collections for people who've been sacked?" Sophie asked with a frown.

"Course we do. Why wouldn't we?" asked Karen. "It's not

as if she's guilty of gross misconduct – although, she probably is – still, people will want to do something, I'm sure."

"Fine, I'll arrange something. I'll need ideas for a gift though, so get your thinking caps on will you?" Anika was already organising the collection in her mind; and then there was the staff rota to do, of course. She wouldn't be stepping into Charlotte's shoes exactly, just keeping them warm for a little while.

She went to the main office. Although it was often the case that Charlotte wasn't in there – the woman wasn't tied to her desk, was she? – but now seeing the empty desk felt like... It felt like someone had died.

Tom Eccles sat at his desk, typing on his computer while talking on the phone.

He saw Anika and beckoned her over with a flick of his fingers. He passed her a lime green post-it note. Anika read it and frowned.

Tom covered the mouthpiece of the phone. "Mr Snømann called. He was out somewhere. Wants you to get on with that."

"Me?" said Anika.

"Asked for you in person," said Tom.

Anika read the task again.

19

CHARLOTTE

On the first full day of being a former Hedgelord employee, Charlotte Mitchell surfed a wave of rage at the injustice of it all.

She rage-cleaned her house, needing to burn off the energy fizzing through her veins, threatening to consume her. She heaved furniture out of the way and got down on her hands and knees to scrub floors and wipe skirting boards. She polished chairs and tables with the kind of aggressive fervour that would fetch off the varnish if she had any grit in her cloth. Not even the bottoms of chair legs escaped her attention. She wanted to eliminate all dirt and gave a vicious grunt of laughter each time she found a new place which concealed dust and fluff. She would conquer it all!

She rage-cleaned the bath by climbing inside and roaring at the limescale as she scrubbed it, daring it to return.

She rage-walked to the supermarket at top speed and did

some rage shopping. She rage-chewed a baguette, gnawing at the end as she walked around the shop. In her mind, she dared someone to challenge her behaviour, but it was a few days before Christmas and the shops were already a battle zone. She'd have to up her game if she wanted to stand out from the crowd.

She needed something else – then she remembered the park with adult fitness stations on the other side of town. She carried her shopping over there and found a stepping machine that overlooked the frosty grass. She plonked down her bags and climbed onto the machine, stepping its mechanism as fast as she could make it go. She yelled her frustration at the empty park. It was moderately exhausting, which was good. Adrenaline kept her going for a long time, then her legs went a bit wobbly and she had to climb down and rootle through the bags for a drink.

She should probably have bought something other than wine, but she would just drink enough to sustain her for the walk home. If she was going to be a cliché then she might as well do it right. She opened a bottle and took a hearty swig before wiping her mouth and picking up her bags. She wondered how quickly she could walk home from here if she put some effort into speed-walking. She took another swig, limbered up, and set off at a punishing pace.

She got home to find a package inside her front porch. She opened it. There was a card that read SORRY TO SEE YOU GO and, inside, more than a dozen signatures from colleagues at Hedgelord. A leaving card! Like she had just switched jobs! Or retired!

There was a plastic gift card inside the card.

Charlotte laughed in disbelief. A Hedgelord gift card. Of all the gifts!

The card's envelope was attached to a jiffy bag on which someone had written. *A small personal thank you for all the time's you helped us. I remember you said how much you liked this.*

Inside the jiffy bag was the brightly coloured Christmas tree brooch Sophie had worn. It was not an attractive thing, but the sight of it nearly brought tears to her eyes. "Oh, Sophie."

Charlotte took the card and the horrible but thoughtful gift inside.

The house was clean now. She had cleaned the inside of the oven, the washing machine's soap drawer, and she'd descaled the kettle. She stood by the kitchen window, staring out at the garden, wondering whether it would be weird to cut the lawn in December and deciding yes, it probably would be. She still needed a way to get the rage out of her system. The rage-cleaning acted like a lightning conductor and she needed to do more of it. If this feeling stayed in her body and mind she was certain it would fry her. She went round the house, looking for something else that needed to be done.

She entered the lounge and smiled at the next task.

She'd put up the Christmas tree in early December, but it was a plastic one she'd bought a few years ago. It brought with it the smell of dust from the loft, which was unsurprising. She snapped on her rubber gloves, removed the decorations and dismantled the tree, carrying the pieces up to the bathroom where she could clean them in the bath.

When she had finished, she huffed with frustration. It still wasn't enough.

She plonked herself down with a cup of tea. Maybe she could fake being a normal person for a while. It would be like roleplay. She could watch television, browse her phone for cat pictures or whatever. She would definitely not obsess on her situation or find ways to indulge violent fantasies.

She pulled out her phone and gazed at social media, looking for something to distract her. One of the first things she saw was Hedgelord's feed. Of course it was. What she hadn't expected was spotting the vacancy for her job.

They had advertised her job already?

It felt like a stab to the heart, but she couldn't help examining it.

Could you be Hedgelord's next Events Manager? This prestigious, senior position invites applicants with several years' experience at planning and hosting large events. Send CVs to Anika Chowdhry.

Of course it would be Anika. Nobody else at Hedgelord would have the wherewithal to get an ad together in such a short space of time. Nobody else would have got the apostrophe placement correct, either.

Charlotte sighed and read through the comments. Mostly it was people tagging their friends and relatives so they would see the ad. There was one that made her sit up and take notice, though.

Bloomers are also replacing their events manager. Good riddance to the two idiots who spoiled everyone's fun at the church nativity!

"Oh, fuck," she sighed. Jack was at the centre of her ball

of weird emotions right now, many of them negative. But he didn't deserve to be fired for the chaos she alone had created the other night.

She immediately switched to the Bloomers feed and saw that they had put up a similar post. In fact, it looked an awful lot like the Hedgelord one, as if someone had spotted Anika's work and cribbed from it.

Charlotte immediately saw where her energy needed to go. It was all very well cleaning the whole house, but there would be bills to pay, and she was currently without a job. If she could divert herself by making the perfect CV and the perfect job application, then that was a positive thing, right? And if she had been a successful events manager at Hedgelord for so long, surely she was a shoo-in at Bloomers?

She thought about how she would lay it all out. There was no doubt that her background and skillset were perfectly suited to fill Jack's shoes, but she needed to explore every avenue and exploit any advantage that she could imagine.

She sighed and typed a text to Jack. *Thinking of applying for your old job. Any top tips on how to pitch to Marcus and Maremba?*

A few minutes later there was a reply. *Hah. I am applying for your job too. Haven't you heard though? Both garden centres have a new boss. Some Finnish guy called Snømann."*

"Well fuck." Charlotte wasn't sure what to make of that.

20

ANIKA

Anika sat at Charlotte's desk, crossing items off her to-do list. She'd kicked off the recruitment process for Charlotte's replacement and the next thing was to address the reputational damage caused by the Christmas tree and nativity debacle. Hedgelord had once again hit the headlines for the wrong reason. It was stunning to contemplate that Hedgelord had brought shame on itself more than once this festive season. There had to be something they could do to elevate their standing in the town once more. If only Anika could think what that might be...

Tom entered the office and waved a brief hello, while Anika twirled a pen and thought about what opportunities might be salvaged from the chaos of Charlotte and Jack smashing things up.

Tom seemed quite unshaken by Charlotte's departure. Anika had never taken him for a callous or cold-hearted man. Maybe he really didn't understand what was going on about him.

After a little research and a phone call, Anika discovered the smashed sleigh had gone for repairs at Bloomers. The rival garden centre had already leapt in to offer a new, albeit smaller Christmas tree to replace the destroyed one.

"Damn," she said. That would have been an easy win.

The next most obvious thing that had not been repaired was the destroyed nativity.

Anika's family were not Christian, and British society, as far as she could tell, was a godless one, but she had been subjected to enough school assemblies and TV shows to remember a bit about nativities. There was the baby Jesus in his crib, plus Mary and Joseph. And the shepherd guys and some kings and, she recalled, a general smattering of farmyard animals. Sheep and cows. Pigs? Maybe. She didn't recall any nativity chickens or ducks, which seemed a bit amiss.

"Donkeys!" she said, suddenly remembering.

And she had half an idea that there was also a camel, but that seemed odd. She wasn't sure why there'd be a camel in a barn.

But yes. That sort of thing.

She googled *life size nativity set* and instantly swore.

Tom looked up at her. "Did you just shout 'fuck me sideways!'?"

"I did," she said. "Apologies. I don't know what came over me."

Tom narrowed his gaze. "Maybe it's Charlotte's spirit haunting that desk."

"She's not dead, Tom."

She looked at the screen again. "Can you believe this? Thirteen thousand pounds for a life-size nativity set."

"Thirteen thousand?"

She read aloud. "'Twenty one elements. A Mary, Joseph, three times Wise Man, one angel...' Thirteen thousand. And it's a three week wait for delivery."

Tom grunted with amusement. "For that money you could just pay people to stand still and play the parts."

She grunted back at his tedious crack, then had a thought.

She thought some more.

The idea had merit.

She jotted some notes and then went to find Daffyd.

The head elf was relaxing in his tiny dressing room at the back of the grotto. The boards making up the scenery backed onto an area that he had converted into his own office and star dressing room. He had the obligatory make-up table with lightbulbs round the mirror. Along two walls were racks of outfits, including the fancy dress priest clothes he'd worn for Charlotte's 'confession' the other day.

She slipped in, knocking on the wood panel wall as she entered. "Daffyd?"

"Entré, sweet ingénue," he said, beckoning her in. He wasn't down for any grotto duty, and yet he was in full elf costume.

"What is it you're doing today?" she asked, gesturing.

"Understudy of course," he replied smoothly. "We never know when we might need another pair of hands in the grotto do we? I can use the downtime to hone my various skills. You know – juggling and so on."

"Yeah?" Anika wondered what he'd really been doing, then decided it was probably better not to know. "Listen, I had an idea."

"Always a fan of your ideas, Anika. From the mouths of babes and wotnot. Tell me what you're thinking."

"Well," she began, not a hundred percent sure what the idea in her own mind was at this point, "you know the nativity that got smashed up at St Stephens church...?"

"Oh I know, right? What a sight that must have been. I can't believe I missed it." Daffyd shook his head in sorrow.

"Well, perhaps it gives us the opportunity to repair some of the damage done to Hedgelord's reputation. If we replace the nativity, I mean."

"Ha! Good luck with that, miss. Do you know how much proper nativity statues cost?"

"Um, yes. I did look it up. Which is what gave me the idea. What do you think to the notion of a live action nativity?"

"Live action?"

Anika frowned at her own choice of words. "When I say, 'live action', there's not a lot of action. I really mean that we'd have some people standing in for the statuettes."

Daffyd stared at her with wide eyes. The longer he stared the more his eyes widened. He stepped towards her and grasped her hand in a way that was intense and slightly alarming. "I do get what you mean, and I think it's a marvellous idea."

"Oh good."

"I can see it now!" He broke away and swept his arms in the manner of an impresario describing a huge production. "A *son et lumière*...!"

"A what?"

"...With a rousing soundtrack to draw in passers-by who will peer at the sleeping infant in his manger. 'Look at him! King of all kings, he is come! He sleeps peacefully, but this is the Son of God! Rejoice!'"

Anika understood. "Ah, yes I see. And the infant Jesus – I suppose we'd need a baby."

Daffyd stepped back and adopted a simple poised position, not unlike a ballet dance. "Peel back the layers of the man and you find the boy. Peel back the boy and the find the baby." He wrapped an invisible shawl about himself. "*Das Christkind's* pure innocence and holiness can be embodied by any actor."

"Oh, *you* would play the infant Jesus?"

"Of course! That's what you're asking, isn't it?" Daffyd said, puzzled.

"Um—"

"That's settled, then," he declared. "We're going to need a massive manger of course. I know a props guy who can do a rush job."

"That's great. I'll call the Reverend Ralph Robertson and set things up," said Anika.

21

GALLAGHER

The following day, Gallagher and Luka were brewing a cup of tea when Snømann entered the shed, all smiles.

Gallagher got to his feet. "Morning, Mr Snømann."

Doing a spot of shooting practice in the countryside the day before had really been good for Gallagher's mental wellbeing. Not only had it cemented in his mind the idea that Snømann had softened towards them a little, but it turned out taking potshots at targets with a range of firearms did something wonderful for one's general stress levels.

"Good morning, Gallagher. Good morning, Luka," said Snømann. "I wanted to see whether the two of you are ready to take the next step in my organisation."

"Next step?" said Luka.

"Yeah, you know. Join the programme."

Luka grunted. "You mean getting dressed up in boiler suits like your other men?"

Snømann waved a hand as though it was obvious. "They are aviator suits. Designed especially for me. They look good, don't they? They would suit the two of you, I think."

Gallagher thought about all the precise and efficient men who had been taking up roles in the garden centre of late. Blond Man Group. They were all Snømann's employees.

"There are other uniform options for different situations," said Snømann.

"Aviator suits." Gallagher thought they sounded rather cool. He wanted to ask about going to the toilet wearing an all-in-one, but that seemed like a thing he could probably figure out in private. He looked at Luka and wondered if they made the aviator suits for the more portly senior gentleman.

"What does it mean 'join the programme'?" asked Luka.

"Oh, I have a full programme of training and career progression. It will start with very basic tasks, but you did well at the informal firearms experience, so I think you will climb the ladder quickly."

A little part of Gallagher wanted to point out that, as plantsmen in an out-of-town garden centre, they really had no ladder to climb, and in many ways liked their lives that way. But he was curious.

"What's it like, further up the ladder?"

"Training is more involved," said Snømann. "Similar to security staff or military skills. Things like defensive driving techniques."

"Cool!" Gallagher loved the idea of defensive driving. Would he get to drive that tank-like SUV of Snømann's?

"It certainly won't involve you offering any more advice

on my love life." The Scandinavian chuckled, pointing at his still-red ears.

"Allergic reaction very uncommon," Luka muttered.

"You are interested in the role, then?" said Snømann. "Good. I will send over some aviator suits in your sizes, and arrange an induction."

With that, he left.

Gallagher and Luka looked at each other.

"I am really not sure what is going on," said Luka.

"Boiler suits," said Gallagher.

"Military training."

"We get to be part of Blond Man Group."

Luka made a noise. "We forgot to ask him about pay rise. We should ask about pay rise."

"Next time," said Gallagher and finished making the tea.

22

ANIKA

Anika found Karen when she had stepped away from the tills for a break.

"Right," she said with a sigh to convey her busy but interesting work. "Work rotas done. Things smoothed over with St Stephen's church. Plan for live action nativity underway. And I've sorted through the current applications for Charlotte's replacement."

"And we can stick a broom up your arse and you can sweep as you go," said Karen cheerily.

"I like being busy. It's all good for the CV."

"Excellent," said Karen, "because we also agreed to help our new boss come up with ideas for how he can spend time with his Sophie."

"We did," Anika agreed.

"And I'm really looking at you," said Karen. "You are the ideas woman, Mine pretty much amounted to Netflix and chill."

"Do you see them as a Netflix and chill couple?" asked Anika. "For one thing we'd need to explain what it means to Sophie."

Karen gave her a look. "Come on, then. Tell me what you've thought of."

They walked together through the store, heading slowly towards the break room.

"What we need is to create a situation," said Anika.

"Situation?"

"Yeah. You know how in films, there is always that part where the two romantic leads are thrust together into a situation. They are forced to spend time together, and it's a chance to see some sparks fly." Anika mimed sparks flying, her eyes wide.

"Huh," said Karen. "I think so. But how do we make it happen?"

Anika tapped her phone. "Well, I have a list. Want to hear them?"

"Obviously!"

"Here we go. Idea number one is really straightforward. We get them booked into the pod at the Granary pub."

"Oh, those dining pods left over from Covid. I hear they're really swanky."

"Right. It's famous for being special and quite romantic."

"I like it."

"We order them the nicest wine, they will be left alone because it's deliberately isolated, and we let nature take its course."

"Okay, that is nice. And it's not my money we're spending, right? So, yeah. Go for it."

Anika appreciated the support. "Here's another idea, but it's a bit more off-the-wall. It's dog walking. The kennels at Little Brockley are always looking for volunteer dog walkers. We get a couple of dogs dropped off for them and they get to go for a nice romantic walk together."

"I mean, dogs!" said Karen with a thumbs up. "Sophie would love that! We definitely must do that one. In fact, do that one first. I'm excited for her, she's going to have a ball." Her expression turned thoughtful. "What if Sophie pays the dog more attention than Snømann?"

Anika shrugged. "Again, we let nature take its course."

Karen narrowed her eyes. "You don't entirely approve of this guy for Sophie?"

Anika tried to put her thoughts in the correct order. "Hmmm. I don't think it's my place to say if someone is right or wrong for her."

"What? Even if he's well dodgy or creepy?"

Anika smiled. "Do I think he's dodgy? Yeah, a bit. No – a lot. He's turned up out of the blue and all of a sudden he's our boss. I feel a fast one's being pulled on us here. But maybe that doesn't matter. I'm just a jumped-up elf. Temporary worker. On the other hand, do I think that he could be good for Sophie? Also yes. She's super old—"

"She's in her sixties, Anika."

"—Right. So her chances for happiness... She's not got many left." She gave Karen an encouraging look. "I want Sophie to be happy, so I will get on and make some bookings for these love traps."

"Love traps? That what you're calling them?" said Karen,

smirking. "You could almost make a crusty old cynic believe in the power of love!"

Out of nowhere, Daffyd appeared, striding into the break room and delivering a lusty version of Frankie Goes to Hollywood's *The Power of Love*.

He grinned at the two startled women. "Well, who could resist?" He swooshed two large pieces of fabric about. "I need an opinion on my outfit."

He draped the white sheet over his front. "White. Pure, holy, humble." He switched it for the gold sheet. "Gold. Striking, regal—" He dropped into an inexplicable American accent. "Aw, truly this man was the Son of God." He looked from Anika to Karen.

"Are you going to a toga party?" said Karen.

"It's for a nativity thing we're sort of planning," said Anika.

"Planning?" said Daffyd. "No, no, no, Anika. It is happening. My co-stars are ready, all in place for this evening."

"This evening?" This was not what she had agreed to or wanted. "I think I'd rather see what you've got planned. Small scale first."

Daffyd's eyes sparkled. "Yes! Yes! Small local provincial run at first and, if it works, we take it national. My one-man nativity wonder showcase on the road!"

"One man?" said Karen. "I thought you said you had co-stars."

The round, bald man chortled. "Ho ho. Just you wait and see!"

Karen tapped Anika on the arm. She looked up. Snømann was approaching.

He pointed a meaty finger. "Anika. I need to have a word with you."

"With me?"

He beckoned her to follow and she did, fearing he'd somehow heard the comments about him being a bit creepy.

"We have work to do," he said, as he led her up the stairs to his office.

"Yes?" said Anika.

"I have an important upcoming event that I will need some help with. It appears you are the person who is best placed to help me."

"Oh."

This was good, surely? She was pleased that she had been recognised for her capability. "Happy to help. What do you have in mind?"

In Cameron's old office, he threw himself back into the comfy chair behind the desk. It wasn't the exaggerated lounging Cameron used to do – more like a small movement to draw her in as he stretched out his arms to illustrate the size of the undertaking. "We will have a lunchtime celebration event on Christmas Eve. All colleagues from Hedgelord and Bloomers will attend and it will be really special."

"Oh, that's lovely. Everyone together."

"I thought so too."

"But don't you think some colleagues might be busy with their families on Christmas Eve?" Anika asked.

"It is lunchtime. No problem. It is important that

everyone makes time for this. We will need to stress this in all communications," said Snømann.

Anika realised she should be making notes. She pulled out her phone. "Right. Got it. Where will the celebration take place?"

"A rented marquee in the place you call the paddock," said Snømann. "The biggest marquee we can possibly hire, heated of course. Decorated in the Scandinavian tradition, please."

"So, an example of that might be...?"

"A Yule Goat is important. Make sure it is as large as possible. It should be isolated in the paddock so that we can set fire to it as part of the event."

"Big marquee in the paddock. Yule Goat. Right."

"As for the other details, I will leave them to you, but I want lavish catering and most definitely a mood of opulence should prevail. Is that clear?"

"It is clear. Can I get some help from other people? It will be a lot to do in a short time."

"Yes of course. The men have been briefed, and they will expect a task list for setup and breakdown. Employ them for any other tasks that seem of a physical nature. For the planning you can of course get help as you need it from other members of staff. Perhaps my Sophie might enjoy the chance to be involved with this, under your supervision?"

"Very good!" said Anika. "I will go and chat with her now."

"Thank you." He waved a hand to indicate she was dismissed.

Anika went down to the ground floor and walked over to

the café to find Sophie. She was serving breakfasts, wearing a floaty silk dress.

"Nice dress Sophie," said Anika.

"Thanks, Anika. Snømann gave it to me."

Anika thought it looked pretty expensive to be splashed with bacon fat, but said nothing.

"Listen, I've got a new thing I'd like you to help me with. Snømann wants a big celebration party on Christmas Eve. There's lots to do, so I wondered if you might help with some of the planning?"

"I'd love to," said Sophie. "You'll need to tell me what to do, though. I'm not as organised as you are."

"Let's get our heads together a bit later. We can work through some of the things we need to get done."

"Lovely!" Sophie grinned. "Oh, do take a mince pie on the way out. We've got free samples today. We're trying to push them in the shop so we don't have loads left over."

"Oh nice, I will."

Anika turned to the table near the exit. There was a sign.

Mince pie's. Take one to try!

She thought about getting Sophie to change the sign, but she'd need her help. She reached across to see if she could discreetly rub out the misplaced apostrophe with a finger while she took a mince pie with the other hand. She was very nearly successful. She sighed – it would have to do.

23

GALLAGHER

Gallagher and Luka faced the member of Blond Man Group in the boiler suit who had appeared outside their tea shed. Gallagher reminded himself that it was an aviator suit, not a boiler suit, although he didn't really know the difference.

"I have your uniform," said the stranger. "Get changed and come with me."

"Pleased to meet you. I am Luka." He shook the hand of the stranger. Gallagher could see Luka was trying to slow things down and assert a little control.

"Sven," said the stranger.

"How long have you been here, Sven? I've seen some of your colleagues around."

"This is my first week. I will now perform your induction. Uniforms please."

Sven was both bossy and polite. It was a tricky

combination to resist, so Gallagher took the uniform with a smile.

"What size is this?" asked Luka, taking his and holding it up.

"It is the correct size," said Sven.

"No," said Luka. "Says here it is XXL. Is not right."

"It will fit. We shortened the legs," said Sven. "Try it please."

Gallagher could see this answer irritated Luka, who was presumably questioning the girth rather than the length.

There was no sensible way of retreating to a private space to change, so Gallagher stripped off where he was. Luka did the same, emitting a constant soundtrack of low grumbles.

Moments later they both stood in their suits.

"Maybe with a belt it will fit," conceded Luka as he paced back and forth in his uniform.

It looked like a perfect fit to Gallagher, but he nodded in agreement anyway. He wished there was a mirror handy so he could see how he looked. He had a feeling it was probably flattering for his skinny frame.

"Good!" said Sven. "Follow me."

They went with Sven out through the overflow carpark. The warehouses off to the side seemed to be a hive of noisy activity. Several of the Blond Man Group – how many were there on site? Thirty? Forty? – seemed to be engaged in large-scale construction activity. Sven led them into the paddock, which was little-used at this time of year, apart from special events which needed the space.

Gallagher saw it had been laid out as some sort of

obstacle course. "What's this? Nobody said there would be running races."

"Relax," said Sven with a smile that did not encourage relaxation. "This is a gentle warm-up. It will get the blood circulating."

Gallagher was very wary when tall, athletic gym-bunny types talked about a gentle warm-up, but he couldn't think of a way to retreat without losing face. He could see Luka wasn't happy with what lay ahead either.

"You see these obstacles?" Sven asked. "You will do a single circuit as individuals, and then you will go round again working as a team. Understood?"

Gallagher nodded, but Luka raised an arm. "There are rules here? Tell us what they are."

"No rules. Your objective is to navigate the obstacles," said Sven. "I will time your efforts, starting now." He tapped his phone.

"Fuck. Come on buddy," said Gallagher.

There was a low wall for them to climb as the first obstacle. It was made of hay bales and both Gallagher and Luka managed to hoist themselves over without too much trouble.

There were two lines of car tyres laid out for them to step through. Was it a test of agility? Gallagher pranced through them, and could see Luka lumbering alongside, much more slowly.

Then they came upon a rope swing, with a long water jump underneath. Gallagher marvelled that someone had built this entire course recently. Was the water jump made from pond liners? It looked like it.

"What the fuck am I supposed to do with this?" Luka asked as he drew up alongside. "I am heavy guy. This swing will not support me."

Gallagher knew what Luka really meant was that he lacked the upper body strength to support his full weight on the swing, but Sven jogged over, grabbed the rope and swung over with ease. He pointed to his back. "I weigh sixty kilos and I have an extra twenty in this backpack. The swing is rated for one hundred. You will be fine."

Luka did not look happy with the news.

"Hey! Buddy!" Gallagher whispered. "He said we have to navigate the obstacles. He did not say how."

Luka nodded in understanding. "This is true." He bent down, removed his boots and socks and paddled through the water. "Is fucking cold."

Gallagher attempted the swing, and very nearly made it straight over, but he toppled backwards at the last moment and sat down in the water. He lurched out, spluttering. "Bollocks! You're right, it is cold!"

They made it over the agility net and through the muddy tunnel, ending up back with Sven at the starting point.

"You have returned. Your time is recorded for your training record. Now you may go round again as a team, see if you can improve your speed." Sven restarted his timer.

"Right. Come with me," said Luka. He made straight for the agility net, where a small ladder was propped up on the far side. "We take this and use it on all obstacles."

"No rules," shrugged Gallagher.

The two of them picked up an end of the ladder and jogged to the first obstacle. Each time they reached something challenging they used the ladder to clear it without difficulty.

When they got back round to meet Sven he gave a small nod of acknowledgement. "An improvement. This bodes well for teamwork. You are wet. We will get you fresh uniforms before your first classroom based session."

"Classroom?" Gallagher was crestfallen. He'd expected something more interesting.

"The stripping down of a rifle."

"Oh. *That* kind of classroom stuff. Sounds alright," said Gallagher with a shivering grin at Luka.

24

ANIKA

Anika and Sophie were in the office. Anika typed into a spreadsheet while Sophie had an A4 pad in front of her which she was filling up with words and squiggles. All this in effort to create a spectacular celebration event for the staff on Christmas Eve.

"What does the word 'opulent' say to you, Sophie?" asked Anika.

Sophie thought hard. "No bones. Definitely no bones."

Anika knew Sophie was capable of mentally swerving in unusual directions, but this one left her confused. "Eh? You'll need to explain that one to me."

"For the catering. Quite often there will be a cheap version with bones, or a fancy version with no bones."

"Sorry? Try again."

"Like you can have a salmon steak with bones or you can have a salmon fillet with no bones. Same with chicken. You can have a chicken thigh with bones or a chicken breast with no bones. If you tell people it's opulent and they have bones they'd be pretty upset, I think."

Anika's hands hovered at the keyboard. "We already selected the catering menu. I don't think there were any bones, were there?"

"Oh no. No bones. But you asked the question," said Sophie.

"What I really meant," explained Anika, "was, 'Are there any aspects of opulence that we ought to be including for this event that we didn't yet cover?'."

"Oh, I see." Sophie pulled a face as she thought hard. "Christmas crackers!"

"Good point. We've not talked about those," said Anika. "I wonder what the opulent version of Christmas crackers is?"

"Well!" Sophie looked really pleased with herself. "Would you believe my neighbour Desiree has a business where she does this?"

"She makes opulent crackers?"

"She makes up party bags, wedding favours – anything you like. I could ask her?"

Anika nodded. "We'd need to tell her what we want, I guess. We'd need to describe an opulent Christmas cracker. I'm just not sure I know what that looks like."

Sophie put her hands on the desk, palms inwards, a foot apart. "From the outside it will look like a regular Christmas cracker. It's what's on the inside that matters. We need a really special gift that's the right size for a cracker."

"Good point." Anika thought hard. "What was that fancy pen Cameron had? You remember how loads of people said it was nice? We could find out what that was and get some of those. If we knew where Cameron was, anyway."

"Oh, I can help with that," said Sophie. "He's in the Alpine Lodge."

"The what?"

"The Alpine Lodge. I've been popping in with his meals."

"I thought he was on holiday."

Sophie paused and frowned. "I might be getting confused. Anyway, shall I get on and sort out the crackers?"

"That would be amazing" said Anika, who was happy to ignore Sophie's occasional diversion into old person ramblings. "You got everything you need to do that?"

Sophie added *Cracker's containing silver-plated pen's like Cameron's* to her messy notepad with a flourish. "Yep! Leave it with me."

Anika was not going to waste time battling with Sophie's rogue apostrophes. "Thanks," she said. "That will free me up so I can source the materials for our Yule Goat artist. I've got someone who can build what we need at the kind of scale Snømann's asking for, but she needs a load of specialist supplies."

By teatime, Charlotte had checked her phone for the umpteenth time that day. She hadn't heard back about her job application for Jack Hartigan's position. Would she even get a response this side of Christmas? She'd assumed that she was the best candidate by a mile and half-hoped she'd be snapped up as soon as she applied. Of course, recruitment didn't work like that. She also suspected she might be immediately disqualified because she'd been part of the same incident which had led to Jack's termination.

She hated all this waiting around. She wanted to be doing something, and ideally it should not involve smashing things.

Christmas was only four days away and she'd already done much of her Christmas planning. Christmas day itself, as always, was dinner with her mum. They were a tidy, two-person family and rubbed along perfectly well. The widowed Mrs Mitchell had not been in touch with Charlotte about any of the calamities that had hit the headlines, which either meant she'd not read the news recently or, more likely, had decided to keep quiet about it.

Charlotte had rechecked the local news on the internet. Fortunately, it seemed the destroyed tree and nativity had been shoved from the top spot by some story about a lorry of smuggled goods or something.

THREE COUNTIES POLICE *are keen to speak to the driver of a transport lorry after he fled during a routine traffic stop. The lorry, believed to contain manufacturing equipment, was stopped on the A31 between Clopton Howes and Canon's Ashby. The driver, Bargus Popovicu, who had brought the lorry over from Europe via Dover, spoke to the police briefly before fleeing across the fields. A police search is underway.*

AN ODD STORY, she thought. At least it was dragging public attention away from her horrible moment of fame.

She had no idea if her mum had seen her shameful appearance in the papers. However, the Mitchell family were big believers in "least said, soonest mended". Problems, scandals and upsets were never dwelt upon. The focus was always on a more positive future. The Mitchells never psychoanalysed themselves. "Bloody navel-gazing" her dad had called it. It was better to just get on with life and accept those upsets that were bound to occur along the way. And, yes, that might mean Charlotte squashed down her emotions at times and, yes, that might mean those compressed emotions might come out in an inappropriate manner, but that was the price to be paid for a peaceful, quiet family life.

Right now, Charlotte had too much energy and emotion bubbling inside her to simply keep it pressed down. She was both bored and irritated. She was a woman adrift. She needed to do something.

And so, wrapping up against the increasingly chilly weather, she decided to go out for some early evening shopping. Some final Christmas presents, some extra bits of food for Christmas day, or maybe just a big fatty dessert and a bottle of wine to cheer herself up tonight. It didn't matter really.

Being thoroughly wrapped up, this time with a large scarf covering her face rather than the distinctive furry hat, she hoped for anonymity and, as she walked through the shopping area, was pleased to go unrecognised. She popped into a shop here, another there, but the truth was she didn't really want to buy anything. She couldn't buy her way out of her current misery.

And inevitably, unwisely, she found her footsteps leading

her back to the scene of the crime. She approached St Stephen's in a circuitous manner, but there was no fooling herself.

The church was currently in darkness. There was a newer, smaller Christmas tree in the place of the destroyed one. The only evidence of the previous tree was a long sooty scorch mark across the pavement.

The smashed nativity had also been cleared away. In its place, a new display shed had been erected (a Tunbridge Slimline she noted, recognising a shed from Hedgelord's own line). One side of the shed was fully open, and from within came a golden light and, oddly, the sound of a man's voice, amplified through a speaker.

"And Lo! the shepherds did heed the angel's words and gathered their flock – Flossy, Dolly, Betty, Jenny and Fluffkin – and set off for the city of Bethlehem."

Charlotte approached the shed cautiously. A smattering of other people were gathered. None stood too close – just watching with heads turned as though they really had no clue what it was they were beholding.

Inside the shed was a new nativity. Well, it appeared to contain some salvaged parts of the original nativity. There was a sooty Mary bent in prayer over the manger. And across from her, a wise man with part of his head crushed looked on benevolently with one eye. And behind them both, tucked into the shed, was a donkey. Oh, God, it was a real live donkey in there!

However, a live donkey in the shed was not the strangest part of the display. That unique accolade surely had to be given to the baby Jesus.

The front of the shed was taken up by a massive manger: basically a plain funeral casket on legs. Within, buried under piles and piles of swaddling white sheets, was the baby Jesus. A giant baby Jesus. Or, to be blunt, a naked Daffyd from work. Well, he looked naked. Certainly, the shoulders and arms poking out of the top of the sheets was unclothed.

Daffyd, lying down in his manger bed, held a microphone connected to a PA speaker and was apparently narrating the birth story of Christ. Christ narrating his own birth. Charlotte had to concede it was a meta version of the narrative unlike any she had previously encountered.

"And the shepherds reached the humble stable where the Christ child lay. The baby saw them and recognised them." Daffyd lowered his microphone, and with wide goo-goo baby eyes reached up his hands in greeting to the imagined shepherds.

It was... Charlotte struggled to find the words. It was both horrible and mesmerising. She stayed far too long, eventually managing to tear herself from the scene and back away into the darkness.

25

ANIKA

Anika had booked the 'love traps' for Sophie and Snømann, as well as sorting out the recent changes to the grotto rotas. She left for the day feeling super productive.

She made a mental note to go and check in on Daffyd's one-man nativity story but, when she got home, she discovered that her Uncle Arjun and his family were visiting. She enjoyed spending time with her younger cousins – Rohan and Priya – and found herself exercising some of her newfound grotto skills to entertain them. Once she'd run through her reindeer facts and cracker jokes, she produced the juggling balls she'd bought so that they could all have a go.

It was a lovely evening, filled with all the right kinds of distractions, and hours later Anika realised she'd had a really good time. She glanced at her phone for the first time in ages and saw there were a lot of notifications.

There was a series of texts from Daffyd.

Here's a pic of me all set up at the nativity, all neatly wrapped in swaddling clothes! I had to get someone to help with that. They left me one hand free to operate my phone and microphone, and they will come back in three hours.

The picture showed him bound tightly and laid out in what must have been a really massive crib.

She read the next text.

I should have put some thermals on under the swaddling clothes, but as you know I am a method actor, so I just have an adult nappy on underneath. It's pretty cold here, there's frost on the ground. If you're around, can you bring a warm drink or a hot water bottle?

Anika checked the time on that message. It was from nearly two hours ago. There were further messages.

I can't feel most of my body now. Please help.

"Oh shit!"

It wasn't even the last message.

Some drunk people came by and decided that this was a urinal. Any other time, I might have enjoyed the experience, but now I'm wet. I just want to sleep. I think I might be dying. Can I text for an ambulance? Going to try

She looked up from her phone. "Mum! Dad! Can you give me a lift into town please!" she yelled, trying to explain as simply as possible.

"Our Anika is very important," her mum cooed to Uncle Arjun. "She is responsible for all their special events."

It took five minutes to get her parents to stop bragging about her; another ten before Anika's dad pulled up outside St Stephen's church. The streets were now deserted.

Anika rushed to look at the nativity scene. It was visually stunning, with Mary and Joseph gazing serenely over the crib. Mary had sustained some damage during the events of the other night, but she'd been positioned so that her good side faced the street. A donkey stood over the crib. Anika couldn't remember seeing it before.

From a speaker to the side came a stammering little voice, every second word punctuated with a tiny sob. *"On the eighth day of Christmas my true love gave to me..."*

Anika went to look in the crib.

There was a fat bald man shivering in it, his face paler than the sheets he was wrapped in.

"Help me..." said Daffyd in the tiniest voice. "So cold..."

The donkey moved and Anika let out a small scream of surprise. It was a real donkey! It leaned over into the crib and she tried to push it away. It pushed its face into her arm and bit down.

"Ow! Fuck you!"

"Language, Anika!" Anika's mum followed behind with the first aid box she'd insisted on bringing, even though Anika had said it wasn't something needing bandages and safety pins.

"It bit me!"

"Me too," came Daffyd's small voice. "But I can't feel it anymore. It's all frozen."

Her mum took one look at Daffyd and called over to the car. "Sunil! Come here and lift him out!"

"I need to move the car, this is not a good place to park," he said.

"Leave the car and come here."

Together, they got Daffyd onto his feet and out of the crib.

"Oh, my God, you're naked!" said Anika, grabbing at his slipping sheets.

"Th-there's nothing to see," Daffyd shivered. "It's all shrivelled up to nothing. I th-think I might have f-f-f-frostbite."

Anika's mum pulled a foil blanket from the first aid box and wrapped it around him. "Why does he smell so bad?" she whispered.

Anika didn't share what Daffyd had said in his last message, and just shrugged instead.

"Into the car, come on," said her mum. "We don't want to be seen. People will think we're kidnapping baby Jesus."

"What shall I do about the donkey?" Anika said, but nobody was listening. She grabbed the rope attached to his halter and tied him to the church's door knocker. She had no idea whose donkey it was.

Daffyd wasn't an easy load to steer, but they got him into the back seat of the car.

"Are we taking him to A&E?" asked Anika.

Her mum pulled a face. "He will sit for a long time waiting to be seen. We will take him home and try to gently warm him."

Anika had been afraid her mum might say that. She was keen to help Daffyd, but she was less keen to bring him into her family home. She didn't want to describe him as a weirdo, and it would be wholly unfair to call him creepy. But there was a selfish and peculiar energy to Daffyd that gave off unnatural goblin-like vibes. She didn't really want that energy or those vibes in her home.

But Anika's mum was insistent. A few minutes later, Daffyd was on the settee in the Choudrys' lounge, still wrapped in his foil blanket.

Anika realised her mum had discreetly slipped a plastic bin bag underneath to protect the settee from what obviously smelled like urine. Now her parents fussed around trying to come up with ways to warm him up.

"I can bring a fan heater," said her dad, "blow it onto him."

"Absolutely not!" said her mum. "We need to heat him gently, not suddenly. He does need to remove any wet garments, though."

Anika realised her parents were looking at her. "What?"

"You must leave the room while we undress your friend," said her mum.

"Oh. Right, yes." Anika scampered out of the lounge as quickly as she could. She had no interest at all in seeing Daffyd without his clothes. This had got weird *really* quickly.

26

GALLAGHER

Gallagher and Luka were on a night-time exercise with Snømann's men.

"Tell you what mate, this is fucking brilliant!" he said to Luka.

This was absolutely not the kind of thing Gallagher had expected to spend his evening doing. Usually, if anyone suggested he do some extra work for free he'd be laughing and telling them to jump in a ditch. But something called a 'night-time exercise' seemed somehow far more exciting. Anyway, the only alternative was to go back to his dingy flat above the Chinese takeaway and stare at the black mould all evening.

Gallagher and Luka had left the garden centre in a small convoy of the fancy Volvos. They were being driven at speed by one of the Blond Men Group. The countryside whipped past as they lounged in the comfortable leather seats.

"What did you say your name was?" Gallagher asked the driver.

"Sven," he said cheerily.

Gallagher frowned slightly. "Are they all called Sven?" he mouthed to Luka.

Luka just grinned. He didn't care.

"Do you know what we're doing on this exercise, Sven?" Gallagher asked. "In case we need to prepare or anything?"

"Er, it is teamwork training. Full instructions will be given upon arrival," said Sven.

There was silence in the car until they pulled up in a lay-by near the isolated and slightly elevated wooded area called Picket's Copse.

Luka and Gallagher joined the group of a dozen Svens who all stood in line. Someone came along the line and gave each of them a head torch, which they all strapped on. They were given a whistle too.

Snømann stood and addressed them all. "What I would like for you all to do is to fan out so that you entirely surround this wooded area. It's a lovely wood. I am bringing my lady friend here tomorrow. Fan out so you will be around twenty yards apart from the next man. You will turn off your head torches, maintain this position and ensure that nobody approaches the woods. If you see someone, you will give two short blasts on your whistle. The exercise will be over when you hear six short blasts from a whistle. Understood?"

They all nodded and marched off. Gallagher couldn't stop himself from smiling. It was as if he belonged to some sort of cool group of commandos or something. As he walked away, he saw someone being taken out of one of the

Volvos. He was not dressed in one of the boiler suits and wasn't tall or blond like the others.

"Bargus, you will come this way, with me," said Snømann, heading into the trees, Bargus stumbling alongside. He had not been given a head torch.

"Mr Snømann sir," the man stuttered in poor English. "I am sorry about the lorry..."

"The lorry is gone," said Snømann, "but our business is not yet done."

Snømann and the man called Bargus were soon lost in the dark woods.

Luka and Gallagher fell into step together as they walked around the perimeter of the woods. "Is it wrong that I want to give the whistle a quick toot, just to see what it sounds like?" Gallagher said.

"Fuck's sake, don't be an idiot!" growled Luka.

Gallagher knew he wouldn't, but he felt giddy with the oddly comforting camaraderie that came from being in this isolated place with a group of well-trained people who had welcomed him into their ranks.

They arranged themselves in position, looking out over the fields, protecting the woods. Gallagher knew it was just an exercise, and that no threat was expected, but he looked out with fierce concentration, determined to be the first to spot anyone approaching. The night was cold, but he was still warm from the walk, and he was certain that he could stay alert for a good long time. The Moon was bright, and Gallagher could see further than he expected, now his eyes had adjusted. He glanced across at Luka, who stood still like a sentry. Gallagher wondered if he could do that, rather than fidgeting with nervous energy, but then he'd stay warmer for longer if he moved around a bit.

A little over twenty minutes later Gallagher heard six whistle blasts. The exercise was over. The head torches went back on and he joined the flow of men making their way back to the Volvos.

"See anything?" he asked Luka.

"Maybe deer in distance," said Luka.

Gallagher was envious. He'd seen nothing at all the entire time. They climbed back into their Volvo as Snømann emerged from the woods. Bargus was elsewhere, and Gallagher wondered what part of the exercise they'd been carrying out under the cover of the trees.

ANIKA'S MUM had insisted on Daffyd staying the night in the spare room, so she could be sure he was fully recovered. It was unsettling how swiftly Daffyd slipped into the role of vulnerable child, and how her mother accepted the giant, man-sized baby. She gave him a pair of pyjamas and tucked him up in bed. For all Anika knew, she'd read him a bedtime story as well.

In the morning, Daffyd was faced with the choice of wearing his swaddling clothes (freshly laundered) or jogging bottoms and a t-shirt belonging to Anika's dad. He chose the jogging bottoms, so Anika ate breakfast alongside the disturbing sight of Daffyd cosplaying her dad.

"Sunil! Come to the table!" called her mum. "We have a guest. You must eat more, Daffyd," she insisted. "You will need your strength after suffering trauma."

"Trauma, yes I suppose you're right," said Daffyd. He was pulling some sort of kicked puppy face especially for her mum, which made Anika roll her eyes.

"You have something to say Anika?" asked her mum sharply.

"Just wondering if you're up to work today, or whether you might need a rest day," Anika said to Daffyd. "Because of trauma?"

"I think I can soldier on," he said, bravely.

"Daffyd, I need to ask you whose donkey that was at the church last night," Anika continued. "I'll have to go and take it back where it belongs."

Daffyd stared at her. "Donkey? I don't remember there being a donkey."

"You've got bite marks on your arms, Daffyd. How do you think you got those?"

Daffyd lifted his arms and stared at the bruises. "To be honest, I quite often get these. I think nothing of it."

Anika walked to St Stephens, hoping the donkey would have been collected by its owner by now. She sighed when she got there and it was still tethered to the door as she'd left it. It drew curious glances from early passers-by, but no one seemed inclined to claim it.

She untied it, mindful of its bitey behaviour the night before. "Who do you belong to?" she asked. "How did you even get here?"

The donkey gave no answer, so Anika led it away, patting its neck, even though it had bruised her arm last night when it bit her.

"Right, come on, then. You can meet the reindeer at

Hedgelord. You can stop in their compound while we work out where you belong."

She led the donkey along the route to the garden centre, getting more toots than usual from the passing traffic as she was dressed as an elf and leading a donkey. It was an eye-catching look, she had to admit.

She was almost at Hedgelord when her father pulled up in his car and opened the window. "What are you doing, Anika?"

Daffyd was in the passenger seat. Her dad was giving the ridiculous man a lift to work.

"I'm taking care of this donkey," said Anika, waving an arm at the annoying, bitey beast. "I couldn't just leave it outside the church, could I?"

"Make sure you wash your hands after handling that thing!" called her mum from the back seat.

"Will do, mum."

27

CHARLOTTE

As another morning wore on without news of her job application to Bloomers, Charlotte decided she just needed to get out of the house. And even if her conscious mind would not admit it, getting out of the house meant going to Hedgelord – or at least going as close to it as she dared.

She might have had her job viciously ripped away from her, but that didn't mean she didn't still belong. It was like those stories she'd read of people who'd had their arms amputated but could still feel them, itching or twitching. Phantom limbs, that's what they called them. Charlotte didn't know if there was such a thing as a phantom garden centre, but if there was, that was what she was feeling.

She felt sure she was persona non grata at Hedgelord at the moment, but there was a good vantage point from near Picket's Copse. The general landscape around the town was flat and dull, but there was a gentle hill and a lay-by near the brow of the hill. She parked her car and stepped out, away from the woods, to survey the land down the hill. From here she could see both Hedgelord and Bloomers. Two garden centres, what had felt like two warring cities when she had been a part of the ongoing rivalry.

Charlotte had brought her binoculars. They had once belonged to her grandfather who said he used them for bird-watching. She didn't recall him actually having any interest in ornithology. She half suspected he had been a dirty old man who made his own entertainment in a time when there had been only three TV channels and no internet. Regardless of what kind of 'bird' her granddad had been interested in watching, he had invested in good quality binoculars and Charlotte had an excellent view of the garden centre compounds.

She swept over the Hedgelord plant area. She spotted Luka and Gallagher walking slowly along the path. One of the elves stood at the check-in for the outdoor grotto. Maybe it was Gillespie?

After a few minutes she switched to Bloomers. The general goings on in the outdoor areas were remarkably similar to Hedgelord. She noticed there was a lot of activity near the Bloomers warehouses. Lorries were being unloaded. There were pallets of boxes, seemingly identical, along with some complicated equipment – lots of metal pipes, funnels and vessels – being moved around too. It hardly looked like garden centre stuff.

It was quite the mystery.

There was movement near Bloomers' front doors. There were plenty of customers going in and out, but a flash of platinum blonde hair and a certain familiar wiggling walk drew her eye. It was Sophie. For a second she wondered what Sophie was doing over at Bloomers, then she saw Snømann walk up to her side and gently take her elbow.

"Hmmm."

She liked to see Sophie enjoying some happiness, but Snømann firing her had entirely soured Charlotte to the man. He might bring a frisson of excitement to Sophie's life, but that didn't mean Charlotte had to like him.

Her train of thought didn't get much further because she heard someone at her side. She lowered the binoculars to see Jack Hartigan, astride a mountain bike.

"Well, this is unexpected," he said, neutrally.

"Following me?" she said, forcing an equally neutral tone.

"Not at all." He pointed at her binoculars. "You come here to spy on your former workplace, then?"

Charlotte was on the cusp of inventing some lie when she spotted a tiny binoculars case at Jack's waist. "Did you come here to do the same thing?"

He paused, as if he too was thinking of lying, then set his lips in a rueful expression. "Yes. Yes, I did."

They both stared out over the two garden centres.

"I miss it," he said.

She thought she'd leave it there. Let him be the only one to admit his sadness, but then she said, "Me too."

He nodded, dismounted from his bike and stepped closer. "See anything interesting?"

"Not really. That Snømann and our Sophie looked as though they were both going out somewhere. They were over at the front of Bloomers."

"They're an item, then?"

Charlotte nodded.

Sophie and Snømann had come as a couple to the Hedgelord staff Christmas party about a week ago. It had been the same night Charlotte and Jack had flown back from Lapland together. For a few short tentative hours, Charlotte and Jack had been a couple, thrust together by circumstance and finding something in each other that neither realised they needed. But Charlotte had ruined it, with her lack of trust and with her foul temper. Snømann and Sophie had been together for barely more than a week. Charlotte and Jack hadn't been able to achieve even that.

Charlotte realised she and Jack were both carefully avoiding eye contact. Their conversation was dull and stilted, but it was more than they'd managed over recent days, so she was grateful. But she had no idea what to say next. Despite her deeply mixed feelings for Jack, could they manage to do something as simple as go get a coffee together and discuss their plans to get back into the workplace?

She had no idea how she'd begin to broach something even as simple as that.

While she silently racked her brain on what to say, a white van pulled into the lay-by.

"Morning!" called the woman from the driver's window.

"Morning," said Jack politely. Charlotte offered her a small wave.

The woman jumped down from the van. "Got some dogs for ya!" she said.

"Pardon?" said Jack.

The logo on the side of the van declared that it was from the Pup's Trust dog re-homing charity.

"Did you say dogs?" said Charlotte.

"I know," the woman grinned and did some jazz hands. "Surprise!"

Charlotte was glad Jack was frowning because she had no idea what was going on here.

"You're the guys from the garden centre, right?" said the woman.

Charlotte and Jack glanced at each other.

"We are," they said together slowly.

"Good! Good! I know I'm a bit early. Thought I might have the wrong people!" the woman grinned. "Your friends set this up. A special little romantic treat."

"Oh, we're not romantically—" began Charlotte.

"What friends?" said Jack.

The woman tapped the side of her nose. "Can't tell you who. Now, let's see who we've got for you..." She went to the back of the van.

Jack looked at Charlotte. "Did you set this up?"

She pulled back. "What? Booked what is apparently a romantic dog walk for me and the man who hates me, then somehow magically pulled you and your mountain bike to this very spot?"

He made a confused face. "Yeah. Point."

"You'll walk them for ninety minutes then I'll meet you back here, yeah?" called the woman.

"Are you sure we're meant to do this?" Charlotte asked.

The woman grinned indulgently. "They told me you might say something like that, but I'm under strict instructions not to take no for an answer. Now, you wouldn't begrudge a couple of rescue dogs a nice walk, would you?"

"I – er, no."

The woman opened up the back of the van. "Come on then. Elsa! Buddy! Come here you good pups, you're going for a lovely walk! Yes you are."

She presented Charlotte and Jack with a lead each.

"You've got Elsa," she said to Jack. "You'll find her a lovely girl, once you get past her grumpy outer shell."

"What kind of dog is she?" Jack asked.

"It's hard to be exact, but I would say she's got a bit of Staffie in her, and definitely some Labrador."

The woman handed the other lead to Charlotte. "You can take Buddy. He's a sweetheart. He will bark at trees, but that's just a thing he does. I think he likes trees, but he barks at them." She pressed a roll of poo bags into Charlotte's hand. "You'll need these."

"Poo bags. Romantic," said Jack.

Charlotte took Buddy who looked like some sort of collie. "Back here in ninety minutes then?"

The woman nodded, climbed back into the van and drove away.

Charlotte and Jack looked at each other.

"What just happened?" Charlotte asked.

"I have no idea. I guess I'm locking up my bike and taking Elsa for a walk," said Jack. "Which way shall we go?"

There was another car in the distance, a large Volvo, coming along the road. The world about them was otherwise empty.

"This way, I guess," said Charlotte.

Within a few short minutes of walking along the woodland path, Charlotte found she was enjoying Buddy's company. "You know what's great about dogs?"

"What's that?" said Jack.

"They just seem to love everything. A patch of grass, Buddy loves it! A lumpy bit in the path, he loves that too. I can't imagine what it's like being in Buddy's head, but I bet it's really nice."

"Yeah," said Jack. "Elsa seems good at hiding any joy she feels. Do you see how she is drawn to the same features as Buddy, but looks peeved all the time?"

Charlotte squatted down and fussed Elsa's face. Her doggy breath misted in the air. "She could be such a sweet girl though, look at her! I wonder why she can't calm down and just enjoy herself?"

Jack pulled a face. "Are you saying this dog is annoying in the same way that you are annoying?"

Charlotte reeled at the casual swipe. She'd been having such a nice time she'd forgotten how mad Jack still was with her. His comment stung her more than she wanted to admit, even to herself. "Maybe," she said, and walked on.

As they crossed a stile into a field, the path grew muddy and ill-formed. The churned-up ground was rich with interest for Buddy. Charlotte glanced across at Elsa, willing her to demonstrate some charm.

"Did you hear back about an interview at Hedgelord?" Charlotte asked Jack.

"No. I can't imagine we'll hear before Christmas now. Besides, I wonder whether they really need two event managers if they're planning to merge?"

Charlotte sighed deeply. "Yeah."

As they approached a tree, Buddy started to bark, so they all stopped on the path.

"What is it boy? Why do trees bother you?" Charlotte asked.

"I don't know if he's bothered exactly. Look at his tail going," said Jack.

It was true. Buddy looked thrilled to see the tree.

"Come on then, let's go and see the tree," said Charlotte. "Maybe your enthusiasm will be catching and Elsa will be pleased to see it as well."

Charlotte had now completely absorbed the idea that Elsa's temperament and fate was tied to her own. She willed the sulky dog to respond to Buddy's explosive joy.

They all paused when they reached the tree. It was a huge oak, with spreading empty branches that filled the sky above their heads. Buddy sniffed the base of the trunk as if he had discovered something rare and precious. Elsa seemed more interested now, pulling at the lead, keen to explore every crevice.

"You go girl!" said Charlotte with a smile. "See, she just needed a bit of patience."

Jack smiled. "People who work with damaged dogs like this deserve a medal. Not everyone has that much patience, do they?"

Charlotte wasn't sure if he was talking about the dog or not. On balance she thought he probably wasn't.

Elsa began to dig frantically at the churned soil by the tree roots.

"Okay, steady on old girl," said Jack.

"Old girl?" smiled Charlotte. "Would you have ever tried that pet name on me?"

"We'll never know— Elsa! Stop now or we'll get told off by a farmer."

But Elsa didn't want to stop, and now Buddy was joining in. The two of them were clawing with heightened interest.

"I think they've found something," said Charlotte.

Elsa began tugging at something tufty she had uncovered. She tugged, growled, then dug further.

"Oh, God, stop!" shouted Jack suddenly.

Charlotte didn't see what it was initially. Jack pulled Elsa back with gentle force and when Charlotte saw what was buried in the soil, she pulled Buddy away.

A face and the floppy brown tufts of a man's hair were visible through the soil.

"Fuck!" Charlotte whispered.

Jack had his phone out. "Christ, my hands are shaking," he said, his eyes wild.

Charlotte took his phone and dialled 999.

28

CHARLOTTE

An ambulance arrived at the scene in the woods first, which was pretty redundant since the buried man was very clearly dead. The paramedics hung around and patted the dogs until the police turned up fifteen minutes later.

The two police officers seemed to spend quite a bit of time confirming the obvious, that there was a dead man buried in the corner of a field by Picket's Copse, then shortly after what must have been nearly every police officer in the Three Counties area descended on the place.

Charlotte and Jack (and their two dogs) were escorted back along the track to the lay-by where they'd first arrived and told to wait there. They dutifully did so. Various detectives, uniformed officers, people in white forensic suits and pretty much every conceivable character off a police TV drama turned up.

One officer came and asked for a statement. A couple more came and asked if they could stroke the dogs.

"Oh, bloody hell, it's you two," said an officer.

He looked familiar to Charlotte.

"Morning, Sergeant Akhtar," said Jack. Charlotte realised he was the officer who had dealt with them both after the tractor/sleigh/Christmas tree/nativity incident.

"Yes, it's us two," said Charlotte and pointed towards the woods. "But we didn't have anything to do with that."

The sergeant's moustache bristled like he didn't believe a word of it and went down to the scene.

"You know what?" Jack said to Charlotte.

"What?"

"Walking dogs and finding a corpse wasn't on my bingo card for today."

"No, mine neither," she said.

"But it's been quite enjoyable," he said.

She raised an eyebrow. "Finding a body?"

He shrugged. "It was exciting at least. Tragic, obviously."

"Obviously."

"But exciting."

"You're not wrong."

Along the lay-by the white van had pulled in. The woman from the dog rescue was in the driver's seat, frowning at all the police gathered about.

Jack and Charlotte wandered over. Jack stopped to ask an important looking officer if they were okay to give the dogs back to their owner.

"Don't see why not," she said.

"Wondered if you needed to take their paw prints or something," said Jack.

The officer looked at him like he was mad. "Why would we do that?"

"No idea. I'm not a police officer."

"And can we go too?" said Charlotte.

The officer nodded. "Yep. We've got your details. We know who the guy is, anyway."

"Oh?"

"That Bargus Popovicu they've been looking for the last couple of days. Smuggler or something. Clearly messed with the wrong people."

And with that nugget of gossip, they went to take the dogs back.

"Had a good time?" asked the woman as they handed over the leads for Elsa and Buddy.

"Yes, they're good company," said Charlotte.

"Well, you know where we are if you want to do it again," she said, handing them each a business card. She waved at the scene around her. "What's going on?"

"Dead smuggler in a field," said Charlotte.

The woman's eyes widened. "Fancy that."

"The world is full of surprises," Charlotte agreed.

OVER THE PAST FEW WEEKS, before he had taken complete ownership of Hedgelord, Snømann had coerced Luka and Gallagher into storing a significant number of lockable crates in their area of the garden centre. Being dubiously in debt to the man meant they had no option. Storing them had been problematic, but necessity was indeed the mother of invention and they had found a way to create a storage space behind their tea shed. It was accessible through a hole in the back, covered up by a large and quite unpleasant poster of a hornet.

Today, they were helping Snømann's Blond Men Group to get most of the crates out of the temporary space to whatever warehouse storage Snømann had elsewhere on the site. Luka counted them off as the boiler-suited men trooped away with the crates, until their secret store was empty of all but three cases.

Gallagher and Luka were still buzzing from their nighttime exercise. They both wore their black boiler suits, somehow feeling a kinship with the fraternity of Svens. Gallagher still wasn't certain whether they were all called Sven, but if he approached any of the Blond Men Group with a raised hand and said "High five, Sven", they invariably complied.

"Most fun and games I've had in the dark for a while," Luka commented over a cup of tea.

"What do you reckon's next on the agenda?" said Gallagher. "I quite want to do the defensive driving thing. Do you think we might be able to do that?"

"Someone still needs to look after plants," Luka said.

"True." Gallagher had forgotten that Luka had a genuine passion for plants. It wasn't a huge focus in the winter season, but in a few short weeks, after Christmas, everyone would need Luka's expertise. "There must be something that appeals to you in all of this new world, though?"

"New world?"

"Come on." He jerked a finger to their nearly empty secret store. "We both know Snømann is a gangster."

Luka blew out his lips. "A free-thinking businessman who is not afraid of the law."

"We were afraid of him," Gallagher reminded him.

"Sure, but we're now on the inside. We don't mind some light drug-smuggling, as long as no one gets hurt."

"Right, right. I guess. So, given that we work for a gangster—"

"Free-thinking businessman."

"—right. Given that, what area of his wider business would we like to be involved with."

Luka though deeply before answering. "Weapons."

"Pardon?"

"Always had soft spot for big dangerous weapons."

"You think they have those things?" Gallagher asked. "Like, you know..." He tried to sketch out formless gun-shaped ideas in the air. He didn't know very much about weapons.

"I think they have a lot of backing and resources, yeah," said Luka.

Gallagher knew he should be appalled, but he was sort of excited. It was good to belong.

Gallagher saw Tom coming down the path. He walked like a man who'd watched a tutorial on how to stride in a confident manner, but failed to grasp any of the key points. He spotted Gallagher and Luka and very nearly jumped. "Ah – hello. Just the fellows I was looking for,"

"That's good," said Gallagher, feeling he should say something.

"Yes. Mr Snømann has asked that you go to his office, please. Some sort of meeting."

"When is meeting?" Luka asked.

"It's now. He made that quite clear. It's the main reason I have taken the trouble to come and find you personally."

Gallagher realised that Tom was furious at this errand boy task, but he would never allow himself to express annoyance. Instead it leaked out of him like a funny smell.

"Yep. We can do that," said Gallagher. Luka stood up as well.

Tom looked as though he was about to say something. Gallagher guessed it was something along the lines of how come they could jump when Snømann said to jump, but would never do anything as simple as shift some bags of compost when Tom asked them to. He thought better of it and kept his mouth shut, giving a nod.

Gallagher and Luka filed into Snømann's office along with a couple of dozen Svens.

How quickly they'd become accustomed to calling it Snømann's office. Gallagher wondered where Cameron was now. There were still various belongings and knick-knacks of Cameron's around the office, including the paper frame stuck onto the window around the view across to Bloomers. The caption declaring them to be twats was probably redundant now they were all one happy family. It was a mind-blowing turnaround.

As if he was attuned to Gallagher's thoughts, Snømann addressed the gathering. "Two garden centres are making the transition to become a single cohesive unit. This is a journey that must be managed. You will form part of that management capability."

Gallagher looked around at his black-clad brethren and felt a swell of pride. He was part of a management capability!

"On December the twenty fourth, we will have a celebration lunch to mark the merger of two companies. There will be an opulent party, and lots of opportunity for people to share their thoughts and ideas on how we might best smoothly navigate this transition. I welcome your ideas on how we might help that process be as painless as possible."

Gallagher nodded. He was *never* asked for ideas or input. This was new!

"I will pass post-it notes amongst you and I invite you to write ideas on them, then stick them to the wall. Take a few minutes to do that now, please."

Gallagher took the block of paper and thought about the task of joining two very different organisations together. He quickly jotted some notes.

- *Make sure job descriptions are the same at both centres*
- *Have a way that we can all ask any questions without feeling stupid*

AFTER A FEW MINUTES he decided to stick these on the wall so that he could take a look at what other ideas were there. He strolled along, reading.

. . .

- *Create a dog-eat-dog room. Make 2 people fight for a role.*
- *Make everyone work for less money so they quit*
- *Pay people off (with cash) then rob them as they leave*

GALLAGHER QUICKLY REALISED there was a big difference in tone between the ideas he'd put down and the ones other members of the Blond Men Group were creating. He glanced at Luka who was doing what he did best: looking busy, scribbling with his pen. It was likely he wasn't even engaging with the exercise, but he looked as if he was working hard.

Snømann was now walking around the room, looking at the notes. He nodded and made noises of general approval as he went. Gallagher was suddenly scared to see how he would react to his lame suggestions, but he moved on without comment.

"You have done good work here," Snømann said to the crowd. "I will make sure that your ideas are harvested and assessed, but it's good to see you are all thinking carefully about how we might handle this tricky situation. Now, if we return to the subject of the celebration that I mentioned, your role will align with this direction of travel. I would like you all to attend to the logistics of the evening, which will include setup, teardown, and of course security and crowd-handling."

The Svens all nodded as if they did this stuff all the time.

Gallagher wondered exactly what would be involved. It wasn't as if they needed bouncers for an event at an isolated garden centre, was it?

"We will issue a task list for the setup and teardown so I trust you will organise yourselves accordingly."

"Yep!" Gallagher raised his hands ready to clap, but saw the rest of the Svens give a simple nod, so he did that instead.

As they all filed out of the room, Gallagher fell into step with Luka. "What do you make of that?"

Luka shrugged. "We turn up, we do as we are told. Is simple."

Gallagher nodded. It was pretty simple. Just another day at work, really. Although the part where they did what they were told was new.

29

ANIKA

Having finally got the bitey donkey to Hedgelord, Anika shut him in with the reindeer. She'd hoped to catch Gallagher so that she could tell him what she was doing, but she couldn't see either him or Luka in the plant area. So she sent Gallagher a text.

Donkey in reindeer enclosure. Not sure whose it is. Need to find owner. Any ideas?

She went inside the building, trying to ignore the noisy braying of the donkey. She really hoped it wasn't going to cause trouble.

"Anika!" She turned to see who was calling her name. It was Tom and he looked mildly annoyed. He walked over. "Anika, I've been asked to send you to Snømann's office. He is conducting a briefing which should have just ended, and he would like to talk to you straight after that."

"Er, right," she said.

"In other words you need to go there now."

"Will do," said Anika. "Is everything okay, Tom?"

"Yes of course," he said, his lips extended over his teeth in the most brittle smile Anika had ever seen. He looked like someone in a dentist's chair, waiting for a polish.

Anika hurried up to Snømann's office, passing Gallagher and Luka coming out with lots of other men dressed in those black boiler suits. She saw Gallagher looking at her text on his phone. He lifted his head when he saw her and pulled a face of mild outrage. She tried to give him a small apologetic smile for lumbering him with a donkey, but then she was inside Snømann's office. There was the lingering smell left by a great many men in a small space, but surprisingly it wasn't sweaty. It had hints of pine, as if they'd all used the same soap.

"Good morning, Anika," said Snømann.

Anika felt a brief pang of nostalgia for Cameron always getting her name wrong and calling her Anita. "Morning. So, how was it?"

He gave her a politely enquiring look.

"The special treat over by Picket's Copse. You took Sophie over there for ten o'clock, yes?"

"I did just that, Anika," he said. "I do not know what the surprise was supposed to be."

"Didn't someone turn up with some dogs?"

"Dogs?" He pulled a face and shook his head. "No. No dogs. We did go for a short walk and then a lot of policemen in their noisy cars turned up. Was that supposed to be part of the surprise?"

"Er, no," she said.

"Good. We moved on and continued with our day. No dogs."

"Oh, sorry."

He waved a hand as though thoroughly dismissing that matter as irrelevant.

CHARLOTTE WAS STRUGGLING with the lack of routine being unemployed brought with it. One bizarre encounter with Jack Hartigan and the surprise discovery of a corpse in a field did not make up for the general malaise she'd been feeling since being fired.

On the twenty-third, two days before Christmas, she'd woken up at the regular time, because her body was programmed to work that way. Which meant the morning was a long, drawn-out chunk of time to fill after she'd eaten breakfast.

She decided to allocate herself some tasks. She grabbed a piece of paper and tried to write down the things she might do if she was an organised person who was going to fill her day with positive, constructive things to help her to get a new job and plan for an enjoyable Christmas.

- *Plan Christmas dinner with mum*
- *Shop for Christmas dinner*
- *Go for a run*
- *Brainstorm what transferable skills I have*
- *Search for vacancies*
- *Buy tree and decorate it*

- *Research churches in the area that I might still be allowed to attend*

SHE READ through the list and huffed loudly. Most of the tasks she'd written down sounded horrendous – either depressing or just unachievable. She knew for a fact that she'd run out of churches, so she scored a line through the last one.

"Fuck," she grumbled. She couldn't face most of these, although getting a Christmas tree might be nice. She had cleaned the house so very thoroughly that a real tree would set it off. She phoned Hedgelord.

"Hi, could you put me through to the plant area please?" she asked.

The phone rang out for a really long time. Gallagher and Luka weren't great at answering the phone. She could picture them both ignoring it, hoping that she would ring off.

"*Yes?*" It was Luka. He sounded impatient.

"Hi. I want to reserve a Christmas tree. It's Charlotte."

"*Charlotte?*"

There was a noise on the line, which sounded like a hand going over the microphone. She could still hear what was going on, it was just slightly muffled.

"*Is fucking Charlotte. I thought she'd gone?*"

"*Mad Charlotte? What does she want?*"

"*Christmas tree she says.*"

"*What? Is that code? Give it here.*"

The phone was handed over with a series of crunching sounds. *"Hello?"*

"Hi, Gallagher. It's me, Charlotte. I wanted to get a Christmas tree."

"Right, yeah. A Christmas tree. And when you say Christmas tree, what is it that you mean?" Gallagher asked.

"A tree? I just want a nice one. I'm stuck at home so if I'm going to be looking at a tree it had better be a good one, you know?"

"Oh right. An actual tree. Yeah, we've got loads."

"I know you've got loads, Gallagher. It's not that long since I was sacked." Charlotte paused, realising why she'd really felt the need to phone. "What's been happening?"

"Oh Christ, it's all change here. The two garden centres are merging, right? There's going to be a big party on Christmas Eve where everyone will either get a nice present or have to wrestle each other for the best jobs. I have no fucking idea to tell you the truth. Luka and me have got cool new uniforms and career progression, so that's nice."

Charlotte smiled at Gallagher's gabbling. He sounded excited. She could hear Luka grumbling in the background. Did she miss these people? It seemed that she did, yes.

"Career progression. Er, right. That sounds good. I think it probably existed before, but maybe Tom didn't talk about it much. What's he doing now, then?"

Gallagher gave a small laugh. *"Far as I can tell he's Snømann's gopher. He doesn't seem to do anything else, really."*

"It is all change," said Charlotte. "What does Cameron make of everything?"

"Hmmm. He's on holiday or something. Not seen him for a bit. Anyway, what do you want to do about this tree?"

"Tree?"

"The Christmas tree you're after. Did you want one delivering or something?"

Charlotte thought about it. "No, maybe I'll pop in. Bag one up for me, will you? A really nice one, about five feet."

"Will do. See you later."

30

GALLAGHER

Gallagher and Luka bagged up a tree for Charlotte.
"I dunno mate, she sounded less stressed than when she was working here," said Gallagher. "Maybe it's this place that sends people over the edge."

"You talking about Tom?" asked Luka. "I heard what you said about him. He is definitely Snømann's little bitch now. It's like somehow that role is exactly what he needs and is also thing he hates the most. He is mad as hell, but also loving it."

"Yeah, you're right, it's like watching him being split in two. No, I was actually thinking more about Cameron. Never known him not to be swanking around at this time of year, pretending he spends time with us all year round and offering us shots of the booze he's been given by suppliers."

"Is true. If he sold the place, maybe he's in fucking Caribbean already?"

"Yeah maybe." Gallagher looked up. "Hey, it's Sven."

It was actually five Svens. The five members of Blond Man Group walked in their co-ordinated way, as if their arms and legs were joined, but once they all stood and faced Gallagher and Luka they relaxed a little.

"You here for work, or just to hang out?" Gallagher asked, after they'd all stood and stared at each other for a long moment.

"We are deployed to assist with finalising plant area tasks so that you may be released to help with setup of the big event. There are many things that need doing here?"

Gallagher and Luka looked around at the eager crowd. Luka grinned, and placed his arms across the shoulders of the nearest Svens. "Welcome! There are always many important tasks here, yes. What is essential though is we are fortified by cup of tea. Plant area brew up is essential part of day. We do not have mugs for all of you, but you will go to staff area inside the building, get a mug, and come back here. Then we will make tea and begin your plant area induction."

The Svens reacted immediately to Luka's words, striding off towards the staff kitchen.

"What will we get them to do?" asked Gallagher.

Luka shrugged. "Not important, but we will find something. Maybe move those pallets of compost from outside the landscaping office."

"We don't want to over-burden them," said Gallagher.

Luka shrugged happily. "Is good to bond with our brothers, no?"

Gallagher smiled. It definitely was. He went into the tea shed and put the kettle on, ready for the returning Svens. It had only just boiled when they trouped back in with their mugs, Luka following them inside. The tea shed was barely large enough to accommodate them all standing, so Gallagher made them all tea, then they went back outside with their steaming mugs.

"Come. We will arrange the stoneware," said Luka.

Everyone went over to the section with statuettes, birdbaths and ornaments.

"What is the required task?" asked one of the Svens.

"Task here is stone benches in this display. We rearrange things to make convivial space for consumption of tea," said Luka, as if it was obvious.

It took no more than two minutes, as the Svens wordlessly moved the heavy stoneware around, resulting in a tiny meeting circle made of stone benches, with all of the other goods packed in the space beyond.

"Sit!" commanded Luka.

They all crowded onto the benches, which were more decorative than practical, especially for larger men.

"Well this is nice!" said Gallagher, looking round at everyone.

"What do we do for plant area induction?" asked the Sven next to Gallagher.

"You're doing it, mate!" said Gallagher, raising his mug in a toast.

"Is there an outcome to this induction?"

"Yep. Ideally we all feel a bit better about things once we've drunk our tea," said Gallagher. "We can call it an ice-breaker, if it makes you feel better. Tell me something about yourself."

Sven gave a small nervous laugh. "Oh. I don't know if people want to know about me."

"I do!" insisted Gallagher.

"I am very fond of the colour green." He glanced around the group. "There, I said it. I enjoy our uniform, but my socks are green. It gives me pleasure when I look at them."

Gallagher looked down and saw a tiny flash of lime green in the gap between his trouser-bottoms and his boots. "Good on you."

Another of the Svens made a noise. "Ah Sven, why don't you get a tattoo if you like it so much? That way it can always be with you."

There was a small rumble around the group. It seemed like a sound idea.

"You have a tattoo?" asked Luka.

The Sven who had spoken pulled up his sleeve to show a large black cat curled around his forearm. "Panther. It's my signature move."

He didn't elaborate, but looked quietly pleased with himself. Was 'panther' a deadly strike in some kind of martial arts? Or maybe a yoga pose?

Luka grunted in approval. "Is like family cat I grew up with."

"Yeah? I mean, aren't all cats like small panthers?" said Gallagher. It was a light and amusing conversation and he grinned at Luka as he said it.

Luka made an exasperated noise. "Absolutely not. This cat was big, like panther." Luka's face was stony and serious.

"Mate, no it wasn't. Panthers are fucking huge. You couldn't have one of those in a house."

"This cat was size of really big dog. Like Scooby Doo big."

Gallagher paused. Luka's bullshit was so fluent and frequent that it was hard to distinguish when he was being serious. "Did you have an actual panther as a household pet?"

"Maybe," shrugged Luka. He looked round at the group. "Who else has tattoo?"

Another two sleeves were rolled up. One of the Svens had a demon riding a motorbike. Another had a skull.

"No skull for me, my wife says it would make me look cheap," said one of the others.

"You don't need a tattoo to look cheap, Sven," laughed another.

Gallagher didn't know whether to be more surprised that the Svens were human enough to laugh at each other, or to find out one of them had a wife. He sipped his tea and smiled at his new group of friends.

31

CHARLOTTE

Charlotte drove over to Hedgelord. She sat in her car for a few minutes, wondering if she might be physically ejected from the store. Now she'd been sacked was she also forbidden from coming back as a customer? She didn't think so, but she hadn't been listening all that carefully once she'd realised what was going on. Off the top of her head she couldn't imagine who at Hedgelord would have the guts to tell her to leave, apart from maybe Cameron himself.

Her plan was a quick in-and-out. She'd pick up her Christmas tree, and maybe some new decorations for it. It would be nice to try and make herself feel Christmassy. Anything to replace the bleakness and grinding, low-level anger.

She walked into the store, taking care not to glance over at the customer service desk to see who was there. She headed straight into the Christmas decorations. It was laid out in carefully-designed areas, like being immersed in a glimmering bubble, where festive trinkets were set at every level to delight and inspire. It wasn't unlike being in a church, Charlotte realised. There was an area dedicated to folksy, rustic ornaments, with lots of wood and painted designs. She walked through to the more glitzy, coloured area and it really did have the same feel as being behind a huge stained glass window. It was both amusing and devastating to consider that not only had she been banned from all the actual churches in the area, but potentially she was also no longer welcome at this weird, commercial substitute.

She selected a few ornaments, choosing the ones that might bring a tiny stained glass vibe to her own home. She carried her basket through to the plant area to get her Christmas tree from Gallagher and Luka. They were not in their usual hangouts, so she poked through the baled-up trees, found one with her name on it, and retrieved a trolley to wheel it through the store.

As she went back inside, Anika walked past, then did a double-take. "Charlotte?"

"Hi Anika."

Anika looked about nervously, as though Charlotte's sudden appearance was some sort of test. She seemed to shake herself out of it almost immediately. "It's good to see you," she said.

"Thanks. How are things here?"

"Erm, good, thank you. What brings you into the shop?"

"Christmas, would you believe?" Charlotte said with a

smile. She was well aware that she looked like someone masquerading as a normal human.

Anika was not fooled. She gave a frown. "Listen, I'm sorry about what happened."

Charlotte pressed on with her fake human persona and made herself smile. "All water under the bridge. But seriously, how are things here?"

"Yeah. Um, they're definitely a bit strange. But probably not as strange as whatever you're—" Anika wafted a hand over Charlotte's trolley. She seemed to realise she was being rather insulting. "Oh! I didn't mean that you'd gone mad or anything."

"I'm sorry?"

"I bet it's a change of pace, that's all."

Charlotte laughed at that. It was a genuine laugh because Anika had probably blurted out some kind of truth. "To be honest with you, I think I have gone a bit mad. I don't really know what to do with myself."

Anika nodded sadly, but then brightened. "Oh hey, I don't know if it's of any interest, but there was a whole box of ceramic clowns which arrived damaged. They are out in the skip area, waiting for disposal." She gave Charlotte a sly look. "If someone was to smash them up, it would be really helpful."

"Ceramic clowns, eh?" Charlotte said, licking her lips. "Sounds like something that could only be improved by smashing."

"You would definitely be doing the world a favour," said Anika. "I think your baseball bat is still out there. You know the way."

"I'm just going to leave my trolley here for a few minutes," said Charlotte, pulling her purchases into the gap near the café.

She walked round to the skip area. As she approached she thought she could hear a smashing sound, but it was probably nothing. She pushed the gate open – and found Tom inside, flushed from the effort he'd clearly been putting into his work. He held her baseball bat in one hand and was plucking another broken clown from a box with the other. He placed it in a pile of crushed ceramic and looked up.

"Charlotte."

"Tom."

She walked over and stood next to him, surveying the work he'd already done. "Thorough. Very thorough. You always had an eye for detail, and I see you have pulverised every last piece into crumbs."

"Yeah," he said. "If a job's worth doing it's worth doing well."

"You're not enjoying the changes here, I take it?" She held out a hand for the bat. "May I?"

He handed it over. "No. I don't think the new regime is interested in the retail side at all."

"Hmmm. Not interested in retail? That's exactly what we're about though, right?"

"Precisely. Mr Snømann is all about big plans. This Operation Yuletide Surprise thing."

"What's that?" she said.

Tom shrugged miserably. "No idea. It's not about improving the customer purchase experience, that's for sure."

She thought about the activity and machinery she'd seen around the Bloomers warehouses on her dog walk with Jack. "There's some big moves afoot," she said.

Tom gave her a sidelong look. "Yeah?"

"A large amount of deliveries to the Bloomers warehouses. Big, big stuff. And I don't think it's garden ware or last minute Christmas stuff."

"No one tells me nothing anymore," Tom pouted.

Charlotte wasn't sure anyone ever told Tom anything before, but said nothing. She put a clown down on the ground. "These things would be crap even if they weren't broken."

"They were supposed to be holding little blackboards, so you could use them to display the Christmas day menu. The arms all broke so the blackboards are gone." Tom shrugged. "They were cheap."

"A traditional Christmas clown to hold up the Christmas day menu?" laughed Charlotte. "Yeah, these need to be pulverised." She brought the bat down on the clown. It made a satisfying crunch. She pushed the pieces back into a pile with her foot. She rained down blows onto the smaller pieces, finding it oddly enjoyable, reducing them to increasingly tiny bits.

She and Tom took turns smashing up clowns.

"What does Cameron make of all this?" asked Charlotte.

"No idea. Nobody's seen him. I don't even know if Bloomers' Marcus and Maremba are around, either. The whole thing feels so peculiar. Snømann has bought the two garden centres up, but seems to have little interest in what we're actually all about."

"It's nearly Christmas, Tom. A couple of days off and everything might make a lot more sense." Charlotte didn't really believe the words, even as she spoke them, but the two of them went back to the important work of pulverising clowns, and Charlotte thought that perhaps things did make a bit more sense, even if just for a little while.

32

ANIKA

Anika was in the midst of a planning frenzy. The tasks relating to the Christmas Eve celebration were spinning out of control. She had run out of colours for her colour coding and thought maybe she was going a little bit spreadsheet-blind.

Her phone rang. It was the dog pound where she'd left a message. "Hi!"

"*I heard your message,*" said the dog woman. "*We definitely did drop the dogs off for their walk. The two people were waiting in the lay-by. We were a few minutes early, but they were there, waiting.*"

"What? Really?" Anika couldn't understand. "And you met them at the end of the walk and they returned the dogs?"

"*Yep. Exactly like we talked about. Obviously, the stuff with the police and the dead body in the woods was a distraction but ... I don't know why the two of them would tell you different. Elsa and*

Buddy had a lovely walk with them, and your friends seemed to like it, too."

"Right. Strange. Thanks for the call."

Anika could make no sense of it. The love trap had been sprung, but Snømann claimed that it hadn't happened. Was it possible someone else had taken the dogs for a walk? Weird.

She sighed, knowing she couldn't possibly know the answer. The next love trap at The Granary was all planned, so maybe that one would be more successful. She would make sure the wrong people couldn't step into that one by making Sophie wear something distinctive, like the eye-watering Christmas tree brooch she had.

There was a specific problem in front of her. Snømann was arranging a Christmas Eve banquet dinner for over a hundred and forty people. That was every single Hedgelord and Bloomers employee – every full-timer, part-timer, and every seasonal hire such as herself. It was a generous gesture by Mr Snømann. Well, sort of generous. Enforced, work-related fun on Christmas Eve of all days was also very selfish, in its own way. Anika could imagine some of the older women like Karen or Charlotte comparing it with a man ordering steak for you at a restaurant, or buying you the dress he wants you to wear. Generous, but controlling. Anika could imagine that's how they would view it. Although she was of the age (and salary level) where she would never turn down free food or free fun.

But a hundred and forty guests meant a hundred and forty meals. In a marquee. In a field. A place with no fixed kitchens. That meant the caterers were turning up with essentially a hundred and forty pre-prepared meals, plus the drinks, and the crockery and cutlery. And Anika needed to find space for it all.

"Tom," she said.

Tom, who was increasingly looking like a husk of his former self since Charlotte had been fired, glanced up from his computer, a grumpy if somewhat blank-eyed look on his face.

"I need to find a significant storage space where the caterers can put the meal prep stuff for the big party."

Tom shrugged.

"Come on," she said. "You're one of the longest serving members of staff here. I need your expertise."

He shrugged again. "I dunno, Anika. I'd say the warehouse, obviously, but Snømann has that all sealed up and full of some other stock he's had brought in."

Her nose wrinkled as she frowned. "What stock?"

"No idea. Those new hires of his have the place all locked down like it's part of some secret operation."

"There's a lot of new hires at the moment, aren't there?"

He nodded. "Well, the merger of Hedgelord and Bloomers... It's a lot of work, I guess."

She made a half-hearted sound of agreement. "Actually, if you merge two places it's usually an excuse to cut numbers."

She looked at the plans in front of her. If she was running both sites, she'd be tempted to slash these numbers. You didn't need a hundred and forty people to run two nearby garden centres. It was basic economics. In fact, with all of Snømann's new eager blond recruits, you barely needed any of the existing garden centre staff. The thought of the two garden centres merging prompted a thought.

"Bloomers have got more warehouse space than us," she said. "And their site sort of backs onto the paddock."

Tom was shaking his head. "They're stockpiling at that warehouse too."

"Really?"

"Something Charlotte told me." He looked about suddenly. "I've not been talking to the enemy or anything."

"She's not the enemy," said Anika. "And how does she know?"

"No idea."

Anika stood. "Well, maybe there's some room over there for the catering things."

En route to Bloomers, she decided to take a walk through the paddock, the site of tomorrow's Christmas Eve event. The marquees were in place, so she could check on progress and see whether she might spot any issues.

She found the two marquees up and joined together, to make one huge marquee. She went inside and looked around the space, counting off the extra decorations she'd ordered to make the inside opulent. There was a wood burner on each side as well, currently being moved into place by the operational team – which is what she'd chosen to call the men in black boiler suits. At some point she would need to have a word with Snømann about his diversity policy, because she hadn't seen a single woman on that team, and the only ones who weren't tall blond Scandinavians were Gallagher and Luka. She'd tried to number the members of the operational team a few times, but it was surprisingly difficult, because they were so alike. Would it be considered offensive to allocate numbered badges to them? She decided it probably would be.

"Gallagher!" she hissed. "Come here a minute, will you?"

He trotted over.

"Listen, I'm trying to get a grip on resources," she said.

"What does that mean? What is a resource?"

"People."

Gallagher pulled a face and shook his head. "Oh dear. It hasn't taken long for you to become management, has it?"

"What? No, I'm not management! I'm an elf. I'm paid minimum wage, remember?"

"Yeah, well. Minimum wage or not, when you start calling people resources, you're management."

Anika was stung. "Right, well that's why I need your help. I can only humanise people if I can tell them apart. Can you tell me that guy's name?" She pointed.

"Yeah sure, that's Sven."

"Good." Anika snapped a picture and made a note. She pointed at another. "What about him?"

"Sven."

They repeated the exercise twice more before Anika lowered her phone. "Wait a minute. Are there any of these people who're not called Sven?"

Gallagher shook his head. "No. All of them are Sven."

Her brow creased. "That can't be right! It's the same as me calling them resources. Someone has decided they should all be called Sven."

"Nah," said Gallagher. "It's a proper name, isn't it? Pretty sure it's just a coincidence."

Anika wondered what the probability of that might be, but decided she didn't have enough information to work it out (and even if she did, she knew Gallagher wouldn't care). "Aren't there a lot of these guys about at the moment?"

"Yeah!" he said happily.

"Why do we suddenly need so many people?"

"No idea."

"Because, thinking on it, I don't think the plans for our celebration dinner even include them. The numbers don't add up. I mean, they wouldn't add up even if I could count them."

Gallagher grunted, uninterested now. It seemed that, in the shifting dynamics of the garden centre, he and Luka had thrown their lot in with the new crowd.

She gestured over to Bloomers, just across the road on the far side of the paddock. "And do you know what's going on in the warehouse over at Bloomers."

He shook his head. "Should I?"

"I'm looking for storage space."

"Storage spaces for your resources," he said, which really meant nothing at all but was apparently an attempt at wit.

Irritated, she swept her hand at the work going on around them. "Well, just enjoy yourself, Gallagher, huh?"

Sighing, she made her way towards Bloomers.

33

GALLAGHER

Gallagher went back to find Luka. He was hammering stakes into the ground for tensioning marquee wires.

"What did Anika want?" Luka asked.

"She's gone all management. Asking questions about people like they're all the same or something. You know what she said?"

"No."

"She reckons that the Svens can't all really be called Sven. Can you imagine?"

Luka unfolded himself from his kneeling position, standing straight so he could meet Gallagher's eye. "What? You think all of these people were called Sven by their fucking parents?"

Gallagher clamped his lips in a straight line to stop stupid words from escaping while he thought harder about the idea.

Truthfully, it was difficult to imagine the Svens actually having parents and coming from regular families. Somewhere, deep in his unconscious, he'd pictured them coming off a production line. "Now that you've put it like that, maybe ... no?"

Luka rolled his eyes theatrically. "Now, as to *why* they are all called Sven, we maybe don't want to be seen asking questions like that."

"Yep. Yep. I hear what you're saying," said Gallagher.

In all the excitement of getting a massive team of cool new colleagues, Gallagher had forgotten that Snømann was terrifying and extremely dodgy. He didn't want to dwell on it, because Snømann also seemed pretty good to work for. Gallagher wondered whether he was in danger of getting carried away with the idea of this all being perfectly normal. He determined to keep his eyes and ears open, and things would probably be fine.

"Should we be called Sven too?" he asked.

Anika walked around Bloomers, heading to the warehouse spaces out back. She just needed to find space for the caterers to put the necessary things for the many meals. Surely that couldn't be too hard?

A large area of the Bloomers car park had been annexed off with high fencing, and she could see the large warehouse buildings behind. A lorry carrying a shipping container pulled up and a pair of the Svens opened a large gate so it could reverse inside.

Carefully, staying out of the way, she skirted the lorry and went inside the building through a huge, roll-up door. There was no sense in getting in everyone's way.

The Svens were busying themselves bringing a forklift truck to the rear of the lorry, so Anika went deeper inside to take a look around. Tom had been partly right. This place was definitely a hive of activity, but it wasn't full. There were towering racks of shelving, only half full, which was good to know. There was plenty of room in here to store things if needed. She made a note to check whether all of the Svens could drive forklifts. It could prove useful with the delivery of the catering goods to the banqueting marquee.

She walked down the central aisle of the warehouse, still keen to see if there was any chilled storage. When she reached the end of the racking, there was a separate area. It was brightly lit and had long tables arranged in a curve. It suggested there was a kind of workflow here, with Svens standing at the table, engaged in some sort of task. Nobody had noticed she was there, so she moved forward quietly, interested in what they might be doing.

So far she had been confident that she could justify being here if challenged, as she was most definitely working for Snømann, doing as he'd asked. So why did she suddenly feel as though she was witnessing something she wasn't supposed to see?

The first group of Svens were opening boxes that were stacked beside them. They pulled out decorations that were in the style of a fat red candle sitting on a holder shaped like a jolly Santa figure. Where his hat would normally be was the candle tip and wick.

Anika was fairly certain Hedgelord did not stock anything like that.

The candles were lined up and pushed along the table to the next group of Svens. They separated the candles from the holders, packing the holders into another box while the candles were moved around the table to the next station.

One of the Svens operated a machine that looked like a drill, but instead of a whirring drill bit, it had a thin blade. Anika wondered if it was heated, because as he brought it down across the base of a candle, it easily slid through. He passed the main body of the candle carefully to the next Sven and tossed the off-cut into a bin.

Anika crept forward to see what happened next and saw that the candle was hollow. As the Sven shook it over a set of scales, white powder poured out.

"Fuck," she whispered.

Anika took a step backwards. This was something very bad indeed. She had limited knowledge of drugs, so had no idea whether this was cocaine, heroin or something else, but it was definitely drugs. Little bags were the next step in the production line, and there were a great many of them, judging by the number of boxes stacked up at the back.

She picked up one of the as-yet-unemptied candles, unable to believe it.

"Hey!"

One of the Svens had looked up and spotted her. She turned, the candle hidden behind her back.

Anika had two choices. Make a run for it, or try to talk her way out.

"Hi, I've been sent over by Mr Snømann to look at your throughput," said Anika.

"Our throughput?"

She stepped forward, stuffing the candle away down the back of her elf costume. "Yes. Can we make this workflow more efficient?" she said. "For example, if we got another of these machines, it looks to me as though it would help a lot. You're a bottleneck." She pointed at the Sven who was cutting the bases off the candles.

He looked embarrassed at this. "Yeah. Maybe."

Anika was emboldened by this. "And you – over here taking the candles from the boxes! You should lift the box onto the table and lie it on its side. It will be much faster taking them out and you won't have to bend over so many times."

The Svens nodded.

"Good. Well, let me go and talk to Snømann about ordering another one of those machines. I will let you know how that goes."

Anika turned to walk away.

"Wait a moment."

She froze and half turned.

The Sven who had challenged her walked over. "We asked for another of these machines three days ago."

"Had you? Good thinking."

"You would know this if Snømann had really sent you."

"Ahh," Anika pulled out her phone and pretended to look at her notes. "Is it coming from er, Gillespie Instrumentation? Yes, he did mention that."

"Wait here please." The Sven made a phone call.

"Snømann? A young woman dressed as an elf is here in the extraction area. She says that you sent her." He looked up. "What is your name?"

"Anika. I mainly wanted to see if you had chilled storage over here. The other stuff was more of a stretch goal."

The Sven nodded as he listened. "Yes. She has seen everything. Very well."

Something about his tone made Anika think she was in a lot of trouble. She held her phone at her back and tried to discreetly make a call to someone. Anyone.

Sven ended the call and looked at Anika. "You need to come with me." He grabbed her roughly by her upper arm and she immediately lost her grip on her phone. It fell to the floor behind her as she was dragged away.

"Hey!" she yelled.

At the tables, the Svens resumed their work as if nothing had happened.

34

CHARLOTTE

harlotte revisited her previous task list over a cup of afternoon tea.

- *Plan Christmas dinner with mum*
- *Shop for Christmas dinner*
- *Go for a run*
- *Brainstorm what transferable skills I have*
- *Search for vacancies*
- *Buy tree and decorate it*
- *Research churches in the area that I might still be allowed to attend*

CHARLOTTE HAD WRESTLED the Christmas tree into her lounge and cut away the netting. The tree pinged back into shape, revealing itself to be as fresh and cute as she'd hoped. She smiled and offered silent thanks to Gallagher and Luka. The tree filled the room with the pleasing, piney scent they'd always struggled to emulate in the grottos. She inhaled deeply before unwrapping the decorations she'd bought.

Adding decorations to the tree was oddly soothing. Charlotte thought about her trip to Hedgelord, wondering if she'd just wanted to go and see that ragtag group of people who knew her one more time.

It was strange that all it had taken for her to finally bond with Tom, after several years of working together, was for her to lose her job and for him to lose his standing with senior management. Smashing things together had felt like a really pleasant moment. With a jolt, Charlotte realised that sharing the clown smashing with Tom had given her more pleasure than the actual destruction. She had no idea what that meant, but for the moment she decided to cling to the idea of it indicating a certain maturity.

She was almost tempted to text Jack and tell him about it, but she sighed and resisted. Whatever was broken between them wasn't going to be fixed with the news that she had taken a baby step towards adulthood.

If she was to celebrate her successes, she'd probably need to do it alone.

She looked at her watch. The sun might be setting outside, but the afternoon was barely over.

She could go visit her mum. That would be nice, but it would hardly be celebratory. Opening a bottle of wine and a box of Christmas chocolates didn't seem to hit the right tone either. That was just continuing the slide into alcoholism and gluttony.

Sophie had mentioned a pub – The Granary.

If she was going there for a meal with Snømann it was probably going to be swanky and popular, especially this close to Christmas, but Charlotte reckoned they might be able to squeeze in a single person.

Dining alone required a certain amount of confidence, but Charlotte had suffered so many knock backs and attacks this year that the thought held no fears. And what to wear? How did one celebrate in a way to bolster one's fragile sense of self after being sacked and rejected? Charlotte gave a small bark of laughter. There was only one answer, of course. It was an occasion requiring a 'fuck you' dress.

Charlotte wasn't a follower of fashion, but even she understood the concept – made famous by Diana, Princess of Wales, after her husband had admitted adultery and she turned up to an event in a fabulous, daring outfit. It was a dress oozing confident sexuality, making it clear that the wearer was undefeated by crushing events. It just so happened that Charlotte possessed such a dress. She'd owned it for several years but had never dared to wear it, in case it was too slutty. Well, tonight it was definitely going to get worn, and Charlotte would dine alone and be fabulous.

35

ANIKA

Anika was strapped to a chair. Ordinarily it would be a nice, comfy chair, but she was strapped to it with cable ties around her wrists.

Having tied her to the chair, a trio of Svens stood watch over her in a corner of the warehouse. She saw two of them had guns holstered at their belts, but they didn't seem to make a big deal of this and she was too frightened, too British, and too unwilling to look uncool in front of the bad guys to mention them.

They were definitely the bad guys. There was no denying it. And she didn't have to wait long before the biggest bad guy came along.

Marti Snømann unbuttoned his winter coat as he walked down the aisle towards her. "Oh, Anika, Anika," he said with what sounded like genuine distress. "I did not want to see you here."

"To be honest, Mr Snømann, I just wandered in and I've

got no idea what's going on," she said. She hoped to play innocent, but Snømann gave her a patient yet sly look. "Okay, I saw a bit of what's going on," she admitted.

Snømann tsked loudly and shook his grey head. "Such a shame. I value my employees, and I value the sort of intelligence and initiative you have shown during my brief tenure as your boss."

"Er. Um. Thanks." She couldn't help herself. She felt a rush of warm pride at his compliment, despite the situation.

"I suppose the very least I can do is offer you an explanation," he said mournfully.

"You're a drug smuggler," she said.

He opened his mouth as though to deny it, then gave a cheery shrug. "That is exactly what I am. An importer and exporter of recreational drugs between numerous countries. I suppose you are wondering about the details of this particular operation."

She'd had time to think about it. "You're currently 'importing' Santa candles. I'm doing air quotes but my hands are tied. Cocaine wrapped— It *is* cocaine, isn't it?"

"It is."

"I knew it! Cocaine wrapped in a coating of wax probably throws off the sniffer dogs if done right."

"Very good."

"You bring them here for unpacking and sorting before shipping them off to dealers and users across the country."

"Correct. But why use a garden centre as a front, I think you're wondering?" he said.

"Well, they're businesses with a large footprint. Lots of space. Lots of opportunity for storage. Also, there's almost nothing they don't sell at some time or another. It's called a garden centre, but really it's a 'garden plus everything else' centre."

"Yes, but—"

"And most garden centres, like these two, are based near key infrastructure points which is good for transportation."

"Quite, and yet—"

"But it's also out of town," she said. "They're often in rural areas, or on the edges of them. Low police presence and few CCTV cameras."

"You have thought about this," he nodded approvingly.

"I've had a few minutes," she admitted. "It's surprising you haven't done this before. Wait – you have? No, you haven't!" she decided. "You've been too focused on Hedgelord and Bloomers. This is a test run, isn't it?"

He gave a begrudging nod.

"That's why you've got all your stooges from the motherland here. You want this all to run super smoothly. And if it does, then maybe you'll expand into other garden centres across the country..."

"It is a possibility," said Snømann with no small pleasure. "The concept of garden centres is almost entirely unknown across much of Europe. Yes, there are nurseries and *jardineries,* but not garden centres. And yet, do you know how many garden centres there are in the UK?"

"A thousand?" Anika guessed.

"Ha!" Snømann barked with laughter. "Over five thousand. They contribute nearly five billion pounds sterling to the UK economy each year. They are huge, yet only recently one of the biggest chains has been forced to close a quarter of its stores due to costs. It is a lucrative but fragile industry."

Anika frowned. "You don't just want to use Hedgelord and Bloomers as fronts? You also want to keep them going as proper garden centres?"

"But of course! Garden centre turnover is five billion pounds; cocaine powder, two billion a year. Combined, that's a seven billion pound industry. My empire of beautiful garden centres, kept financially steady by the ever-reliable demands of cocaine users!"

"You're mad!" she said, then thought about it. "Actually, it makes a lot of sense."

"I know!" he chortled. "I have worked very hard for this. And, as I say, it's such a deep, deep shame that an intelligent and hard-working employee such as you had to find out about it in this way."

Anika could not help but feel a pang of admiration for this entrepreneur, and she had to keep reminding herself that illegal drug dealing was illegal for a reason.

"I would have been much happier if you had just been a cannabis dealer," she said.

"Oh?"

She shrugged. "You know: the overall health impacts, the low addiction."

"True."

"Obviously has its own problems – on memory and mental health."

"Obviously."

"And logically it just sort of fits in with the garden centre vibe. Growing plants, nurturing crops."

He clicked his cheek ruefully. "That's the problem. It's too obvious."

"But cocaine?"

"Good profit margins."

"You're the scum of the earth."

He stuck out his bottom lip, unfussed. "Kills fewer people than smoking and alcohol. Or fast food for that matter. Popular at all levels of society. And it provides employment for people in some of the poorest regions of the world."

"Oh, I'm sure you can justify it to yourself'." She had another thought. "There's just one thing I don't understand..."

"Just one?" he said. "And you were doing so well."

"Sophie. This pretend infatuation with our Sophie. I'm sure it fits into your plans and she's key somehow, but I don't see how..."

"No, not at all," said Snømann. "I am genuinely fond of her. We Finns are slow to admit to our emotions, but I think I might be willing to love that woman." He clicked his fingers, suddenly remembering. He took out his phone. "Damn!"

Anika understood. "Your surprise date at the Granary," she said. "You're meant to be there."

He screwed up his face in irritation. "But you have caused me to be delayed. Distracted." He sighed, tapped on his phone and put it to his ear. "Sophie! Sophie, my love!"

Anika thought about shouting out for help at that moment, maybe somehow conveying her location and her predicament in just a few short words. But one of the Svens had stepped forward and casually placed his hand on the pistol at his belt. Anika decided silence was the better option.

"I am so sorry," said Snømann. "I must cancel our dinner date tonight. Something has come up at work." He glanced at Anika. "A little, little problem. Soon fixed. My apologies, *mi amore*." He made noisy kisses and ended the call. He glared at Anika. "See?"

"See?" she said.

"You not only make me miss a delightful date with the beautiful Sophie but you remind me again why I am so sad to lose you."

"You don't have to lose me..." she suggested faintly.

Snømann's head bowed in miserable resignation. "Sven ... Sven. Take her to the Alpine Lodge."

Two of the Svens came forward and, one at each side, bodily lifted up the chair with Anika still in it.

"What's the lodge?" she said.

Snømann made no explanation. All he said was "We shall try to make you as comfortable as possible," before walking away.

36

GALLAGHER

While Gallagher and Luka were still applying the tensioning wires to the marquee, one of the Svens called them over. They approached, but he held up his hand to stop them as he spoke into his phone.

"Yes, sir. I can redirect half a dozen operatives. I will send the English too, yes?" He nodded as someone spoke on the other end. "Sure, straight away."

Sven looked at Luka and Gallagher. "Please can the two of you go and report to the Alpine Lodge?"

"What?" said Luka.

"We've had a security breach at Site A. We need you over there."

"Sure," said Gallagher. "Alpine Lodge." He frowned. "Where is that?"

"It's on the edge of the Bloomers site. If you ask at Customer Service they will show you."

Luka and Gallagher walked over to Bloomers.

"You ever been over here before?" asked Gallagher.

"I came to look at their plant area a few times," said Luka. "Is inferior in many ways. Populist."

"What does that mean?" asked Gallagher.

"Playing to fucking gallery. You can give people what they want or what they need. Bloomers concentrates on what people think they want."

Gallagher nodded. "And you think that at Hedgelord we give them what they need?"

"Only if they fucking ask," said Luka, rolling his eyes in exasperation. "And nobody ever asks, but the possibility is there."

It was a classic piece of Luka logic, so Gallagher left it well alone. The evening air was crisp and pleasant, so the two of them dawdled slightly, shooting the breeze as they went.

When they entered the shop they got directions to the Alpine Lodge, which led them through the plant area. They took their time checking it out.

"Are there some fellas over here that are like the equivalent of you and me?" Gallagher wondered, looking around.

"You think every garden centre needs pair of handsome plant experts?" asked Luka, flashing his movie star grin.

"Well yeah! Not sure about handsome, but someone's got to hoik the fucking gravel around, haven't they?"

As if in answer, they passed a path up between some sheds, where they caught a glimpse of two people who looked as if they were moving heavy bags off a pallet.

"Is that them?" Gallagher asked. He felt like David Attenborough spotting a rare animal at a watering hole.

"Don't know." Luka was whispering, as if he was afraid of spooking them.

"We could go and have a look, maybe say hello?" Gallagher said.

"We should do job we were sent to do," said Luka.

The two of them glanced at the distant figures with a mix of curiosity and regret, then carried on to the Alpine Lodge, where they both halted in surprise.

"This is fucking mad!" said Gallagher. "When they said Alpine Lodge, I assumed it would be the name of a shed, like the Highland Hideaway."

"Is actual fucking Alpine Lodge!" Luka walked around the large building in the fading afternoon light, prodding and inspecting. It was made from sawn logs, as if someone had felled a small forest to construct it.

The windows were too high to see inside, so they walked round to the front to find the door. There was a large porch with a swing, which would probably be fun in the summer. The windows overlooking the front had shutters across them, so they still had no idea what was inside. Gallagher tapped on the door.

A Sven opened the door. "You are taking the next shift, yes?"

"Er, yes. What do we need to do?" asked Gallagher.

"Come in, I will explain."

They stepped into a comfortable room, where the furnishing reminded Gallagher of the grotto, except this was the grown-up, deluxe version. Comfy chairs, sheepskin rugs and tartan throws made the place look inviting.

"You will remain in this room unless summoned elsewhere," said Sven. "One of you will patrol the perimeter twice an hour, and you will also inspect the CCTV monitoring from the laptop on the table. Nobody goes in or out without direct say-so from Snømann. Is this clear?"

"Yes?" said Gallagher, looking round. "Yes." He grinned and looked at Luka. It seemed simple enough, and looked like a nice place to sit and pass the time for a while.

37

CHARLOTTE

C harlotte wore the 'fuck you' dress and agreed with herself that she looked fucking sensational. She'd had a momentary wobble when she'd first put it on and looked in the mirror, wondering if it was too raunchy, but a hefty glass of red had strengthened her resolve. The dress was made from a richly embroidered fabric. It had a playfully short skirt with decorative ruching at the top of the bust, featuring a daring low back that plunged right down to the top of her bum. She accessorised it with the garish and kitsch Christmas tree brooch Sophie had given her. What was a decent 'fuck you' without a touch of the ridiculous?

She caught a taxi to The Granary. The pub sat on a quiet country road, tucked between rolling fields and a small copse of winter-bare trees. The building had thick stone walls and a pitched slate roof. Warm light spilled out through arched windows. A few cars were neatly parked by the side.

Charlotte walked into the bar. She held her head high,

went to order a drink and find out about a table. She saw several heads turn as she walked through and hoped she wasn't going to get pestered by blokes out on the pull. She had pictured an empowering meal, not a fight for personal space.

The bar was busy, so she waited for a few minutes, looking at the wine list. Someone slid into the space next to her and she groaned inwardly. She turned to glare at her new neighbour, keen to set the tone before he'd opened his mouth.

"Fuck!"

It was Jack Hartigan. He raised his eyebrows. "Charlotte."

"What are you doing here?" she asked.

"It's one of my favourite places. I think I mentioned that to you."

Her face coloured. Did he think she'd come here to find him? "Oh. Oh shit. You did."

She briefly wondered whether she should call a taxi and go somewhere else, but a woman in a suit squeezed between her and Jack and clapped her hands. "Aha! I've found you."

"Found me?" said Jack.

The woman pointed casually at Charlotte's brooch and smiled. "Would the two of you come with me please?"

Charlotte glanced at Jack, but he looked as confused as her. They both turned to ask a question, but the woman was already moving through the room, beckoning fiercely.

Charlotte sighed and followed, along with Jack, just so they could correct whatever misassumption the woman had made.

"I am delighted to tell you that the two of you will be

dining in our exclusive pod and will be served our special tasting menu," said the woman.

"Wait a minute, is that the tasting menu with the wine pairings?" asked Jack. "I thought that was suspended over the Christmas period?"

She winked at him, making Charlotte roll her eyes. "It is indeed, but we are making it exclusively available for the two of you this evening."

"Yes – but why?" asked Charlotte. "Are you sure this is for us?"

The woman looked taken aback. "I am very sure. We were definitely told to expect you. It has been arranged for you at considerable expense, and all been prepaid. If there is some concern, then—"

"—No concern," said Jack smoothly. He leaned in and whispered to Charlotte. "This menu is to die for. You will not want to miss it. I suggest we just roll with it and set aside our differences or the evening."

She gave him a look. "Set aside our differences?"

He gave her a look in return. "I can if you can."

Charlotte huffed. "Fine."

The woman led them back through the door and outside the building. Charlotte threw a confused look at Jack. How could this be right? They went round the side of the building, and there was the pod. It was an actual pod: like a transparent acrylic egg on its side. Fairy lights twinkled around it, and inside was a single table, already laid for them.

"Oh. This is … unusual," said Charlotte.

They stepped inside. It was warmer than Charlotte had

imagined it might be in the depths of winter. She had no idea how it was heated, but it was very cosy. There was even a tiny Christmas tree in the end of the pod.

"Welcome to your private dining experience," said the woman. "As you can see this space is very much your own for the evening. Every course is one of our chef's special creations and will be matched with the finest of wines by our sommelier. Your waiter will bring the courses for you, but otherwise you will not be disturbed. There is a console to operate the temperature control and the opacity of the pod itself. I shall bring the mulled gin and tonic aperitifs if that suits."

The woman withdrew and they were left alone in the pod.

"Well, I've got to say that this evening has taken a turn I did not see coming," said Jack, settling back in his seat. "First of all there's you in that dress—"

"You've got thoughts on my dress?" Charlotte's insides had given a small lurch of unexpected pleasure. He'd noticed the dress. Obviously, that was its purpose, but he'd noticed it!

"Only positive ones."

She crossed her arms, amused. "Oh, do tell!"

If she was going to enjoy the evening, then watching Jack stumble into a trap as he tried to compliment her dress was a perfect start. What could he possibly say? Gosh, Charlotte, it really shows off your tits and ass? My my, Charlotte, it's a lot sexier than the other things I've seen you wear?

"Er, your dress?"

"Yes. My dress."

He raised his chin. "Wearing that, the act of wearing that, you seem to have come ... *alive*."

She wasn't expecting that.

"I've always, mostly, known you as Charlotte the Fighter," he said. "You've lost some of that in the past few days."

"Really?"

"Really."

"The business with the Christmas tree and the Santa sleigh. Wasn't that me being a fighter?"

He twisted his mouth. "Honestly? That looked desperate. You were like... You were like a caged animal biting at any hand that came near."

"I'm an animal, huh?"

"You asked. Since..." He cleared his throat. "Since things went horribly wrong between you and me after Lapland, you've either been this miserable snarling beast, or just look like you've given up on life. That dress. It's a statement, right? A sort of 'I'm here, I'm not going away'."

She huffed.

"I'm wrong?" he said.

"It's my 'fuck you' dress."

He laughed loudly. "Oh, so I got it. Well, good for you, Yeah, 'fuck you, world'. It's great. It's great to see you come out fighting again. I get to see you in that dress, which gives me hope, and then we're to be fed the best food and wine available. I might buy a lottery ticket tomorrow."

"I still think there's been an error," she said.

He spread his hands. "If the universe wants to give us a nice gift then who are we to argue? Worst case scenario is we face a grovelling apology from that nice lady who will find us somewhere else to sit. In the meantime we should enjoy ourselves."

"Well that was my intention when I came out this evening. I wanted to stick two fingers up at all the stuff that's gone on in my life. Hence the 'fuck you' dress."

"Ah, I see. Well I approve."

Their aperitifs arrived. Orange and clove infused gin with tonic water.

Jack raised his glass. "To you and your 'fuck you' dress."

She chinked her glass against his. "You're in a much better mood than when we last spoke."

He nodded. "Yes. I mean, I'm not sure I have forgiven you for what you did, but let's put this down to a combination of my naturally sunny disposition and my excitement at having a crack at their famous tasting menu, shall we?"

Charlotte grinned. "Can't say fairer than that."

ANIKA WAS STILL TIED to a chair but was now inside the 'Alpine Lodge'.

Despite being on the Bloomers site, in a very non-alpine piece of England, it was very obvious why it was called that. It was like one of those swanky chalets where people stayed to go skiing. Anika's family were not at all interested in winter sport, but the aesthetic was familiar. Warm, woody tones glowed from every corner. Cushions and throws invited lounging and snuggling.

There were several things that made this Alpine Lodge interesting. One that it was here at Bloomers. Anika was astonished to think that while Hedgelord had noticed a few minor changes since Snømann had taken over, he'd been building entire buildings over on the Bloomers site – including a drugs-processing warehouse and a luxury prison. Yes, it was definitely a prison: Anika had seen the doors she'd been taken through, and they were fitted with fancy bolts that went deep into the frame.

Another thing that made this Alpine Lodge interesting was the presence of the former Hedgelord boss, Cameron Clasp, sitting in a nearby chair, relaxed, sipping whisky and watching...

There were no two ways about it. He was watching porn.

He was so transfixed by the oversized buttocks pumping enthusiastically on the huge screen before him that Anika was certain he hadn't even noticed her.

"Cameron," she said.

"Hmm?" He didn't look away.

"Cameron!"

He paused the film with a sigh and turned. "Good lord, Anita. What are you doing here?"

"Same as you, I guess," she said.

"Splendid! Well pull up a chair, eh? If you don't mind, I would like to see the rest of *The Adventures of Bootygirl*, but you can choose the next one."

"Right, I see," said Anika. "Maybe it's not quite correct to say I'm doing the same as you."

"No?"

"I have no massive inclination to watch porn, but— What adventures does *Bootygirl* have, exactly? Has she got a superpower?"

"Her superpower is having a massive booty. There's an

action sequence where she whacks a couple of baddies off a train with a side-swipe, on her way to seduce the hero in the sleeper carriage. Want to see it?"

"Erm, maybe later..."

"I mean, given the choice I'd be out on the driving range, practising my swing. Not with the weather as it is though, obviously. Shame. I need to work on my teeing off. My biggest weakness Patty Fufu used to say."

Anika looked about the place, at the roaring open fire (gas fired, not real, she thought) and the big sheepskin rug before it. She looked at the hampers of food on the kitchen counter, and the very well stocked drinks cabinet in the corner.

"How did you come to be over here?" she said. "Nobody knew where you'd gone."

Cameron swirled the whisky in his glass and looked pensive. "To be honest, Anita, it's a bit of a blur. There was a business deal where I signed over a portion of the garden centre, then the celebration happened. There was a very nice Laphroaig, a lap dancing club, and at some point I ended up here."

Anika looked around at the luxurious surroundings, at the quality drinks, nibbles and porn on offer, and only then did it occur to her that maybe Cameron didn't even realise he was being held captive.

38

CHARLOTTE

The gin and tonics were delicious (although Charlotte wasn't sure a drink needed a massive sprig of rosemary in it), and were swiftly followed by smoked salmon roulade starters with a carafe of Sauvignon Blanc. It suddenly became very, very easy to let this unlikely good fortune carry them through the evening.

"I visited Hedgelord you know," said Charlotte as they both took a spoonful of the second course's crab and herb risotto. "After I got fired, I mean."

"You did?" said Jack. "Would you believe I went into Bloomers? Very much on the low-down, mind you."

"No!" Charlotte had assumed she was the only one with the inexplicable urge to know what was going on – like some sad muppet who couldn't let go. "What did you find?"

"So, obviously there's been a takeover."

"Yep."

"People are nervous about what happens next. Men in

weird black outfits are doing all the work. No sign of Marcus and Maremba." He jabbed his spoon. "But probably the maddest thing of all is the outbreak of enormous new buildings that have appeared, literally overnight. I have no idea how that even happens."

"Enormous buildings?"

"Yep. One of them's a new warehouse or something."

Charlotte put her own spoon down. "What could that be for?"

"I have no idea. I could maybe see a model where you'd buy up bankrupt stock or something. Having space like that gives you some opportunities, but it's so big. Like an aircraft hangar."

Charlotte sighed. "We can't let go, can we?"

He shook his head. "What sad sacks we are. Defined by our work."

She made an amused hum.

"What?" he said.

"I'd assumed you were a much more well-rounded human being than that."

"Oh?"

"That you had a whole life going on outside work."

"Oh, we can't all be like you. A woman of faith."

"You're mocking."

"I'm not. I know you've had your ups and downs with your church, but you have always wanted to devote your life to something bigger than yourself. Church, hymns on Sunday, good deeds through the week."

"Your view of my Christian faith is far too rosy. It's been a battle."

"Tell me."

She chased a last piece of rice around the bowl, then gave up.

"Seriously," said Jack. "Tell me. I'm not a man of faith. There's a whole lot of fierce Catholic guilt in my family tree, but it seemed to just pass me by. You... You actually believe."

"I do."

"So, tell me. I want to know."

She grunted. "Faith is not an on-off switch. There are good days and bad days. It's like..." she swirled her glass "... alcohol is bad for us. Alcohol is the bad choice."

"Is this about your faith?"

"It is. Shut up a minute. We know alcohol is the bad choice for us. Just as I know – I *know* – that God exists and he came to earth as Jesus. Put himself down here in the shit with us, because he loves us and wants to bring us into his love. But sometimes you forget that alcohol is bad for you and you get utterly pissed on—" She looked at her glass. "What is this?"

"A pleasantly herby Vertmentino," he said.

"Right. That. Some days I let the good choice – God, staying off the booze, whatever—" She hesitated, unsure.

"No, I'm still following the tortured metaphor. Go on."

"Some days I let the good choice slide because it seems almost everyone else is not making the good choice either. And sometimes I don't want to make the good choice. Some days I want to tell God to fuck off." She sighed. "Some days I *do* tell God to fuck off. It's like alcoholics never call themselves a former alcoholic. Once an alcoholic, always an alcoholic."

"Right."

"Same with God, with Jesus. I have doubts and I have battles and it's never over." She sniffed. "And I know I'm not a good person."

"Charlotte—"

"No, I'm not, Jack. Just because I can see what goodness is and because I've touched goodness, briefly, it doesn't mean I'm not a bitchy, angry, selfish and vindictive woman." She looked at the wine again. "The tasting notes, does it say this stuff makes you feel guilty and maudlin."

"It does not," said Jack. He reached across the table and took her hand.

She didn't flinch. She thought she ought to flinch. They were enemies, right? She didn't want to flinch though. She was clearly verging on drunk but the touch of his hands made a liquid shiver run through her: cold and warm at the same time. A contradiction, like hot ice-cream.

"You are not a bad person," he said.

"Fuck you, I am, Jack," she said. "I got you fired."

He tilted his head. "Yeah. Yeah, you did. I can't deny it. And I'm probably still pissed off about that. But the fact that you have doubts means you put more effort into being a good person than any of us. Some of us don't even think about being a good person."

"Really?"

"Really."

"Because I assumed that, when you weren't at work, I assumed you were out delivering soup to poor orphans or helping, I dunno, helping fallen women or something."

"Yes, that's obviously right," he said. "Clearly, I spend my weekends travelling to Dickensian England to help— Sorry, did you actually say fallen women?"

"I have been drinking, you know."

He sat back, releasing her hand. She didn't want him to.

"What do I actually spend my time doing?" he said. "I spend my free time sniping with my ex-girlfriend over the most pointless things. We've still not sorted who gets to keep the rug and who pays for it. Petty stuff. And I visit shopping sites to buy things I don't need. I've started watching *Love Island* on ITV. That's how low I've sunk."

"Is *Love Island* on at Christmas?" she said.

"Repeats of *Love Island*. I'm not even watching empty headed bimbos and himbos copping off with each other in real-time. Repeats. I tell myself I'm going to learn the guitar again. I won't. I've ordered a home gym that I'm too lazy to open. Oh – and I've started browsing dog rescue centres because, after our walk the other day, I appear to be deluding myself that owning a dog will fix the hole in my life. There's not a single altruistic thought in my head."

She downed the rest of her wine. "Adopting a dog is good thing to do."

"For selfish reasons, though." He shook his head and smiled. "I'm as much of a mess as you are."

The pod door opened and the waiter came in to collect their plates.

"How are we doing?" he asked.

"Oh, we're complete messes," said Charlotte with a bright smile. "What's next?"

"Hearty and indulgent duck breast with a port and cherry

reduction, served with caramelised parsnips and potato gratin."

Jack rapped the edge of the table. "Bring it on!"

The duck was indeed delicious.

As they ate, Jack's expression went from neutral to thoughtful to wryly amused. When she looked at him directly his face crumpled with laughter.

"What?" she said.

"I was just thinking about that time – what, less than three weeks ago? – when we drunkenly broke into Mickey Bubbles' house."

She laughed too. "Oh my God, that was so fucked up!"

It was no wonder Jack was thinking about it. The last time they had been in a pub and drunk as much as they had done tonight, the two of them had cooked up the idea of reviving the fortunes of their garden centres by breaking into the house of much-loved Christmas crooner, Mickey Bubbles, and pressuring him into performing in a customer's garden.

"Yeah, it was fucked up," Jack agreed. "It was somehow both a terrible thing to do and the most amazing adventure!"

"We are a bad influence on each other."

Charlotte looked at him. It occurred to her that the pub, and the alcohol, and the fact they were together again, in this moment, was not the only reason he was thinking about the Mickey Bubbles thing. "Are you thinking what I think you're thinking?"

He gave her an impish smile. "What? Are you thinking we should go and take a look at what they're really doing in those warehouses over at Bloomers?"

"I'm asking you if *you're* thinking it," she said.

"But is it what you're thinking too?" he said.

"It's probably a very bad idea," said Charlotte.

"What are they gonna do? Sack me?"

Charlotte laughed at that and immediately felt bad. "Sorry. I shouldn't laugh. It's not funny that you lost your job."

"We both lost our jobs," said Jack, slapping the table for emphasis. "And yet here we are, both still caring about our ex-workplaces. It could be a useful act of closure for us."

"Closure, huh?"

"Closure."

"And fun," she said. "You definitely don't need to convince me, I am totally up for a little bit of light breaking and entering."

"Oh, actual breaking and entering, is it?"

"Probably. And on that subject, how will we get inside?"

"Well, here's a funny thing. Bloomers has a whole set of cast-iron procedures to cover all eventualities. When a person leaves, they must hand over all of their assets, including passes and keys, to the designated handler. Trouble is, because Marcus and Maremba haven't been around, nobody has ever been assigned to do that, so I still have all mine."

"Then the only thing stopping us is this open bottle of wine," said Charlotte. "Do we neck it or take it with us?"

Jack grinned and picked up the bottle. "Let's see how soon we can get a taxi, shall we?"

39

ANIKA

"Cameron," Anika asked. "Have you tried going outside at all?"

He wrinkled his nose as if she'd said something odd. "Can't say that I have. Weather's been atrocious, apparently."

He changed channel and on the TV screen was a red weather warning, saying that snowfall had immobilised much of the country. "See? Why would I want to go out there? Looks terrible."

Anika shook her head. "What even is that? It's not a regular TV channel, is it? Has it just been showing this same image all the time?"

"Yes," he shrugged. "It's just an information jobbie, isn't it? Like Ceefax."

Anika had no idea what Ceefax was, but she knew this thing on the screen was fake. "The weather is not at all like that. It's just a little bit drizzly."

"Well it will probably refresh shortly," said Cameron. He switched back to the porn film and settled down to enjoy it. "It's been very entertaining here in this delightful lodge. They even sent me a quirky escort. Desiree her name was. Lovely woman."

Anika turned the name over in her mind. Desiree. Wasn't that the name of Sophie's neighbour who was making fancy gift bags for the big celebration party? She was supposed to be asking Cameron what kind of pen he had, so it seemed strange that Cameron had decided she was a sex worker. Anika thought it probably spoke volumes about his general attitude towards women.

She was definitely done being polite. "You're a prisoner, Cameron. We're both being held prisoner here."

"Really?"

"I'm strapped to this chair, for God's sake! Didn't you notice that?"

Cameron shrugged. "I try not to judge people. We all have our kinks, don't we? You ask Desiree! She did this thing with modelling clay. I tell you..."

"Yeah, well this is not something I chose. Is there any way you could release me, please?"

Cameron paused the film with a sigh and got up from his chair. He walked over to Anika and bent over to inspect the cable ties around her wrists. "Cable ties? Women can normally open these with their fingernails can't they?"

"Not when they're tied down, Cameron."

"Well, I will need some scissors, then."

He drifted around the room, gazing at the empty occasional tables which were arranged between the chairs.

He searched as if he had no real idea of how searching was normally done.

"Look in the drawers!" yelled Anika.

Cameron made a small noise of surprise when he discovered some of the tables contained drawers, but they also seemed to be mostly empty. He pulled a second remote control out of one.

"Well hello! Do we have some other channels we can access here?" he said, and plonked himself back down into his chair to investigate.

"Cameron! You were going to release me!" Anika shouted.

"No scissors, sorry," he said, poring over the buttons on the controller.

Anika gave a muted roar of frustration. "Break a leg off one of those little tables. I think we could use it to snap the arm on this chair."

Cameron turned to her in horror. "I can't go breaking things! We're not animals, are we? Good lord, that's just not cricket."

Anika growled in protest as he went back to pressing buttons, but she went quiet and began watching the screen. It had changed to show a view of the room they were sitting in. She swivelled to see where the camera was. It was small, but just about visible. The two of them were on CCTV.

IN THE SECURITY office of the Alpine Lodge, Gallagher checked the time. "One of us needs to patrol the perimeter."

"I will go," said Luka, fetching a joint from his pocket as he moved towards the door.

"Yeah, we can take it in turns. I'll look at the CCTV," said Gallagher.

He opened the laptop, and found the feed. He sat down, scrolling through the various images on display. There was one trained on the outside, so he watched Luka lighting up his joint before strolling off. The outside was lit up with floodlights, and the feed showed each side. Gallagher located some navigation buttons, and found he could either toggle to the feed he wanted, or let them all play in rotation. He skipped back to see where Luka had got to, but he'd barely moved. At this speed it would take him ages to go right round the building.

Gallagher looked at some of the interior feeds, wondering how many rooms were in the Alpine Lodge. There were a couple of empty ones set up for meetings, each with a large central table surrounded by chairs. Then there was a huge, lounge-style room with two people sitting in chairs. He wondered who they were, then realised there was a massive screen in view, playing a soft porn film.

"Oh cool!"

Gallagher wondered whether he could zoom in, so that he could watch it too. After a few moments of investigation, he figured out how to do it. He zoomed in so that the film filled the laptop's own screen and sat back to enjoy *The Adventures of Bootygirl*. When Luka eventually returned, Gallagher pointed at the laptop with glee.

"Mate! Look at this! They're watching porn in the big room over there, and we can watch it too."

"Huh. Is cool." Luka pulled a chair over and got himself

comfy, just as Bootygirl executed her signature waggle on screen, making Gallagher hoot with laughter.

40

CHARLOTTE

Charlotte and Jack arrived at Bloomers.

The taxi driver had zero interest in them wanting to be dropped off at a locked-up garden centre after dark. He drove away, leaving them by the tall, padlocked car park gate.

"Right, I have some good news and some bad news," said Jack.

"Yeah, what's that?" Charlotte asked.

"The bad news is that out of all the keys I still have, the one which opens this padlock is not amongst them. I'd forgotten they locked them after hours."

"Fuck. What's the good news?"

He gave an apologetic smile. "I am *really* going to enjoy watching you climb over it in that dress."

Charlotte whirled on him, suddenly furious. "What? Not on your fucking nelly! Why is it that in films and telly, when dresses get ripped in the name of adventure, nobody ever mentions how expensive they are! There's no way I can go climbing in this without splitting the skirt or snagging the embroidery."

"Oh. Yeah, of course. My bad. I'd hate to see it spoiled."

Charlotte shook with frustration, knowing there were limited options available to her. "Right. This is what's going to happen. You're going to turn around and I am taking it off."

Jack laughed and then looked askance. "What? No, really? You can't be serious?"

"Which part? Me taking it off or you turning round?"

"Well, both! I mean, we're on a main road for one thing. Anyone who drives past will get a better view than me."

His plaintive tone made her want to smile, but she inhaled deeply. This was not the time to be sidetracked by lust. "Stop whining and turn around."

She pulled off the dress, which was a completely ridiculous thing to do in December, as if she wasn't already cold enough. She folded it into a neat package, put her bag on top, and hoisted herself up onto the gate. Her shoes had heels, but not massive ones. She muttered a small prayer of thanks to her earlier decision to choose the less punishing option.

"I could do with a little light so I can see to climb over," she said.

"I can do light, but I will need to turn around," said Jack.

"Fine. Turn around."

He shone the torch from his phone to illuminate the bars of the gate. Charlotte climbed up and straddled the top. A small noise of appreciation came from Jack.

"What did you say?" she demanded.

"Nothing. You look like some kind of warrior queen, riding her gate into battle. Just stay like that for a minute though – I want to make sure I commit it fully to memory." He moved the light across her body, lingering more than was necessary on her underwear. She was pleased she'd worn the fancy matching stuff in black lace.

"Fucking perve," she grumbled as she climbed down the other side and found her feet on the floor.

Jack pushed her dress through the gate and she pulled it back over her head as he climbed over the gate to join her. Shivering, she stamped her feet to warm them.

He dropped down onto the ground and draped his jacket over her, his hands lingering slightly on her arms. "Let's get you warmed up, then we'll go take a look round."

ANIKA'S CHAIR HAD WHEELS. She couldn't believe it had taken her so long to realise and take advantage of the fact. She wheeled it over to the smallest of the occasional tables. Cameron glanced at her, but his eyes were very much on the film.

She hooked a foot underneath the table and used her other foot to scoot the chair backwards, dragging the table after her. She was on a thick rug, so it was slow going at first, but she sped up once she got onto the polished floor at the edge of the room.

She positioned herself and the table so that she could squeeze the most impact out of a single move, because she had a hunch Cameron would not approve of what she was about to do. She wanted to kick the table against the wall with such force that one of its spindly legs would break off. Could she deliver a kick like that, or was she kidding herself? She raised the table with both feet, swung her legs back as far as she could manage (which was not far) and shouted as she pistoned her feet forward with maximum effort. The effect was not quite what she'd intended. The table caught on part of her chair, and the transfer of momentum caused by her magnificent kick flipped the chair over onto its side.

"Oh fuck!" she yelled as she hit the floor. She was not only winded, she had also bashed her arm hard as she landed. She wiggled her fingers. They worked fine, so hopefully she hadn't broken anything.

"Anita? What in blue blazes are you doing down there?" asked Cameron, standing over her.

41

CHARLOTTE

C harlotte followed Jack as he unlocked the gate which led into the rear of Bloomers. They had no need to pass through the main shop: they could simply walk through the plant area.

"I can already see the building you're talking about, even in the dark," whispered Charlotte. "It's huge!"

"Yeah! Come on."

They crept through the plant area and out to where the new building stood.

"I'll see if my pass opens it," said Jack. "It should do – I had the highest security clearance."

Charlotte rolled her eyes. "Highest security clearance? You do know it's a garden centre, not MI5?"

"Hey! Security is important." Jack offered his pass to the door lock in the side of the warehouse. The light flashed green and the door clunked open.

"Cool!" Charlotte gave him a thumbs-up.

They went inside. Lights came on at their approach, which was both handy and also slightly terrifying. Charlotte saw warehouse racking, stretching away into the shadows.

"What's all this for? Most of it's empty," said Jack.

"Suggests that whatever it's for is not up to full scale yet," said Charlotte. "Looks a bit busier down that end. Let's go and look."

The lights continued to turn on as they approached and turn off as they moved away. It was probably really efficient, but it brought an unsettling horror movie vibe.

"Boxes and boxes of candles." Jack pointed up at the racks. There were hundreds of identical boxes. On a nearby bench one was partially open; he pulled it closer.

Charlotte joined him as he bent over to see what was inside. He took out a candle and novelty holder. It was a Santa figure with a candle for a hat. He turned it over in his hands.

"Well this is very odd. Obviously I know what stock we ordered for Christmas, and I swear I never saw these ugly things," said Jack. "If you'd twisted my arm, I *might* have bought a box or two, but they'd have ended up in the discount section. Guaranteed." He gazed up at the racking and the piles of boxes. "There must be thousands and thousands of them here."

Charlotte walked around the benches. "What do you suppose they do here? It's all been tidied up, but it's like the candles come out of the boxes where you are, then are moved here."

Jack followed her. "Oh yeah. What's in that box on the floor?"

They both stooped down. It was filled with discarded terracotta Santa bodies.

"So the holders go back in boxes and just the candles get passed on round the benches," said Charlotte, moving on. "So – I'm standing here, and I get a candle…" She picked up a portable machine. "I don't know what this is, but it's got red wax on its blade."

Jack scrabbled on the floor and picked up a disc of wax. "You're cutting the bases off the candles."

They looked at each other, understanding dawning.

"Fuck," said Charlotte. "This is a smuggling thing."

There was an enormous plastic bin at the end of the bench, filled with red wax. Jack picked a candle out of it and peered inside the hollow base, using his phone to light up the inside. "Can't exactly see a lot, but is that powder, would you say?"

Charlotte looked and nodded. "Fuck. What do we do? This was supposed to be a funny, silly end to the evening."

"But it's not."

"No."

Jack took her hand. "We should probably return the way we came and figure out what to do," he said quietly.

As they moved around the far end of the workstation, Charlotte noticed something else on the floor, almost underneath the bin of red wax. It was a phone. She picked it up and tapped the screen.

"Oh fuck!" She showed it to Jack.

The phone's lock screen had a picture of Anika, Charlotte, Sophie and Karen, all snarling in fury at the camera as they pointed at a pile of shattered crockery on Karen's patio.

"What the hell is that?" he said.

"An evening of slightly drunken destruction," said Charlotte. "I think this is Anika's phone."

They looked at each other.

"What would Anika's phone be doing here?" Jack whispered.

"It's not good, whatever it is," she whispered back.

Charlotte was torn between pondering that question further and getting the hell out of the warehouse, then a set of lights snapped on in the darkened end of the warehouse where they had yet to look. She shoved Anika's phone into the top of her dress.

"Fuck!" she mouthed silently to Jack.

Someone else was in the building.

Without further discussion, the two of them hurried back round the workstation, towards the shelving and the distant door.

"Please stop. I do not want to send my men to hunt you down like dogs."

Charlotte looked back. Snømann stood a few feet away, with several of his black-clad companions advancing towards them.

"Jack—" she said.

He squeezed her hand.

They were never going to outrun these people, so they turned and stood their ground.

"This is a popular venue tonight," said Snømann mournfully, walking towards them. He gestured about. "Are you impressed with my operation?"

"To be honest," said Jack, "we're both a little drunk and we came in here looking for fairy lights, for a joke. We'll get going now, and stop being so irresponsible."

"Oh Jack. Charlotte. Please do not take me for a fool. I watched you on the cameras and I saw you put the pieces together. The only part you didn't inspect was my recycling facility. Come."

Snømann indicated they should follow as he moved deeper into the warehouse. He grabbed a handle on the massive bin of red wax and dragged it behind him. Further along was another open area, with a large, open-topped vat standing in the centre, around eight feet tall. It was flanked by a step ladder and a scissor lift. Snømann hefted the bin of wax onto the scissor lift and stepped back.

Charlotte saw drips of hardened red wax running down the sides of the vat and guessed it was some sort of heater to melt down the candles.

"Mostly we make small candles using the moulds you can see behind," said Snømann. "I am proud to say that this operation operates a zero waste policy."

Charlotte couldn't help but give a bitter laugh.

"What, you are amused at that?" said Snømann. "You think that just because I smuggle cocaine I cannot hold myself to my own personal ethical standards? All holders are exported for re-use and all wax is melted down to make new candles. It is admirable, no?"

"It's good to hear about your ethical standards," said Jack. "I guess that means you won't want to hurt us, so we can just agree to say nothing and walk away. How does that work for you?"

Snømann's face twisted in a sad smile. "I'm afraid it doesn't. You two will come with me to the Alpine Lodge while I prepare for Operation Yuletide Surprise."

"Yuletide Surprise?" said Charlotte.

"Yes. I am effecting great changes here, at both Bloomers and Hedgelord, but sadly, there cannot be great change without sacrifice."

"Er, what kind of sacrifice?" said Jack.

"In many ways, this is the ideal time of year for it," said Snømann. "You know the story of the Winter King?"

Charlotte shook her head slowly.

"In certain European tribes, long ago, there would be a special feast at this time of year. One of the villagers would be chosen at random to become the Winter King. For a day he would be feted and fawned over, treated like true royalty, and then the next day..." He drew his finger across his throat and made a squeaky Donald Duck noise. "A sacrifice to ensure the prosperity of the tribe during the difficult months ahead. So it is here."

"Here, how?" said Charlotte, sure she wasn't following.

"Yuletide Surprise," said Snømann. "In the wonderful enterprise to come there will not be room for all of the current garden centre employees. And so tomorrow, there will be feasting and joy at our celebration brunch and then sadly..." He drew his finger across his throat again and repeated the duck noise.

"You're going to slit their throats?" said Jack, stunned.

Snømann laughed. "No. No, God, no. I am speaking metaphorically. I thought you British were masters of figurative language. No, in this day and age there are far simpler and less painful ways of getting rid of unnecessary people. In one act, I will make sure everyone is taken care of." He was still laughing. "Slitting people's throats? Oh, that sounds like far too much hard work. Come. The Alpine Lodge awaits."

42

GALLAGHER

Gallagher and Luka were transfixed by *The Adventures of Bootygirl* on the big screen via their CCTV cameras.

"You know what's good about this?" said Gallagher.

Luka offered a questioning grunt in response.

"It's that Bootygirl is in charge. She's not being exploited or dominated by men. She's kicking ass.

"She is also wobbling ass," said Luka, pointing at her onscreen jiggling.

"I can't pretend that's not enjoyable, but she's an actual adventure hero as well. I want her to recover the ... what is she recovering again?"

"Who fucking cares?" Luka asked. "I want her to get naked again."

"It's not microfilm, is it? We don't have those anymore. It's important anyw—"

The door flew open and several Svens marched in, with maximum choreographed swagger.

Gallagher slammed the laptop shut and smiled up at them. "How do, guys!"

Charlotte and Jack were amongst the Svens, and Snømann followed. Gallagher was surprised to see so many of them, but he smiled politely. "Hi Charlotte. Er, Jack."

Charlotte gave Gallagher and Luka a stern look. "Really? The two of you are henchmen now? I'm surprised at you, I really am."

"Oh no, we're not henchmen," said Gallagher. "We're just doing some security work."

"We not henching for anyone," said Luka.

Charlotte looked incredulous. "You're literally wearing the henchmen uniform!"

"Silence," said Snømann to Charlotte. "No more talking." He opened the door to the interior of the lodge and pushed Charlotte and Jack inside.

Gallagher, still surprised by the arrivals, followed them through, uninvited.

Inside was the space he'd seen on the CCTV camera. The soft furnishings, the luxurious rugs, the rustic wood panelling. On the wall, *The Adventures of Bootygirl* was playing. Cameron Clasp sat back in a recliner, sipping a tumbler of whisky.

Anika was strapped to a chair and lying sideways on the floor.

Gallagher automatically went to her. "Fuck me. Let's get you up."

"Oh, the gang's all here!" said Cameron in cheery drunkenness.

Gallagher righted the chair and crouched down in front of Anika. "Are you all right?"

She gave a small nod.

Snømann clicked his fingers. "Gallagher, out!" He pointed at the door.

As Gallagher left, he heard Snømann giving orders for the Svens to tie Jack and Charlotte up and take their phones.

The door was closed and Gallagher saw no more. However, Luka already had the laptop open and was staring at the CCTV screen. Bootygirl no longer filled the view, but the camera inside the room showed what was happening.

Charlotte, Jack, Anika and Cameron, all locked up in the Alpine Lodge; three of them bound to chairs.

Gallagher's mouth wanted to form words, to discuss what he was seeing, but before he could begin, Snømann emerged. He leaned on the desk by Gallagher and Luka, took a deep breath and released it, as though a difficult task had just been overcome.

"I suppose that could have been quite confusing for you, yes?" he said. "Surprising, even?"

"That was Charlotte. And Jack from Bloomers."

"Exactly, yes. Even though they had both been fired from their respective jobs, they decided to break in here in order to cause trouble and put all our business operations in jeopardy."

"Did they?"

"I think they were drunk as well. You might have noticed."

"We did," said Luka uncertainly.

"They were a danger to themselves rather than anyone else," said Snømann.

"That's why you have to restrain them?" suggested Gallagher.

"Precisely. Very good."

"And young Anika?" said Luka. "The little elf?"

"Very much the same story," said Snømann.

"Really?"

"Yes. I'm afraid so. People who seem to be our friends, who cannot become part of the new organisation we are building here ... they become disruptive forces."

"I see ... I think," said Gallagher.

Snømann gave him a fatherly pat on the shoulder. "Confusing and surprising. I know."

When the two Svens who'd been tying people up came out into the security office, Snømann beckoned them forward.

"Sven and Sven here will stay with you. Keep you company. We need company when things are confusing and difficult. Yes?"

One Sven sat down on a chair and gave a supportive smile to Gallagher. The other leaned against the frame of the entrance door.

"Of course, yeah," said Luka.

Another warm shoulder pat from Snømann and he made for the door.

The Svens smiled at Luka and Gallagher. "Hey," said one. "Who would like to hear some Christmas jokes?"

"Er, sure," said Gallagher.

The Sven pulled a thin book out of his inner pocket and began flicking through it.

Gallagher leaned over to Luka. "So, *are* we fucking henchmen now?"

Luka looked at him.

43

ANIKA

Anika was pleased to be upright again. Cameron's efforts to help had left her with even more random bruises. She was less pleased to see the prisoner count was growing.

She wondered at the significance of Charlotte and Jack being captured together, with Charlotte wearing a seriously revealing dress. She hoped it signalled an end to the hostilities between them. She noticed the Christmas tree brooch Charlotte was wearing.

"Why are you wearing that brooch?" said Anika.

"Really?" said Charlotte. "*That's* the question you want to ask right now?"

"It's Sophie's brooch."

"Yeah, I know. She gave it to me."

Anika noted a certain wobbly drunkenness to Jack and Charlotte, and an irrelevant but wild suspicion popped into her mind. "You've not ... you've not been at the Granary pub, have you?"

"How did you know?" said Jack.

"And you didn't...?" She cleared her throat. "By any chance, did you get a surprise meal in the dining pods. The full, um, tasting menu thing."

"Actually, we did."

Charlotte scowled. "Okay. It's spooky how you've gone psychic all of a sudden, Anika, but we've got significantly bigger fish to fry at this moment."

"You're right," said Anika. "Tell me what you know."

Charlotte opened her mouth to speak, but Cameron interrupted. "Hold your horses, Anita. As the most senior member of staff I think I should perhaps conduct this meeting, don't you?"

Anika sniffed, trying to ignore her aches and bruises. "Sorry Cameron, but we all need to ignore you." She addressed the others. "He thinks this is some sort of luxury spa, whereas I think we are in quite a lot of *actual* danger. Snømann is drug smuggling."

"Nonsense!" roared Cameron, but all three shushed him loudly and he slumped back with a loud *harrumph*.

"We took a look in the warehouse," said Charlotte, "and saw his operation. Unpacking the drugs. And he has other plans up his sleeve. Worse ones."

"I know. He plans on rolling his drugs processing operation to garden centres across the country."

"I meant that he plans to kill—"

"We *think* he plans to kill," put in Jack.

"—he plans to kill all Hedgelord and Bloomers

employees at some big celebration event in the paddock tomorrow," Charlotte continued.

"Operation Yuletide Surprise," said Anika.

"Yes!" said Jack. "He mentioned that. A winter sacrifice. But how do you know?"

"I saw some plans on his desk in Cameron's old office the other day."

"Cameron's old office?" said Cameron, alarmed. "This old boy might be taking a winter break, but he's not dead and buried yet."

No matter how they spun it round or retold it to themselves, Snømann's plan appeared in equal parts to be devious, demented and very, very bad.

"It must be gone midnight now," said Anika when it seemed they had already gone over it too many times to make a difference.

"Christmas Eve," said Charlotte. "Barely more than twelve hours until the celebration lunch and..." She looked round. "Cameron's taken himself off for a bit of a sleep, I think."

Their erstwhile boss had gone. After the erotic adventures of dubious superheroes had concluded and the whisky bottle was empty, he'd said something incoherent and stumbled into a side room from which he had not returned.

"Okay. Enough chit-chat," said Jack. "Time for action."

Anika gave a demonstrative tug on the cable tries around her wrists. "Action?"

Jack jerked his head back towards the door. "Those were your plantsmen on guard duty out there."

"Luka and Gallagher," said Charlotte.

"Right. Surely, they're not okay with all this."

Anika considered this. "I reckon there's a chance we could get them to help us, if we can isolate them from the others." She looked round to the CCTV camera up in the corners of the room. "Hey! Hey! Luka! Gallagher! Can you come in here?"

Charlotte joined in for a bit but there was no response.

"Maybe it's not wired up for sound," said Jack.

"Okay, okay," said Anika. "We get help another way."

"They took our phones. I told you," said Charlotte.

Anika grumbled. "I lost mine."

Jack rocked with excitement. "But you've got that, Charlotte."

"Hmm?"

He swivelled as best he could towards her. "You picked Anika's phone up."

Charlotte began to protest before clearly remembering. "Oh, fuck. It's … it's tucked in the top of my dress." She tried to give a bit of a wiggle.

Charlotte's dress was a small thing. A low cut top and a short hem. Anika couldn't see a sign of it in there, and there wasn't much space for it to hide in. "You sure?"

"Yeah. Yeah. In between. It's... I don't know how we're going to get it out."

Anika felt a wave of relief wash over her. "It's voice controlled." She called a command to her phone. "Call emergency!"

Beneath the fabric, Charlotte's chest glowed, like partly-ready Iron Man.

"It's ringing!" said Jack.

Charlotte and Anika shushed him.

They all fell silent. The phone was on speaker, nestled somewhere in the top of Charlotte's dress. It rang out, then a woman's voice answered.

"Hello?"

Anika recognised the voice and realisation struck her. The phone had dialled her emergency contact. "Oh ... Mum?"

"Hello, Anika. What time is it? Are you all right?"

Anika paused before answering. "Er, yes, all fine. Just ringing for a bit of a chat really."

"What are you doing?" Charlotte hissed.

"I'm not going to panic her," Anika mouthed viciously, then said in a normal voice, "I'm here with some friends, by the way."

"Oh? Hello everybody!"

There were embarrassed greetings from Jack and Charlotte.

"It's half past midnight," said Anika's mum. *"It's an odd time to call."*

"Listen, I have an idea," Jack whispered. "If I shuffle over towards you, Charlotte, I can use my face to try and get the phone to do what we want."

Charlotte pulled a face. "You want to stuff your face into my boobs, hoping you might accidentally dial the emergency services?"

"What was that, Anika?" came her mum's voice.

"Oh, my friends are just being a bit loud," said Anika.

You know I was hoping we could mend things between us, but all I see from you is this obsession with sex," Charlotte hissed at Jack.

"What? No! I'm just trying to be practical."

"What is going on?" said Mrs Chowdhry.

"Fine!" said Charlotte and thrust her chest at Jack. "Do your worst!"

"Sorry, mum," said Anika. "Jack and Charlotte. They're a little, er, drunk."

Jack shuffled towards Charlotte then leaned forward, levering himself with his strapped-down arms to gain access to her dress.

"Charlotte from work?" said Anika's mum.

"Yes, mum."

"I thought she'd been fired."

Her voice became muffled as Jack literally shoved his face against Charlotte's boobs in an attempt to dislodge the phone.

"It was unfair dismissal," Charlotte said, then laughed. "That tickles!"

There was a gargled response from Jack, who was still working his way towards the phone.

"What is going on?" demanded the muted voice on the line. *"I'm going back to bed, Anika."*

"Gok eek!" yelled Jack, emerging with the phone between his teeth. He withdrew and carefully sank back into the chair, allowing the phone to fall onto his lap.

"Sorry about them, mum," said Anika.

"*And that's the Jack who you said she'd been going out with?*" said Mrs Chowdhry.

"Not exactly going out with..."

Charlotte addressed the phone in Jack's crotch. "It's a bit complicated, Mrs Chowdhry. This is Charlotte by the way."

"*Hello, Charlotte. We met.*"

"Yes. I remember. At the Mickey Bubbles concert. Jack here and I have known each other professionally for a long time, and only recently found out we were attracted to each other."

Anika groaned. "You are not telling her everything!" she said through gritted teeth.

"We were attracted to each other," agreed Jack. "Hi Mrs Chowdhry. You have a wonderful daughter. The best elf at Hedgelord."

"*You don't need to tell me about that. I know.*"

"Anyway, Mrs Chowdhry," said Charlotte, "after Jack and I got together there was a ... misunderstanding, and I did something unforgivable."

"*Oh, the Santa video thing.*"

"Yes. That. Now there's this awful thing between us and I don't know if it's fixable."

"*I see,*" said Anika's mum. "*Jack, why don't you tell me how that made you feel?*"

"Mum, no!" Anika moaned.

Jack sighed and looked up at the ceiling. "Honestly, Mrs Chowdhry, I was devastated. I can't begin to tell you. I'd recently been dumped by my previous girlfriend, and I guess I was still hurt from that experience; but I really thought Charlotte and I had a future. I never expected to be stabbed in the back like that. I guess I was so angry and hurt that I just wanted to shut her out of my life."

"The two of you are clearly in some pain, and yet I think you both want this. Jack, tell me why you thought that the two of you had a future."

"Gosh. I dunno."

"What is it about Charlotte that makes you want to be with her?"

Jack gave a small laugh. "She's known for being a massive potty mouth and always angry."

"So, I've heard."

"The thing is, I can see what drives that. She's so full of passion for shaping the world to be a better place. Sometimes she's misguided and often she gets frustrated, but things are never boring when she's around."

Anika watched Charlotte's face, as it crumpled with emotion. Was that a tear? It was hard to tell.

"How about you, Charlotte? Why do you want Jack in your life?" asked Anika's mum.

Anika realised she no longer wanted to shut her mum up. She wanted to know these answers.

Charlotte sighed. "He both grounds me and lifts me up," she said, her voice cracking slightly. "He sees through my bullshit defences. I think he sees the real me. He makes me better than I am on my own."

"I see."

Charlotte coughed and her voice returned to normal. "I mean, it doesn't hurt that he's sexy as all fuck and I was a little bit sorry when he finally got hold of the phone just now."

"*I don't think I understand that last bit...*" said Mrs Chowdhry.

"Yeah, you don't need to, mum," said Anika.

"*...But the two of you sound very much as if you belong together.*"

Jack and Charlotte both gave a small, only slightly reluctant nod of acknowledgement.

"Thank you, Mrs Chowdhry," said Charlotte.

"Yeah mum?" shouted Anika. "Is there any chance you could find another phone and call the police?"

"*Why would I call the police?*"

"You need to get the police out to Bloomers."

"*Are you still in that silly rivalry with them? Listen, Anika. We're very proud that you—*"

The phone gave a little bloop. A dead battery symbol flashed on the screen.

"You are fucking kidding me," said Charlotte.

"Out of power," whispered Anika.

"We could have had the police here, but instead we spent our time—"

"I thought we made great progress," said Jack with a smile.

44

GALLAGHER

Gallagher and Luka were playing it cool. The sight of Charlotte and Jack Hartigan being marched into the lodge and tied up alongside Anika had been disquieting to the say the least. But with two Svens sitting close by throughout the night, it was nearly impossible to discuss the matter.

Also, when Cameron had drunkenly staggered off, it rapidly became clear there would be no more adventure of Bootygirl on the big screen.

Both bored and worried, Gallagher had tried giving Luka some very meaningful looks. Luka had given him some looks in return – but if they had any meaning, Gallagher wasn't sure what it was.

Gallagher then tried messaging Luka. The first message had been simple.

What do we do?

Luka's phone didn't buzz. Luka didn't look at his phone.

"I've sent you a message," Gallagher whispered.

Luka shrugged. "Not got my phone on me."

Gallagher carefully showed him the message on his phone.

"Cup of tea?" suggested Luka.

"What are you talking about?" said Sven.

"The making of tea," said Luka.

"Ah. This is very important," one Sven told the other. "The British habit of consuming tea in a convivial manner."

"Exactly," said Luka. "It's very important that we all do it."

"What if I do not like tea?" said the Sven.

Luka shook his head. "It does not matter if you actually like the tea. The tea is unimportant. It is just brown leaves in hot water with milk."

"Mate!" said Gallagher. "You love tea!"

"I love the having of tea," said Luka. "The sitting around, the warmth, the talking bullshit over a brew. In the old country, we drank coffee, dark and thick. Tea is not the same. But – and it is a big but – the act of having a 'nice cup of tea' is the greatest pleasure. No – having 'a nice cup of tea and a biscuit' is the great pleasure of all."

The Svens nodded at this sage piece of cultural advice.

Luka looked about. "We don't have any biscuits, do we? A rich tea, maybe? A couple of ginger nuts?"

The Svens shook their heads. Luka patted Gallagher. "Come on, mate. We've got some at the shed." He stood.

"We will come," said Sven, standing at once.

"You need to mind the fort," said Luka, waving generally at the CCTV. "And someone needs to make the teas. Big question for you – test, if you will – when you make tea, which goes first in cup? Milk? Or tea?"

"Tea," said a Sven instantly.

"No, it is milk, I think," said the other.

"Ah. See if you can work it out," said Luka, pulling Gallagher towards the door.

It was the middle of the night. The skies overhead were clear, the stars bright and the air cold.

Luka waited until they were halfway across the car park before speaking. "Now we talk," he said.

"We're fucking henchmen and on the wrong side in this thing," said Gallagher.

"Tell me about it."

Gallagher groaned with frustration. "What we gonna do?"

"Mate. We are going to light up a joint and think carefully," said Luka. "Never failed me yet."

Luka already had a pair of roll-ups and a zippo lighter in his hand.

Once they were both walking along with their joints, Luka scratched his head. "Snømann has charmed us into buying his bullshit. He is not our friend. He is still dangerous, though. We must not forget this."

"No, but he's *got* our friends!" said Gallagher.

Luka's face twitched. "Colleagues, maybe." He drew deeply on his joint and exhaled into the night air. "Okay. We must do something. We have two choices. We either overcome two Svens, release prisoners and sneak away before he returns..."

"Right?"

"...Or we wait until he returns with shit ton of Svens and overcome them all."

"Oh, I definitely prefer the first one of those," said Gallagher.

"Right. Then all we need is way to whack those two guys. What weapons do we have?"

Gallagher patted down his pockets, wondering what he might have. "Are we actually going to the shed to get biscuits?"

"Of course."

"Because there's a whole load of tools and weapons there. Do we think the Svens have weapons?" Gallagher asked.

"Probably," said Luka. "But we have brains. We can do this. We need to think of something good is all."

"Brilliant!" said Gallagher. He grinned, confident that Luka had a plan. They crossed over from the Bloomers site and the little lane which led onto paddock and the Hedgelord property. "So, do you have any ideas?" Gallagher asked.

"No."

"Fuck."

"You got plans?"

"Course I haven't."

Luka made a deep and troubled noise. "We need Anika – Smartypants the Elf. She's the one with all the ideas."

"She is."

45

CHARLOTTE

Charlotte kept glancing at Jack. Every time their eyes met, the two of them would look away like bashful teens. She couldn't decide if it was maddening or cute.

Anika certainly seemed to find it maddening. "Okay, so we need to get Gallagher and Luka to come in here," she said. "Ideas?"

"Yelling didn't seem to work," said Jack.

"Clearly we need something more subtle. We need to look like we're doing something that automatically needs their attention. Ideally several people's worth."

"We could pretend to be ill," said Jack. "Clutch our bellies."

"We can't move our hands," said Charlotte.

"Okay, then we just look ill."

Charlotte pulled a sickly face.

"You just look sad," said Anika.

"What else do you want me to do?"

"Can any of us vomit on cue?" asked Jack.

"Can you?" said Charlotte.

"I don't know. It just seems like a thing we ought to be able to do. Just think of really revolting thoughts and…" He let his mouth hang open and produced a long gargling sound.

"Are we really waiting for you to throw up?" said Charlotte.

He closed his mouth and swallowed. "No. It's not happening."

"Then we do something else," said Anika.

"Like a fight?" Jack said.

"Hell, yeah!" said Charlotte.

"Right," said Anika, "So to be clear, we need to look riotous for the cameras, but we don't want any actual violence, yeah? No broken bones."

Charlotte felt that comment was aimed at her. "I can dial it down. I'm not a naturally violent person. Besides, I'm tied up. So are you."

"I think we can make this work," said Jack.

"Right then," said Anika. "Let's begin on one, two—"

Charlotte went on two, because it was always the best way to sneak an advantage. She roared and began to drag her chair over towards Jack. She kicked off a shoe – it flopped onto Jack's lap – and stretched out her foot to slap him across the face.

"Fight!" yelled Anika, bouncing around enthusiastically.

Meanwhile, Jack had managed to snag Charlotte's foot. As he grasped it, he brought his little finger round to tickle it. She screamed loudly with the exquisite torment of it.

At that point, the door Cameron had disappeared through some time earlier flew open and the Hedgelord boss came through at speed, waving a ripped off shower curtain rod.

"What? What?" he roared, in equal parts drunk, terrified and enraged.

He swung wildly at nothing. Charlotte, screaming and giggling, flung out her other foot. Her shoe went flying into the TV. It left barely a mark, but the image on the screen fizzled and went black.

"Bootygirl!" yelled Cameron in dismay. He swung his curtain rail weapon in indiscriminate anger. It was a wild and ineffectual swing, though enough to alarm Anika.

She ducked. "Cameron, that's fucking dangerous!" She retaliated by bringing a foot up into his groin, which sent him sprawling backwards across the floor.

The door burst open and two men in black ran in. To Charlotte's annoyance, neither was Luka or Gallagher.

"Stop it!" yelled one. "Stop it or you'll hurt yourselves."

One grabbed Anika's chair and tried to pull her away from the melee. Another reached over to stop Charlotte's chair tipping over.

If there was no Luka or Gallagher, Charlotte reasoned, then they would have to engineer a way out of this all by themselves.

"Oi! Cameron!" she yelled. "Did you really use that

shower rod on Anika, you maniac? I mean, if you *whacked someone really hard with it*, you might do them some damage." She turned to Jack. "As for you, what the actual fuck? Tickling? I take my *shoe* off and that's all you can fucking think to do?"

Both Cameron and Jack seemed to understand Charlotte's meaning at the same time.

Cameron raised the metal rail, grunting as he swung it hard into the chin of the Sven grappling Anika. The Sven's jaw slammed closed with a loud crunch and he toppled backwards with barely a sound.

Jack grabbed Charlotte's shoe with his fingertips, held it with the heel pointing outwards, and scooted his chair towards the Sven who had grabbed Charlotte. He lacked the momentum to give him much more than a sharp prod, but it was enough distraction for Charlotte to bring a knee up into Sven's face.

Charlotte grinned with satisfaction as another Sven bit the dust.

Two unconscious goons. An actual success.

Cameron looked proudly at what he had done. "How's that for a golf swing?" he grinned.

There was a noise at the door and Luka and Gallagher rushed in. Gallagher held a garden fork out as a weapon. Luka was carrying a garden hoe.

"What? What are you two doing?" said Charlotte.

"We've come to rescue you," said Gallagher, surveying the scene.

Luka nodded. "I was going to take them out." He gave

several swipes with his hoe. "And then go, 'ho ho ho.' You know? Hoe."

"Uh-huh," said Anika. "I see."

"Bit late though," observed Charlotte.

Gallagher hoiked a thumb at Luka. "We wasted a bit of time thinking up that 'ho ho ho' line."

46

GALLAGHER

"Right," said Gallagher, addressing the room of freshly-released captives. "Erm, hello everyone. I realise this looks kind of bad, with us dressed as the enemy and everything..."

"Hey, we all make mistakes," said Jack.

"By the way, there's loads of cameras in here. I don't know how many people can see the picture, but we should assume we're being watched."

Luka looked up at the nearest camera and took a moment to pull down his trousers and flash his bum.

"What the fuck you doing, man?" Gallagher asked.

"We are swapping sides, no? I wanted to mark the occasion."

Gallagher shook his head. "Shall we fasten these two Svens into the chairs and be on our way?"

Luka was already checking them over and preparing to tie them up.

There was a light cough from Cameron, who had flopped back down into his comfy chair. "Why so hasty?"

Gallagher and Luka stared at him. Charlotte, Jack and Anika stared at him.

"Because they are bad people who have a massive drug smuggling operation and they plan to kill us?" said Anika.

"Anita, they've always treated me with the utmost respect," said Cameron. "Look at this place, it's like a home from home."

"Did you not hear the part about them planning to kill us?" Anika asked.

"Yeah, but we've saved you now," said Gallagher.

"No. They plan to kill all of us." Charlotte spun her arms to encompass everything.

"Everyone in the world?" whispered Luka in awe.

She scowled. "No. Everyone at Bloomers and Hedgelord, you numpty."

"Operation Yuletide Surprise," said Anika. "It's his plan to get rid of everyone."

"Something at the celebration event in the paddock," said Jack. "In..." He wheeled around. "Is there a clock in this place?"

"Time is an illusion," said Cameron with a dismissive flap of his hand. "And as for these threats... I've been in business a long time. If I had a tenner for every time someone has threatened to kill me, I would have even more money than I do now. I think I'll stop here and finish the film, if it's all the same to you."

He looked at the broken TV screen, gave a childish groan,

and reached for a fresh whisky bottle, drinking straight from it.

"Right," said Charlotte. "While Cameron is relaxing, let's think about what we're going to do about Snømann's plans to kill everyone."

"Our priority should be raising the alarm," said Jack.

"You heard how my mum reacted, though," said Anika. "This situation sounds so very unlikely. Will anyone believe us?"

Charlotte pulled a face. "True."

"How about raising the alarm and also warning everyone at the big party that they should get out of there?" said Anika.

Charlotte nodded.

"There is additional problem," said Luka, grabbing Gallagher by the arm and pointing at the camera. "These fucking Svens will rain shit ton of fucking shit down on us all. Someone needs to deal with them."

Cameron's head bounced onto the arm of the sofa and he began to snore.

Gallagher nodded. "Luka and me will deal with the Svens."

"Deal with them?" said Luka.

"Distract them, okay? Everyone else will raise the alarm and try to warn the party guests." He spoke the words, but didn't dare to think how they might carry them out.

"And Cameron?" said Anika.

Gallagher shrugged. "There's probably a wheelbarrow outside you can use."

Everyone nodded. It was as good a plan as they were ever going to get.

. . .

WHEN THEY CREPT OUTSIDE, Charlotte realised dawn had broken. The piercing low winter light of a Christmas Eve morning shone across the Bloomers site.

With much arm flapping, Gallagher encouraged everyone to crouch down behind a set of bins by the Alpine Lodge. Off to the side was the Bloomers warehouse, the heart of Snømann's drugs operation.

Luka scuttled off, coming back with one of the garden centre's customer trolleys, one of the low ones for piling on DIY equipment and garden supplies.

"Look at this!" he whispered in excitement.

"Great," said Charlotte. "Let's get Cameron on there."

"No, I meant wheels aren't wonky," said Luka. "Not one of them. This is some strange magic."

"Why would our trolleys have wonky wheels?" said Jack as he helped Gallagher lower the drunk and snoozing Cameron onto the trolley.

"Is just not natural," said Luka.

"The coast looks clear," said Gallagher. "We can all just head out, through that gate, across the car park and away."

"We find a phone and call the police," said Charlotte. "While you, Anika, go and warn the people at the party. If Snømann plans to cull our staff – fucking psycho that he is – then your job is to get the people out of there."

"You sending little girl into the lions' den?" said Luka.

"Who are you calling little?" said Anika.

"And she's not a girl," hissed Charlotte.

"Um, English is not my first language," said Luka

uncomfortably. "Not even my second or third. You know what I mean? Anika is brilliant at the little things she does, but—"

Anika tugged fiercely at the elf outfit she'd been wearing all night long. "Luka Sibersky, I am an elf! More than that, I'm a Hedgelord elf! I've spent the last three weeks dealing with rampaging hordes of children. And their families, who are usually far worse. I've had reindeer vomit on me. I've had donkeys bite me. I could show you the scars. I've dealt with moronic head elves. And with dead Santas. Whenever there's been trouble, I've been in the thick of it. I meant that in a good way – not that I cause the trouble."

"No, no, we got that," said Jack. "Brilliant speech."

"Er, guys..." said Gallagher.

"There's nothing you can't ask an elf to do," continued Anika, defiantly, "because there's nothing we haven't already been asked to do."

Gallagher was making umming and erring noises while tapping both Anika and Charlotte insistently on the shoulders.

"Fuck's sake," hissed Charlotte. "She's in the middle of her big speech."

"Guys," he hissed back and pointed.

Across the way, a pair of Svens had come out of the rear of the warehouse and were making their unhurried way towards the Alpine Lodge.

"Fuck, we've got to go," said Charlotte.

"They'll see us," said Jack.

"We'll go nonchalantly. Casual."

"We've got an elf and an unconscious man on a trolley!"

"It's Christmas," Charlotte argued. "There's always elves around at Christmas. And..." she glanced about and pulled a rough tarpaulin out from among the bins "...we'll cover Cameron."

"Won't he suffocate?" said Gallagher.

"A risk I'm willing to take."

With an arm-flinging flourish, she managed to get the tarpaulin over Cameron in one go, then stood up to push the trolley out from their hiding spot and towards the gate. Hurriedly, the rest fell in behind her.

Charlotte didn't dare look back to see if the Svens had spotted them. "Walk casual," she said softly. "Just walk casual."

From the lodge to the gate was less than fifty metres, then it was all car park. The store would be open soon, if it wasn't already. The car park would soon be filling with an eager public for the last shopping day before Christmas. Charlotte instinctively felt that being among the public would make them safe. She hoped so.

"Hey! You!" came a shout from behind.

"Might not be talking to us," Charlotte said from the side of her mouth. "Just walk casual."

"Hey! You with the trolley!"

Okay, that seemed more directed. As one they glanced back. The two Svens were running towards them.

"Go!" yelled Gallagher. "We'll distract them."

Charlotte wanted to ask exactly how they were going to do that when Luka threw aside his hoe, reached inside his boiler suit outfit, pulled out a pistol – an actual fucking pistol! – and fired it twice in the Svens' general direction.

The Svens ducked.

"Shitting hell!" swore Anika in surprise.

"Mmmmfucker," burbled Cameron from beneath the tarpaulin.

"Where'd you get that?" Gallagher yelled.

"Off one of the Svens when we tied them up!" Luka shouted back gleefully. "I got you one too!"

Charlotte only had a moment to take in the stunned look on Gallagher's face before she remembered she should be running. Jack had hold of the trolley handle beside her and together they got it up to speed. Anika was ahead and the first through the gate.

There was more shooting from behind as they raced into the car park. A man and woman by their car glanced up and around at the sound.

"Fireworks?" the woman suggested.

"Aye, probably," the man replied.

Anika had squeezed between parked cars and was hugging the car park's border. There was no such option with the trolley and the drunken Cameron. They turned along the path running down the front of the garden centre building.

"Damn it," said Jack.

Charlotte followed his gaze. At the car park's vehicle entrance a pair of dark Volvo SUVs had driven in. Several men jumped out there and then. It very much looked like someone had raised the alarm.

"We sneak past them," said Charlotte.

"Not a chance," said Jack. He gripped the trolley bar and

turned towards the garden centre entrance. The automatic doors slid open.

"Into Bloomers?" she said.

"Home territory for me," said Jack.

"Controlled by Snømann. Staffed by his goons."

"We can do this," said Jack. "And there's a phone in my office where we can call the police."

47

GALLAGHER

Gallagher ducked low as he and Luka ran into the Bloomers warehouse. There came sounds of gunfire from behind as they scarpered along a row of shelves.

They tucked into an alcove to gather their wits. Luka might have been a big strong man, but he was not shaped for speed. He clutched his chest as he tried to regain his breath.

Gallagher couldn't help but admire the twenty feet high shelving units. "This is RX7 poly-stacker. We did the same ones over at Hedgelord. Tricky to put up."

"What are you talking about?" hissed Luka.

"The shelves. I'm just saying these Svens are quick learners."

"Pfff. They've used wrong pins for securing them to the wall. Rookie error. Here." Luka passed Gallagher a pistol.

Gallagher held it in both hands and stared at it. "What am I supposed to do with this?"

Luka gave him a wild-eyed look and shook his own pistol in a mime of shooting it.

"I don't shoot people," said Gallagher. "I've never fired a gun."

"Snømann literally taught us the other day!"

"Yeah, but that was like fun shooting, not actual, deadly shooting."

"This situation is kill or be killed!"

"No one's actually going to kill us."

"Come out, come out!" called a Sven. "We won't hurt you!"

"See?" said Gallagher. "This is all just a big game gone wrong. Sure, Snømann is a drug dealer, but he's a businessman first and foremost. Killing people is bad for business."

"Luka! Gallagher! Brothers!" called a Sven. "This is all a big mistake!"

"See?" said Gallagher. "We've distracted them enough. The others have got away. The police'll be here soon enough. Game over for them and they know it. No need to kill anyone. Come on."

He stepped out of their little nook. Down towards the entrance were half a dozen Svens. Gallagher called out a "Hey, guys" and was about to give a little wave when he saw they were all carrying AK47s slung under their arms.

Muzzles flashed and the warehouse was filled with the roar of automatic gunfire. Gallagher yelped and jumped back into the narrow alcove.

"They're shooting at us! They're shooting at us!"

"Dick," said Luka. He leaned out and fired his pistol blindly towards the Svens. Five, six, seven shots.

There was return gunfire. Sparks flew off shelf supports. The concrete floor exploded in little crater puffs.

"Oh God Oh God Oh God!" yelled Gallagher. He put his hands to his ears.

"Gave away our fucking hiding place," Luka muttered.

The automatic gunfire continued.

"And they've got us pinned down," Luka added.

"I'm sorry!" Gallagher yelled. "I'm not used to this kind of situation."

"Well, you better get used to it quick. You need to man up!"

"Bit sexist."

"We need to be like … like Bodie and Doyle in TV classic, *The Professionals*. You know?"

"I've never watched it!" Gallagher wailed.

Luka gripped his arm. "Then when we get out of here, you will come to mine for Christmas and we will watch *Professionals* all day. Superior Czechoslovakian version voiced by Petr Oliva and Alois Švehlík."

"If we get out of here! They're coming."

Luka gave him a hard look, then grabbed a long-handled broom from the back of the alcove. He used it to reach behind the shelves and with two sharp thrusts knocked out the bolts and washers securing the lower levels to the breeze block wall.

"Oh, man…" said Gallagher.

"We push, then we run. That way, yes?"

"Is this going to work?" said Gallagher.

"Would work on *The Professionals*. Push!"

Luka levered with the broom handle. Gallagher grabbed the frontmost uprights and pushed. The huge shelves barely moved. They wobbled forward and back.

"Rock them, rock them," urged Luka.

Back and forth they wobbled, two inches, four, a foot.

The Svens gave a shout in alarm – then the shelves were tipping forward of their own accord. Metal sheeting and containers above rained down. The shelves pitched beyond a point of no return.

"Run!" Luka yelled.

Gallagher ran. He needed no further prompting.

Behind them, several sections of warehouse shelving came down in a cacophonous tsunami of metal and wood. Ahead was a door through to the next section of the warehouse.

48

CHARLOTTE

It was hard to move casually through the aisles of Bloomers when the drunken man on the trolley you were pushing had woken up a bit and was singing an almost wordless version of *Deck the Halls*. Several customers looked up as the lump under the tarpaulin shifted and sang "Fa la la la la" in an endless loop.

A Sven working the till two aisles over clearly heard them and looked their way. As one, Charlotte and Jack crouched low.

"My office is over there," Jack whispered.

"I know where your office is," Charlotte whispered back.

"You think about me in my office a lot, don't you?"

She gave him a look. He was smirking. Jack Hartigan trod a fine line between smug and charming. She rolled her eyes at him and smiled. This was possibly their last day alive on planet Earth and she was in a forgiving mood.

"You share an office suite with Marcus and Maremba, right? Are they in on Snømann's plan?"

"No one's seen them for days," said Jack. "I half expected to find them locked up in that Alpine Lodge with Cameron."

Hearing his name, Cameron kicked. "Musizzy puff, ma monkey queen," he burbled.

"Quick. Before he really wakes up," Charlotte said.

They dashed forward, through the alcove into the staff area, then Jack scooted ahead to reach the office door. Charlotte wheeled Cameron inside and was relieved when the door clicked shut behind her.

The office was empty.

"Everyone's over at the celebration," said Jack. "Bloomers and Hedgelord are one big happy family now, I guess?"

"Until Snømann kills them all," said Charlotte.

Jack went to his desk. A red light winked on his phone. He pressed play.

"Hey, Team! Marcus here. We've made it to the Yule Forest bathing retreat, and it's very ... spiritual. Lots of earthy vibes and talk about 'reconnecting with nature's rhythms.' Maremba says it's a bit out there, but I think we might just find our zen. Anyway, just wanted to check in—"

Jack clicked the next one.

"Gordana, Team. It's Maremba. Things are ... evolving here. We just finished something called a 'sacred soil ceremony,' where they encouraged us to bond with the mud – literally. Marcus is convinced this will awaken something within us, but I'm not so sure—"

He clicked next.

"It's Maremba. We've been locked in a tent with no

explanation. They're coming to take our phones. Starting to feel like we've signed up for a scam. You have to find Jack. Get Jack back. He'll know what to do—" The call was interrupted. There were muffled sounds and a shout from Marcus, then it went dead.

"Fucking hell," whispered Charlotte. "Maremba and Marcus too."

Jack picked up the phone. "Time for us to call the cavalry."

"Toot toot!" squeaked Cameron under the trolley.

ANIKA SLOWLY CREPT across the pitted concrete area called the Rumble Yard which separated Bloomers from the a nearby country road. From there she crossed into the field next to the paddock which itself backed onto Hedgelord.

In the middle of the paddock stood a large and expensive looking marquee. Through the plastic windows, Anika could see the glow of gas heaters and lights. Immediately outside, by the gated entrance to the paddock, was the Nordic Yule Goat Snømann had insisted on as part of the celebrations. It was thirty feet high, an edifice composed of tightly bound hay bales and wood.

Staff from Hedgelord and Bloomers were already arriving, some inside the marquee already. Soon Snømann would have them all where he wanted them and he would unleash his devilish Operation Yuletide Surprise and be rid of unnecessary employees once and for all.

Several of the blond Svens were positioned around the marquee.

"Damn."

She needed to get in, but they'd surely be on the lookout for her. She needed a disguise and some way of sneaking in.

She was currently dressed as an elf, which was a disguise of sorts, but one more likely to draw attention than deflect it. She needed... She needed a mask. They sold elf masks, along with snowman masks and Santa masks in Hedgelord. They even had some in the grotto.

She edged round the paddock and slipped over a corner fence to get onto Hedgelord property. There were Svens over here too, providing a skeleton crew for the last shopping day before Christmas, but Anika was able to sneak into the plant area, round to the grotto, and go in search of a suitable mask to wear.

As GALLAGHER and Luka ran through the warehouse, there was more gunfire and pinging ricochets. Gallagher pointed his pistol behind him and fired without looking.

"Don't shoot me!" yelled Luka.

They ran through the next door.

There were benches laid out. Piles of boxes. A packing area. A tall vat connected to some complicated piping stood nearby. Gallagher could see trickles of red wax around the top. This was clearly part of the candle and drugs processing operation.

The few Svens working here looked at Luka and Gallagher in surprise as they barrelled through.

"Keep running!" shouted Luka.

One of the Svens grabbed him as he ran past. The two of

them tumbled against the wax vat. A gloopy splodge poured over the side and splashed down on the two men, smearing Sven on the face and splashing down the back of Luka's neck. Both roared in pain.

Luka leapt away. Sven clawed at the wax burning his face.

Another Sven charged forward. Gallagher shot him in the foot. He couldn't say he was aiming at the man's foot, but that was where he shot him.

As Luka yelled and ripped open his boiler suit to get the top half away from his wax-scalded back, there came the sound of their pursuers. Gallagher grabbed his friend and pulled him through the next door. He shut it behind him, turned to look around and, seeing a heavy tool bench nearby, dragged it across the door just as someone slammed heavily into it.

The place was something like a workshop. It was fitted out with benches and racks of tools. At one end were double doors. While Luka pulled clods of solidifying wax off his neck and shoulders, wincing and gasping, Gallagher checked the double doors.

"Locked!"

Luka swore expressively in a language Gallagher didn't know as he looked desperately around.

In the centre of the room was a tractor, with a trailer attached. The trailer had clearly once been a beautifully crafted Santa sleigh, but had suffered some major damage which was only partially repaired.

"If I am not mistaken this is vehicle that Charlotte and Jack fucked up at nativity," said Luka conversationally.

"I don't know if you got wax in your ears," said Gallagher. "But we're trapped."

There was hammering on the door as the Svens tried to get into the workshop.

"We are safe for now," said Luka.

"For now, yeah. For now. But how the hell are we going to get out?"

Luka was deep in thought. "Did you see where they got those automatic weapons from?"

"No. And I don't care."

"From those crates we stored for Snømann in our secret shed. SMGs, assault rifles, fucking grenades. I knew it! We still have at least three crates over in our shed at Hedgelord."

"How handy!" said Gallagher with bitter sarcasm. "But we're pinned down like rats in a trap. We've no way out!"

Luka chuckled. To see a man stripped naked to the waist, chuckling, while people who wanted to kill them hammered on the doors was horribly disconcerting.

Luka grabbed a metal sheet from a stack by the wall and experimentally held it up against the side door of the tractor. "Tell me," he said. "You have not watched *The Professionals,* but did you ever watch a thing called *The A Team*?"

49

CHARLOTTE

Charlotte and Jack clustered together by the office phone as it rang the emergency services.

"Emergency. What service do you require?"

"Police," the two of them said together.

"I thought I was doing the talking," said Charlotte.

"Why did you think that?" said Jack.

"Putting you through," said the operator.

When the police operator came on, there was a brief, silent argument between Jack and Charlotte, carried out mostly with eyebrows, sarcastic looks and pouty mouths. Jack conceded the floor to Charlotte.

"Hello, we need to report a crime," she said.

"What crime are you reporting?" said the operator.

"Well, a lot of crimes actually. Kidnap, drug dealing, murder. Probably murder, right?"

"Probably murder," conceded Jack.

"Can you tell me what's happening?" said the operator. *"Are you in danger?"*

"Very much so," said Charlotte. "We're holed up in Jack's office. That's at Bloomers garden centre."

"The one by the double roundabout near the big supermarket?"

"That's the one. And everyone's searching for us."

"Everyone?"

"The staff. They used to be Jack's staff. Before he got fired."

"Why do you have to mention that?" said Jack.

"Background info."

"Did you also want to mention you've been fired from Hedgelord?"

"You're ex-employees?" said the operator.

"We're all about to be ex-employees," said Charlotte. "Snømann has got them all at a marquee in the paddock and we think he's got a horrible surprise for them. Like he's going to kill them or something."

"The snowman has a surprise? I'm sorry. You're not making sense."

"Snømann replaced all the workers with his goons since we got fired and now we're hiding from them."

"You're hiding in the place you've been fired from?"

"I was fired from Hedgelord. It's Jack who was fired from Bloomers. But we had to do it."

The tarpaulin on the trolley lifted up as Cameron awoke like Frankenstein's monster arising from his operating table. "I say!" he groaned. "I feel as if I've got the mother of all hangovers."

"And he's back in the room," muttered Jack.

"*Hedgelord?*" said the operator thoughtfully. "*Is that Charlotte Mitchell?*"

"It is!" she said.

"*Weren't you arrested the other day?*"

"I'm surprised you knew."

"We both were," added Jack.

Cameron looked at the trolley he was sitting in and tried to get up. The thing wobbled with every one of his movements. "Boats! Could never stand the bloody things!"

"*And who's that?*" said the operator.

"That's Cameron Clasp. My old manager," said Charlotte.

"Get me onto shore would you, my good man?" said Cameron, holding out a hand to Jack.

"*And he's hiding with you?*"

"He was kidnapped," said Charlotte.

"I was bloody kidnapped," Cameron said loudly for the benefit of the phone.

Charlotte waved a silencing hand at him. "Any chance you could fucking shut up a bit Cameron?"

"*Is there anyone else with you? Anyone in danger?*"

Charlotte tried to think. "Luka and Gallagher are in the warehouse, I think. There's been some shooting."

"*Shooting?*"

"I don't know who's been hurt. And Anika, but I think she managed to escape."

"*Is there anyone else with you?*"

"Oh! Marcus and Maremba," said Jack. "My old bosses. They've been captured too."

"*I see,*" said the operator. "*And what do you want?*"

"We want help, obviously."

"I understand. And by help, you mean...?"

"Police. Lots of police," said Charlotte.

"Of course. Of course. You want people to come along and see. You want public attention."

"Er, if that's how you want to phrase it," said Charlotte. "I guess."

"And do you want money, or do you want your job back?"

"Both those things would be lovely but—" She shook her head. "What do you mean? We're calling the police."

"That's right, Ms Mitchell. We understand. You're angry and upset. We get that. I'd just like to know what your demands are."

"Demands?"

"We don't have demands!" said Jack. "We haven't done anything! It's not us!"

"I thoroughly understand," said the operator in what was clearly her 'talking to crazy people' voice. *"You've kidnapped Cameron and Marcus and – Maremba, was it? You mentioned two other people who might have been shot. We are taking this very seriously indeed. We understand you feel aggrieved."*

"Aggrieved?" said Charlotte, feeling her temper rising. "I'll be feeling fucking aggrieved in a minute, lady! I'm talking about a major drugs operation. Cocaine inside Christmas candles! We've got a whole Scandi-Noir crime gang, armed to their teeth, ready to kill all of the employees and probably any members of the public who get in their way."

"I understand," said the operator. *"We are taking you very seriously indeed. Now, you mention weapons. Can you tell me what you've got?"*

"Us?"

"Oh, Christ, you've made a pig's ear of this," said Jack.

"Me?" snapped Charlotte. "I don't see you doing any better. Damn it. Cameron's crawling out the door. Stop him!" She turned back to the police operator on the phone. "Listen. We're not the important thing here, okay? It doesn't matter about us—"

"I'm sure you have so much to live for," said the operator, *"people who love you—"*

"Shut up! Shut up! I'm trying to tell you about the drugs and the guns."

"We're ready to listen to everything you have to say."

"I'm telling you. There's an industrial scale cocaine processing operation in the warehouse here. You need to believe me."

"We believe that you believe that," said the operator smoothly.

Jack had grabbed hold of Cameron and was trying to stop him going back out into the shop. Cameron, half on the floor, was reaching for the door handle.

"I can send you evidence," said Charlotte. "This whole operation. I'm serious. Jack! Grab his hand! Listen, lady, I will send you photographic evidence if you need it. Whatever bits you need."

"Please don't send us any bits," said the operator. *"We understand the seriousness of your intent. Please leave Mr Clasp's hand as it is."*

"What?" Charlotte scowled at the telephone in disbelief and revulsion and stabbed a button to end the call.

"She didn't believe me," she said to Jack. "She didn't take me seriously."

"I heard."

"We're taking you very seriously," said the operator.

"Fuck!" said Charlotte. "Thought I'd killed the call."

"Stay on the line," said the operator. *"Let's deal with this calmly and quietly."*

Charlotte stabbed several more buttons to try to end the call, then tugged the cable out of the back of the unit for good measure.

Jack was sitting on Cameron. "So, they're coming to arrest us," he said.

"For kidnapping and possibly murder."

"And they don't really believe that Snømann is running a drugs operation out of our warehouse?"

"Not at all."

"Hmmm." Jack thought on this. "And you're not going to deal with this calmly and quietly, are you?"

"I'm fucking going back into that warehouse. I'm going to find all the cocaine, get all the evidence we need, and then I'm going to rub it into the police's stupid faces."

Jack considered this. "I think it's the way you phrase things, you know. It's very easy to misconstrue the things you say."

Charlotte huffed and straightened her dress. "You're going to help me, right?"

Jack laughed. "Throw myself back into danger? Of course!"

50

ANIKA

There were elf masks in the grotto.

At the beginning of the season, Charlotte Mitchell, ever the champion of easy inclusivity, had bought a range of rubbery felt elf masks in a mixture of ethnicities. They were on sale in the shop at the end of the grotto experience. There had been pink-skinned elf masks with yellow hair at the temples, printed on below the festive hat, and there had been brown-skinned elf faces with printed on black hair. That simple purchase had created an unintentional survey of who was coming through the grotto and buying the playful elf masks. Now, on Christmas Eve, there were a lot of brown-skinned elf masks left over.

Anika didn't know how she felt about being an Asian woman wearing a brown-skinned elf mask. Obviously, she should feel fine about it, and yet she couldn't shake two lingering qualms. That a) in terms of a disguise she'd not really transformed her appearance all that much, and b) she was now complicit in some sort of morally grey act of blackface.

But she had a mask, and it was as much of a disguise as she was going to have. She headed over to the paddock.

She paused briefly as she approached the paddock. The way to the marquee was lit with strings of fairy lights, with other lanterns spiked into the ground to create paths. It looked quite magical, right up to the point where a solid cordon of Svens stood guard all around the marquee. She'd organised the décor, before going on to make an enemy out of Snømann, so none of it came as a surprise, but now she was here, she needed to get inside with minimum fuss. With a donkey.

"Oh hey!" she called to the Sven who stood at the marquee entrance.

"Who are you?" he said.

"Smartypants the elf, obviously."

The Sven looked sceptical but clearly didn't care and gestured for her go in. As she stepped forward, she thought she saw the bulge of a gun under his boiler suit. These guys were equipped for violence.

Inside, there were long tables set amongst the décor that she'd specified. She couldn't help feeling a pang of pride, as she saw how effective it all looked. The organza lining in the marquee roof twinkled like a starlit sky with the rows and rows of fairy lights behind it. The floor and walls were covered with straw-coloured jute matting, and there were tartan accents picked out on the chairs and tables. The entire thing was cosy, warm and very enticing. It was also the intended site for Snømann to enact the finale of his Yuletide

Surprise masterplan, which put an entirely different spin on things.

Within this space were the hundred plus employees of Hedgelord and Bloomers – the *expendable* employees of Hedgelord and Bloomers. Mimosas and non-alcoholic alternatives had been served up and the guests mingled in pre-brunch groups.

Anika loitered by a polystyrene column near the entrance, casting around for a familiar face. She saw Sophie, looking a little bored. She was probably feeling neglected because her so-called-beloved would rather go off on a criminal rampage than spend time with her, although she didn't yet know that. Karen was with her, which was good. She tried to catch their attention from the doorway.

"Karen! Sophie!" she stage-whispered, beckoning them over. Karen glanced across and frowned.

Anika lifted her mask and waved. Karen waved back. Anika made her beckoning motions larger, sighing with relief when they finally got up and walked over.

"Anika! Now don't make too many demands on Soph. She's got her 'fuck me' shoes on today, haven't you love?" Karen laughed, nudging Sophie playfully.

"I haven't even seen my Marti," said Sophie. "I thought he'd be here by now."

"He'll have to go a long way to top the first surprise for our guests," said Karen, pulling a face.

"What first surprise?" Anika fostered some small hope that Snømann had already somehow revealed his awfulness, which would make it easier to lay out some of the things she needed to explain.

"Oh, the cracker gifts?" Karen said. She hooted with laughter and opened her bag. "There'll be one for you, Anika. A memento you'll definitely treasure."

Both Karen and Sophie dissolved into fits of giggles as Karen reached into her bag and pulled out a shiny silver object and slapped it into Anika's palm.

"Um." There was a feeling of wrongness in both its weighty smoothness and its very suggestive shape. "This looks for all the world like a penis."

"Yes?"

"Where did it come from?"

Sophie shrugged, her eyes wide. "My neighbour Desiree sourced them. She was supposed to get pens."

"The pens for the gift bags? The pens like Cameron's—? Oh. My. God." In her mind's eye, Anika saw the pieces fall into place. "I think I know what happened."

"You do?" Karen asked. "Go on then, it's a mystery to us. I mean, it's got the whole place in fits, I don't think I've ever seen so many willies in one go. Not since my cousin's hen night, anyway."

Anika didn't ask Karen to elaborate. She wasn't certain she needed to know. "When you wrote the order down for Desiree, what did you put, Sophie?"

"Pens like Cameron's."

"And did you insert an apostrophe in pens?" asked Anika.

"Of course I did," said Sophie, affronted. "It's plural. We have to keep our standards up, don't we?"

"Oh fuck!" said Karen, understanding. "It wouldn't take much for the apostrophe to look as if you wrote 'penis like Cameron's', would it?"

Sophie gave a slow nod of understanding. "Well, that is one way of looking at it, yes. But we don't really know that Desiree got the wrong end of the stick because of that, do we?"

"I think we do," said Anika. "Cameron told me that he had a visit from a sex worker called Desiree over at the Alpine Lodge."

All three of them stared at the silver-plated penis in Anika's hand.

"This is moulded from Cameron's actual penis?" Karen said. Her face was a mixture of disgust and fascination. She ran a fingertip along a vein which ran prominently up the side.

"Karen!" said Sophie. "What are you doing? That's Cameron, that is! And what's Alpine Lodge?"

"Ah, well that's the thing," said Anika drawing them in closer. "I need to tell you some stuff. It's bad."

51

GALLAGHER

Gallagher realised that his role in armouring up the tractor and sleigh was mostly fetching and carrying, with a bit of hammer bashing on the side. Luka was masked up and had a welding rig going full tilt, adding sheet steel fortifications to the sleigh.

The wax had hardened on Luka's overalls, totally stiffening them, and with a pragmatism that paid no heed to general decorum, he'd kicked them off entirely and finished off the welding in his Y-fronts, socks and thin vest. The site of the grey-bearded papa bear in his undies and a welder's mask was disconcerting to say the least.

"I'll find you something else to wear," said Gallagher.

He set about finding something suitable. He saw an outfit wrapped in plastic on the back seat of the sleigh. He hesitated. It was certainly big enough for Luka, but was it too much?

No he decided. It definitely wasn't.

"Here you go mate!" he said to Luka, holding up the red and white outfit.

Luka pulled a face as he turned off the welder. "You are fucking kidding me. I am to dress as Santa?"

Gallagher shrugged. "It's either that or put your overalls back on."

"Fine. I can be fucking Santa. Ho, ho, motherfucking ho." Luka put on the Santa suit.

Gallagher laughed, but quickly straightened his face when Luka glared at him.

"What is so fucking funny?"

"It's just all those times that Charlotte and Anika tried to get you to be Santa, and you said no. Now I see you in the outfit, you're fucking perfect mate. That's all. You were definitely born to be Santa."

Luka scowled. "At least I don't need to play nice for any kids. Were there any more outfits there?"

"Er, yeah. Why do you ask?" Gallagher asked.

Luka rolled his eyes. "We look like Santa Claus is coming to town then maybe we have the edge."

"Me as an elf? Fuck no."

"Trust me. Will be good for morale. Like bullet proof vest."

"I think I'd rather have a real bullet proof vest." Gallagher huffed in annoyance. He had enjoyed the black jumpsuits, but Luka had a good point. Looking like a sleigh full of weirdos could only help if they were to capitalise on the chaos.

The banging at the door continued.

"Right. You know how to drive tractor?" said Luka.

Gallagher nodded. He'd helped an uncle with harvesting as a teenager. Once you'd got the hang of it, it was no different to driving a car.

"Good. Give me your pistol."

Gallagher gladly handed it over and then climbed into the tractor cab. It was hard closing the door with metal armour plate on it, but he managed to wedge it shut.

"You rev engine and ram the doors," Luka called to him.

"I think I grasp the very simple plan," Gallagher shouted back.

"Good! Then we go to tea shed and stock up on some real weaponry, yes?"

"Buckle up, Father Christmas!"

Gallagher started the engine. He pumped the accelerator, testing the revs. The Svens bashing on the doors might have been drowned out by the sound of the engine, or maybe they'd heard the tractor start up and were starting to worry.

Good, thought Gallagher, and released the clutch.

The tractor lurched forward in powerful first gear and immediately struck the double doors. They buckled, resisting for a fraction of a second before giving way. The tractor jolted forward into the warehouse proper again.

Seconds later, there was the clap of gunfire and the much, much louder rattle of bullets against the armour shields Luka had welded around both tractor and trailer.

In the back, Luka roared like a beast and opened fire with his pistols. Gallagher glanced back and saw Santa standing up in his sleigh, a pistol in each hand, laughing madly while shooting at the Svens.

"And a present for you! And you! And you!"

Struggling to see his way through the narrow vision slot Gallagher had been granted, he steered towards the daylight that marked the exit.

52

ANIKA

In the marquee tent, Anika had done her best to catch up Sophie and Karen with what she understood: Snømann's nascent drugs distribution centre and the upcoming Operation Yuletide Surprise where he planned to rid himself of all the employees at the party.

"No, that can't be true," said Sophie. "My Marti's a lovely man. I've seen him with dogs, and they're always a good judge of character."

Anika put a hand on Sophie's arm. "Out of all the possible reasons you might have for defending him, that one's just not gonna fly in a court of law, is it, Sophie?"

"Well, he was always so nice to me."

Anika hoped that Sophie already knew, or at least suspected the truth, but couldn't face the loss of someone who'd cared for her.

"Okay, this Operation Yuletide Surprise?" said Karen, pulling out her phone. "We can just call the police, right?"

"We can try," said Anika.

There was movement and noise at the far end of the marquee. Marti Snømann had entered and there was a light scattering of applause. He'd actually shown up. That surprised Anika. She'd feared the man had gone completely psycho and was going to seal the exits and, she didn't know, maybe flamethrower everyone inside. But he was here, dressed in a sharp suit and being the genial host, laughing and clinking glasses with his guests.

"See?" said Sophie. "That is not the face of an evil man."

Snømann looked their way. Anika hurriedly pulled the mask back over her face.

"Trust me, he's a bad 'un," she said.

Snømann waved Sophie over. She made her way through the crowd towards him.

"You believe me, don't you?" Anika said to Karen.

"What? That our new garden centre owner is a power-crazed drug lord who is using his purchase of both garden centres as a front for his attempts to expand cocaine distribution in the UK?" She made a seesaw motion with her hand. But she took out her phone and called the police anyway.

Snømann made his way to a little stage and podium placed next to one of the marquee's long walls. The podium was draped with golden and tartan fabrics. This whole event really looked lovely, and Anika felt it was a crying shame that her efforts were forever going to be overshadowed by this nightmarish turn of events.

Snømann waved and smiled at the crowd, and when he

spoke into the microphone, his voice was smooth and charismatic.

"It is so nice to see you all here," he said. "Soon we will be sitting down to a luxury brunch together. And I see many of you have opened your Christmas crackers with such ... unique party favours inside."

There was laughter, and quite a few people waved their complimentary silver-plated penises.

Karen tapped Anika's arm.

"What?" Anika whispered.

"The police have already been called. Apparently 'two recently fired ex-employees' have taken hostages over at Bloomers."

"What? No. That's not possible. Really?"

"It's what they say."

"But are the police coming here?"

Karen shrugged and handed the phone to her.

Anika crouched down low by a table to speak to the police.

"This is Anika," she whispered.

"*Ah, Anika,*" said a male voice. "*Am I right in saying you managed to escape from them?*"

"I did escape, but now I'm over at the marquee in the paddock."

"*But are you safe?*"

"I don't think so."

"*The kidnappers have made some threats, specifically about 'bits' of Mr Clasp.*"

"Bits?"

"*As in body parts.*"

She had no idea what they were talking about. "Do you mean his penis?"

"Do you have information about Mr Clasp's penis?"

She looked at the weird gift in Karen's hand. "I mean, I'm staring at it right now."

"And it's not attached to Mr Clasp."

"No. Absolutely not. It's silver-plated."

"That's..." The officer on the line sounded queasy. *"That's unusual."*

"We were all commenting on that. We need help! Are you coming to help us?"

"We are sending cars to you right now."

"Good. Good."

She passed the phone back to Karen and carefully stood. Snømann was still delivering his speech, Sophie by his side.

"Well, I think we can all agree that this Christmas season has been a roaring success," he said. "And none of it would have been possible without each and every one of you."

He raised his glass and there were hearty cheers all round.

"Ladies and gentlemen!" Dafydd had climbed onto a chair, his face flushed with excitement. "I'd like to take a moment to talk about my performance as Baby Jesus in the nativity play earlier this week."

A ripple of laughter spread through the crowd, but Dafydd seemed undeterred. "It was a role that truly spoke to me," he continued, gesturing dramatically.

"For fuck's sake," muttered Anika. She needed to act. Even if the police were coming, their lives were in imminent danger. She needed to get everyone out. She should just seize the microphone and tell everyone.

Still crouched low, she made her way forward. She squeezed between Tom Eccles and her fellow elf Gillespie, shushing them when they started to ask what she was doing.

Dafydd was trying to give a fulsome description of his nativity performance while Snømann attempted to genially shut him up.

"It is true this has been an unusual Christmas too!" said Snømann loudly. "A tragic sleigh accident the other week. Two sleigh accidents, actually. And collectively Bloomers and Hedgelord have hired, fired, and said emotional farewells to more Santas than might normally be expected. But we have pushed through to the end."

There were further cheers and Snømann gestured for more, if only to drown out Daffyd's unwanted speech. With Snømann distracted, Anika rushed to the stage, slipped up beside Snømann, took the microphone from its stand and spoke.

"Listen everyone!" she said. "Listen! This is very important!"

"And now an elf wants to do a speech," said Snømann drolly.

Anika ripped her mask away. Snømann's eyes widened in surprise.

"You have no idea what's going on here," she said to the crowd. The two garden centres' many employees looked at her. "Marti Snømann brought you all here for a secret reason."

Snømann gave her a frankly surprised look.

"Operation Yuletide Surprise," she said.

"I was going to tell them," he said, arms outstretched to the crowd. "I wanted every employee here because—"

"He's going to kill us all," said Anika.

"—everyone's getting a year's paid holiday, plus training opportunities and relocation packages," said Snømann at the same time.

They looked at each other.

"Kill them?" said Snømann.

Anika's mouth formed around a question. "A year's holiday?"

"With retraining and relocation packages," said Snømann. "We're expanding our commercial operations."

She had no idea what to say.

"That's Operation Yuletide Surprise," said Snømann. "Investment in people."

"You're lying," she said.

"It would have included paying for certain people to attend business school or finish their university degrees."

"No, no, no. He's lying," she said into the microphone. "He said he was going to get rid of everyone."

"Relocation and restructuring."

"You said you were going to 'take care of them all'."

He nodded. "Yes, Ms Chowdhry. Take care of them." He took a step towards her. "I don't know what you expect in terms of management style here, but where I'm from, we nurture and respect our employees."

"A free year's holiday?" called out someone from the crowd, who was just catching up.

"For everyone," said Snømann. "Starting tomorrow."

"But..." said Anika.

Snømann held out his hand. "Just give me the microphone, Anika, and maybe we can discuss how you can reap the benefits of what we're offering."

"But..."

"A chance to be rewarded for all your efforts and hard work, yes?"

He took another step.

MAKING their way back through Bloomer's shop was a lot easier for Charlotte and Jack without a drunken Cameron on a trolley.

"Do you know how hard it is to crawl in this tight dress?" she whispered to Jack as they crouched in an aisle of discounted books and jigsaws.

"It's fascinating to watch," he said.

She gave him a light slap on the arm. "If we're going to get evidence of the drug stuff in the warehouse, one of us is going to need a phone."

"Or a camera."

"Well, yeah," she said irritably. "Obviously. But which is going to be easier to find? Someone's phone or a digital camera?"

Jack pointed ahead. "In our audio visual technology department."

"Your what?"

"We sell tech. Cameras, TVs, Bluetooth speakers."

Charlotte didn't know that Bloomers sold electronic goods. Hedgelord didn't sell electronic goods. "Really?"

"Growing market for us. Was, I mean, until they fired me."

She nodded. "Fine. Let's go."

She followed him, still crouched low. As they passed near the front of the shop, there was a muffled crunch from outside, followed by a series of pop-pop-pop bangs. Charlotte looked out and saw something trundle by at high speed.

"Fucking hell, it's the Bloomers sleigh," said Charlotte, staring.

"It's had some modifications," said Jack.

It was true, it now featured slab-like sheets of metal fitted to the side of the tractor and sleight.

"Holy fuck!" She was lost for words as she saw Luka rolling around in the back, dressed in full Santa costume with a huge grin on his face.

And as soon as the bizarre sight had appeared, it was gone.

53

GALLAGHER

There were a number of reactions one might expect from seeing an armoured tractor and Santa sleigh cruising at top tractor speed through a garden centre car park. There was the obvious level of surprise from customers, which doubled when one of the Svens chasing them out of the warehouse door let off an injudicious gunshot in their direction. Surprise, fear, panic were all to be expected.

What Gallagher really hadn't expected were the coos and gasps of wonder that even this shabby battle sleigh drew from people.

"Look, it's Santa!" Gallagher heard one parent tell their children.

"I am not real Santa!" Luka shouted back from the trailing sleigh.

"Hold on, mate!" Gallagher yelled.

He hit a kerb at the edge of the car park, rode up the

short embankment, ploughed through the low wooden fence and hedging, and continued onto the road leading towards Hedgelord.

Cars braked sharply and horns were honked, but there was nothing cars could do against the progress of the battle sleigh.

The tractor cornered worse than Gallagher's own shitty car. He mounted the far verge as he turned fully onto the road and swung a left towards Hedgelord. Two minutes later they were drawing all manner of attention from the shoppers at their own garden centre.

"Look! Santa!" cried someone.

"Still not Santa!" shouted Luka. "In my country, it is Grandfather Frost. Much better!"

Gallagher knew exactly where he was heading. At the far end of the car park he swung round and powered through the gates to the recycling area. He rarely remembered to lock them and the sliding bolt snapped under the tractor's momentum. It was short journey from there through plant area lanes that weren't quite wide enough to their tea shed.

Gallagher drove straight over a pallet load of compost bags left outside the landscaping office.

"Stupid place to leave them," he muttered as the bags exploded under the tractor tyres. He braked to a stop by their shed.

There was an 'oof' as Luka fell forward at the sudden stop. Gallagher fought with the tractor's armoured door and jumped out.

Luka stumbled from the sleigh with a grin on his face. "That was fun."

"What now?" said Gallagher.

"I say we open the crates, see what presents Snømann has left us, then go fucking save the day over at the paddock."

Gallagher was buzzing with too much energy to disagree.

He followed Luka in. Luka ripped aside the ugly giant poster of a hornet they'd put up to hide their secret storage shed and ran inside. The crates which they had been so careful to treat with respect and not open were pulled into the centre of the room and the latches thrown.

"Fuck me!" said Gallagher.

Luka lifted a weapon from the foam. "Fucking Heckler and Koch 416 assault rifle." He passed it to Gallagher with a bunch of ammo. He removed a pistol and put a clip of ammo in it with apparent ease. "SIG Sauer P226. Very reliable."

"You know your guns," said Gallagher surprised.

"I read a lot of magazines," said Luka simply.

He stuffed one pistol in his thick Santa belt and passed another to Gallagher.

Crate after crate was opened, Luka moving with the increasingly frenzied speed of an overwhelmed child on Christmas day.

"Take these," he said.

"What are they?" said Gallagher.

"Fragmentation grenades, of course."

Luka arranged a bandolier of grenades over his shoulder and opened another crate. He gave a deep and worrying laugh.

"What?" said Gallagher.

Luka held up what looked like a long tube.

"A bazooka?" said Gallagher in a wobbly voice.

"The RPG-7," said Luka. "Classic anti-tank weapon! This baby is Russian engineering at its finest."

"Said no one ever. Who the fuck would want one of those?"

Luka shrugged. "Someone who doesn't like tanks? Come! Now we go save the day."

They hurried outside. Despite the trail of damage they'd left across the Hedgelord plant area, no one had yet come running. A family of four were gathered cautiously by the winter tree selection, peering at Luka and Gallagher as they piled bundles of weapons into the sleigh.

"Last minute presents!" Gallagher shouted to them before getting into the tractor cab.

Luka climbed in the sleigh, shoved a clip into his rifle and pulled back the slide. "Some people on my naughty list!" he shouted to the wide-eyed children. "Be good, children!"

Gallagher started up the tractor. It was time to ride into battle.

54

ANIKA

On the stage in the marquee, Snømann held out his hand for the microphone. "You should be part of our team," he said to Anika. "We can discuss this."

She wavered.

"Your parents are very proud of all you've achieved so far, in such a small amount of time," he said.

Anika made her decision. She had no idea if it was the right one. She took a step away and spoke to the crowd.

"This man is an international drug dealer. No, it's true. He's set up a cocaine distribution centre in the Bloomers warehouse. We're nothing but a front for the terrible trade in addictive narcotics."

Snømann gave her a patient and condescending look. "Please. These lies."

Anika reached inside her costume and took out the candle she'd stuffed in there from the warehouse.

"Where...?" said Snømann.

Anika smashed the candle against the podium edge. The end sheared off and white powder flew out in a cloud.

"It's snow!" said someone joyfully from the crowd.

"It's cocaine, you muppet!" said Anika.

Daffyd, still standing on his chair, made a soup-sucking intake of breath. "It *is* cocaine!" he said. "I mean, I guess," he added in a much quieter voice.

Snømann stared at Anika. She met his gaze levelly.

"My brother," muttered Snømann, "he told me. Don't do Britain, Marti. The British are crazy. They fuck up everything. Look at Brexit. They eat Brussel sprouts for Christmas, for fuck's sake. You cannot rule such people, Marti, he said."

He sniffed unhappily, fixed his mouth into a hard line, then reached into his jacket and pulled out a pistol.

There were gasps from the audience and a very heartfelt "Bloody hell, mate!" from Tom Eccles.

Snømann fired his pistol into the air, putting a hole in the marquee roof.

"So," he said loudly. "It seems that no one is leaving at all!" He glanced fiercely at Anika. "We were going to have holidays and jobs for all, and a real boost to the local economy, and no one needed to be any the wiser!"

"Yeah, way to go, Anika," said a snide voice from the audience.

"Gillespie?"

Snømann waved away the lingering cloud of cocaine and gestured for his henchmen by the doors. He rattled off something in Swedish or Finnish – some language Anika didn't have a hope with – and the Svens aimed their weapons at the crowd.

"It seems everyone needs to sit down now!" Snømann said into the microphone.

The crowd hurried to behave.

"Is it sit by your name plates or just anywhere?" asked Daffyd. He caught Snømann's look and dashed for the nearest chair.

On stage, Sophie backed away from Snømann. "Marti...?"

He looked at her mournfully. "Sophie, my love. I didn't want it to end this way. I had such hopes for us."

"So, it's true?" she said. Even now she clearly didn't want to believe.

"If it is any consolation, I believe I truly loved you."

Sophie blushed.

"Sophie!" said Anika. "He's a murdering drug-dealer!"

"Well, no one's perfect," Sophie shot back.

Svens were coming into the tent and placing something close to one of the gas-powered heaters that dotted the large marquee. That didn't look good.

"What are you doing?" Anika whispered.

"Tidying up after the mess you've made," said Snømann. "Again."

From outside there came distant sounds. At first, Anika thought it sounded like fireworks, tinny and distant. But it was gunfire and the sound of vehicles. Through the marquee's crinkled plastic windows, Anika saw something large smash its way through the gate leading into the paddock.

It was a tractor pulling what looked like – well, what was

definitely a red sleigh of the traditional Christmas variety. And on the back of it was Father Christmas. He appeared to be toting a large gun and shooting at the SUV that was chasing him.

"What the fuck?" she whispered.

GALLAGHER SHOULD HAVE REALISED the Svens would be mobilising their fancy Volvos in pursuit. They'd followed them down the lane and now their tyres screeched as they turned into the paddock.

The shocking sound of gunshots rattled the sheet steel behind his head. Gallagher tried to make himself as small as possible.

They drove past the large, straw-filled Yule Goat. The thing's giant blocky head seemed to look down with critical concern at Gallagher.

"You and me both, mate," he muttered.

There was more rattling gun fire.

"Go faster!" yelled Luka.

"This is top speed!" Gallagher yelled back. "Shoot them!"

Luka made a low growl of frustration and Gallagher heard him unleash a volley of shots at the vehicles pursuing them.

Moving from road to grassy paddock did not give the tractor any advantage. If anything, it just provided a wider space for the Volvos to spread out and try to overtake and encircle the tractor. One, bouncing over the uneven ground, came racing up the left side.

Gallagher tried weaving from side to side to stop it.

In the back, Luka's gunfire stuttered, came and went.

"Stop swerving!"

Gallagher glanced back. Luka was sprawled on the back seat of the sleigh. As he tried to get himself upright, he fell against the PA system at the back. Lights came on and *Holly Jolly Christmas* by local singing sensation Mickey Bubbles came through the speakers.

Luka cackled madly at the incongruous music.

"Fuck this shit!" he yelled, as though to defy the gods themselves.

He crawled across a floor littered with munitions and picked up the rocket launcher.

55

CHARLOTTE

Jack and Charlotte stood by the glass case of digital cameras and camcorders in what Charlotte had to concede was a fine display of electronic goods.

"We've got the Sonys over here," said Jack. "Great functionality and decent battery life." He pointed elsewhere. "Those are the unbranded Taiwanese ones. Obviously not the same spec, but really good value for money."

"Okay, okay," she said. "Just pick one."

They were in a quieter corner of the shop, but there was no knowing when one of the Svens manning the store might appear, might even recognise them.

Jack reached for the lock on the glass door. "These were never fitted right. You can just jiggle them open if you move the pane."

"I say, what are you two up to?"

Charlotte whirled. Cameron stood behind them, looking

exactly like a man who'd been drinking all night, fallen into a drunken stupor and had somehow pulled himself out of it. His eyes were wide, like he was fighting to keep them open, his normally swept back hair was a mad tousle, and he was, for some reason, eating a whole turkey leg like some medieval lord.

"Where the fuck did you spring from?" said Charlotte.

He gestured hereabouts and everywhere with the turkey leg.

"And where did you get that from?" she demanded.

"They've got a lovely little restaurant here. The, er, Lighthouse. Charming place. We should have a restaurant over at Hedgelord."

"We do have one," said Charlotte and then screwed up her face furiously. "Had! *I* don't work there anymore."

Cameron nodded like this was all very interesting. "So, what are we doing, gang?"

"We are stealing a camera so we can film evidence of the drug manufacturing operation in the Bloomers warehouse," grunted Jack as he lifted and pushed the glass front of the display case. It slid back and he was able to take a couple of cameras from the shelves.

"I have to say this is all very resourceful," said Cameron. "You know, you two should come work for me."

"You fired me," said Charlotte.

"Did I?" He appeared genuinely surprised. "Well, that was bally stupid of me, wasn't it?"

Jack passed one of the cameras to Charlotte. She turned it on. The screen awoke. There was a data card already installed.

"Let's do this," she said.

"Yeah. Go us!" said Cameron, taking another bite of juicy turkey.

ANIKA WENT to the nearest window of the marquee to watch the chase.

A tractor, clad in metal panels, was dragging a sleigh around the horse paddock at juddering speed. Meanwhile, at least three black and silver Volvo SUVs were trying to intercept it. Blond-haired henchmen leaned out of the back windows and, rather ineffectually, were trying to stop the tractor and sleigh by shooting it. Meanwhile, the various Svens at the entrance to the marquee were adding their own bullets to the chaos. And, from somewhere, Anika was sure she could hear the sound of a Mickey Bubbles Christmas song.

Wiser people in the marquee were hiding beneath the tables, but many, like Anika, were hypnotically drawn to the spectacle outside.

Wobbling on the back of the sleigh, Father Christmas hoisted something up in his hands, and Anika realised two things. First, that Santa was Luka bloody Sibersky; second, the thing he was holding looked a heck of a lot like a rocket launcher out of an action movie.

"Oh. Shit."

Luka wobbled as he tried to aim the rocket launcher at the SUV immediately following them. The tractor driver – surely that must be Gallagher! – turned a sharp left, throwing Luka off his balance for a moment. For a second the rocket launcher was pointing straight at the marquee. For a weird, detached moment Anika found herself thinking that would be a bloody stupid way to die.

And then the tractor straightened, Luka found his feet and, without pausing, fired.

He had the angle all wrong. The rocket struck the ground in front of the SUV. There was a boom and a shower of soil. Anika recoiled. The SUV swerved aside to avoid the eruption. The vehicle following drove straight through it—

—And nosedived into the crater created by the explosion, pivoted on its bull bar bumpers, and cartwheeled across the paddock. It came down hard on its roof.

Santa and gunfire had stunned the partygoers, but exploding rockets and Volvos sailing high into the air finally snapped everyone inside into a far more human reaction: screaming panic. Several barged past the Svens at the door and ran for the field. Dozens more rushed to the catering counter and sought shelter against the metal trolleys. There was a huge amount of running and screaming.

Snømann glared at Anika. "This is all your doing."

She blinked and worked her mouth like a goldfish before finally saying, "You think I'm capable of engineering all this?"

His vicious gaze narrowed and he aimed his pistol at her.

"Marti! No!" cried Sophie.

She said it in a sharp tone, and Anika managed to tear enough of her mind away from the fact that someone was pointing a gun at her to realise it was probably the very same tone of voice Sophie had used with her late dog Douglas when he was misbehaving.

"Put that gun down at once!" Sophie snapped in her most furious 'bad dog' voice.

Snømann looked at her.

"Don't you *dare* shoot that young woman!"

Snømann growled, literally stamped his foot in anger and whirled away. "This whole thing is fucked up!" He grabbed Sophie's hand and made to storm from the stage. "Come with me, Sophie!"

Sophie pulled back. "Marti. Marti, I can't."

He looked at her with a distressed surprise. "No – you must. I know that today has not gone as planned, Sophie my love. But you and I..."

She pulled her hand from his. "Oh, Marti, love. You are the best thing that's happened to me in years, but—"

"Then come with me!"

From outside there was a storm of automatic gunfire, followed by the sound of what Anika saw was an SUV ploughing into a wooden fence, a hedgerow and, ultimately, an unyielding oak tree.

"Marti," said Sophie gently. "You are a clever, handsome and loving man, but there are a number of – what do you call them, Anika...?"

Anika blinked, rather distracted by the carnage outside and the panic inside.

"Red flags!" said Sophie. "There are a few red flags."

"Red flags?" said Snømann.

"The drugs. The guns. The murder. That sort of thing. And I'd be a bit silly to ignore them."

"Oh, Sophie!"

"Marti."

Distraught, and with one final look for her, Snømann pulled away and fled to the nearest exit. He raised a radio to his mouth as he left.

56

CHARLOTTE

J ack and Charlotte ran back round the outside of Bloomers, towards the fenced off warehouse area. They hugged the wall closely, mindful of being spotted. It didn't help that Cameron was following casually behind, nibbling on his turkey leg and belching. He put his curled hand to his lips as a burp threatened to become a retch.

"Usually my tum-tum is fine after a night on the scotch," he said.

"Maybe you need to stop eating, if you're feeling ill," said Jack.

"Rookie error," said Cameron. "The grease lines the stomach. Oil on troubled waters and all that."

"Or maybe you want to sit down and let us get on with our job," Charlotte hissed.

"No, no, sweet Caroline. A good manager is always behind his people."

"Good grief," she muttered.

Jack peered round the corner at the warehouse. "Something's clearly up," he commented.

"What?"

"Hard to say..."

She gripped his waist and peered round him and the corner.

He was right. Something did seem up. There were Svens running to and fro about the warehouse. There was a lot of arm waving and shouting. Charlotte was very much put in mind of an ant colony that had been trodden on: angry soldiers and workers milling about in confusion.

"They're panicking," she said.

"Maybe they know the police are coming," said Charlotte.

"Maybe..."

"Come on," she said. "Let's get in there and grab some evidence before they hide it all."

She pushed him ahead and together they snuck through the gate, using dumpsters as cover. The Svens seemed entirely pre-occupied with whatever had got them rattled.

WHEN SNØMANN FLED THE MARQUEE, it seemed like most of his henchmen had gone with him. There were shouts and bangs from outside, countered by the screams and hollers inside. From somewhere a light, jazzy Christmassy number was playing.

Anika jumped down from the stage and ran to the tall outdoor gas heater at the centre of the room. A black package with wires sprouting from the top was taped to the gas cylinder.

"Fuck me, that's a bomb, isn't it?" said Karen, clutching Anika's elbow.

"I mean, it looks like one."

"C4 plastic explosives wired to a remote detonator with fragmentation nail-bomb configuration," said Tom numbly.

Anika looked at him. "You know this stuff?"

"I participate in a lot of combat simulations," he said.

"Does that mean you play a lot of *Call of Duty*?" said Karen.

"*Modern Warfare III* is my favourite," said Tom.

"Christ's sake," muttered Anika. "It's a bomb." She cupped her hands to her mouth. "There's a bomb! Everyone needs to get out!"

Some people started to move. Outside, there was an explosion and an SUV cartwheeled with balletic grace across the paddock. Half of those planning to flee hesitated. Half the terrified partygoers were rooted in place.

"We have to leave!" Anika shouted.

"Listen to the elf!" yelled Gillespie.

In the chaos, few seemed to listen.

"Damn it, we have to do something," said Anika, feeling panic rising within her.

"Leave it to me," said Daffyd. He positioned a festively decorated chair by the bomb. "It has been a pleasure serving with you, ladies and gentlemen."

He stood on the chair, put his hands together, and began to sing: a loud yet tuneful a cappella.

"*In the bleak midwinter, frosty wind made moan...*"

"Fuck," Anika hissed, thinking if she was going to die soon, she might as well get an above average amount of swearing in beforehand. "We are not going out like this."

The flaps at the marquee's main entrance flapped open as a tractor, swerving unsteadily, drove in, the festive sleigh behind it. The abrupt arrival of heavy farm machinery drew yet more screaming from the crowd.

"Sorry! Sorry!" yelled Gallagher. "Wasn't looking!"

"... *snow on snow*..." Daffyd persevered.

Anika waved at Gallagher. "Over here! Over here! Gallagher! We need you!"

57

CHARLOTTE

Jack started filming as he and Charlotte crept through the warehouse. There were sounds of urgent activity elsewhere and, to a degree, Charlotte felt that as long as the sounds were somewhere else then they might as well explore further.

Since Jack was doing the filming, she also felt that she had the role of providing commentary.

"This is the warehouse that Snømann took over when he bought control of Bloomers," she said, trying to both keep quiet and project for the benefit of the camera. "While they've maintained a front of running this place as a garden centre, this warehouse has been turned into a drug processing facility. Follow me as we take a closer look." She beckoned Jack to come with her as they moved down the aisles.

"Take a closer look?" said Jack.

"You think we shouldn't?" she said.

"I'm more concerned that you've gone full David Attenborough. You know this isn't a documentary we're filming?"

"I'm only doing the soft voice because we don't want to be discovered."

He nodded like he didn't believe a word of it. "You'll want a co-director credit for this too."

She was about to shake her head, then had a thought. "If there's a film adaptation..."

"Of this shitshow?" said Jack sceptically.

"I just want it on record that I, Charlotte Mitchell, should be co-credited with devising this ... this exposé."

"Christ, you *do* think you're doing a documentary," said Jack, grinning despite the situation.

"I think it's magical," said Cameron, who was still following them. He had lost the turkey leg somewhere and exchanged it for a garden fork. "It's got really powerful vibes, like that documentary where they all get lost in the woods."

Charlotte scowled at his nonsense. "*The Blair Witch Project*?"

Cameron clicked his fingers, then pointed and touched his nose. "Bingo."

"And why are you carrying a garden fork?" Charlotte asked him.

"In case we bump into some evil goons," he said, giving the fork a not very threatening jab. "Now, let's take it from the top, eh? Back to positions!"

"I'm just going to keep filming," said Jack and continued forward.

Charlotte tried to stay slightly ahead of him all the time.

The noises were closer. There were clangs and shouting. Ahead, four SUVs had pulled up and parked. The back doors were open and several Svens were transferring open topped boxes to the vehicle boots.

"They're packing it up," whispered Charlotte.

"Are the police on the way?" said Jack hopefully.

One of the Svens was in constant conversation on a radio while make big arm gestures for them to hurry up.

"I think the police are coming," said Jack. "What's that?" He pointed at the vats and pipes against the wall.

Charlotte took in the cooling red splodges of wax on the floor, and the waxy rim around the vat. "It's the candle wax. Melt and re-use?" She positioned herself in front of the camera lens. "These dastardly criminals are using hollowed out candles to secretly transport their drugs into the country." She mushed her lips together. "I should have said 'cunning criminals'. That sounds better. Good alliteration. Can we go again?"

Jack looked up from the camera screen. "Again, we're not making a documentary."

"Not yet," said Charlotte.

ANIKA COULDN'T BELIEVE they were having a stand-off while holding a bomb. Tom and Karen had wrestled out the cylinder with the bomb still attached and had lifted it up to put in the sleigh, but Luka was blocking their access.

"No bomb on my sleigh," he said. "Gallagher, we're going."

"It's not your sleigh," said Anika.

He tugged the white trim on his Santa jacket. "Today, I am Santa. One time only." The hand grenades strung across his front rattled as he spoke.

"And Santa is meant to be helpful," Anika pointed out.

"Santa gives," said Luka firmly. "He does not receive."

"We're going!" said Gallagher and started up the tractor engine again.

Anika grabbed the cylinder and bomb and, before Luka could do anything about it, stepped aboard the sleigh with it.

"No!" said Luka firmly.

"Gallagher! Let's go!" she yelled. As the tractor lurched forward, she stumbled and put the deadly cargo down clumsily on the seat.

Gallagher circled the tractor, pushing aside tables or crushing them beneath his wheels.

"I do not want to die in Santa suit," said Luka moodily.

"We just need to get it away from here," said Anika, who similarly did not want her death to be in an unnecessary sleigh-based tragedy.

As the tractor pushed through the flaps and out into the paddock (ripping several supporting guy ropes from the ground as it did), an SUV swung through the shattered gate. There was a burst of gunfire.

Luka picked up what looked like a machine gun and pulled back the bolt. "Stay low little elf," he said. "Try to shield bomb with your body if necessary."

"Really?" she said.

The tractor accelerated. Anika clung to the bomb.

The SUV closed in alongside the rumbling tractor. A Sven leaning out the passenger window raised his gun to shoot at Luka. Luka responded with a rattle of gunfire at the SUV's tyres. The vehicle slewed right then left. The passenger door swung open, the Sven clinging to it in fear. When the trailer and the SUV collided, the Sven lifted his legs to avoid being crushed between the two, scrambling quite unwillingly into the back of the sleigh. He stumbled against Anika, squashing her, then stood, looking for his weapon.

Luka threw his arms around the man's neck from behind and started to throttle him with his machine gun.

There were gurgles and shouts from the two men. And also, rising in volume, she could hear the sound of approaching sirens.

58

CHARLOTTE

Box after box was being loaded into the rear of the SUVs.

Charlotte tried to figure out the amount of cocaine going into the backs of those vehicles, all of which had their seats down. "How much is cocaine worth?" she said.

"About fifty quid a toot," said Cameron instantly.

"And how many toots are they putting in there?"

"Those bricks and bags – they're about a pound in weight each. Worth about a grand a piece on the street," said Cameron.

"Fucking hell," she whispered.

Box after box after box...

"That Volvo's nearly full," said Jack. "That must be..." He waved his hands, clueless.

"Damned fine SUV like that," said Cameron, "carrying capacity of about eight hundred kilos..."

Jack gave him an incredulous look. "How could you possibly know that?"

It occurred to Charlotte that the street cost of middle class drugs and the stats of high-end status vehicles were probably two things someone like Cameron Clasp might know. *How much cocaine can you get in a Volvo SUV?* was at the intersection of a Venn diagram in Cameron's weird mind.

Charlotte wasn't about to try to do the impossible conversion of 'toots' to kilos, but she was sure the number had lots of zeroes at the end. "Millions of pounds worth of drugs in each vehicle," she whispered.

"It's crazy," whispered Jack, still filming.

The Svens finished loading one SUV and the flow of boxes was urgently diverted to the next one.

An idea occurred to Charlotte. It just leapt at her out of nowhere, a mad and impulsive and deliriously dangerous and seductive idea. She didn't know if she should say it out loud. She licked her lips—

"We should steal one of those vehicles," said Jack.

"Hey!" she said. "I was going to suggest that."

"What are we doing now?" said Cameron.

"*We're* doing nothing," said Jack. "*I* am going to steal that nearest SUV. They left the keys in the ignition, the door's open. It's only a few metres away."

"I'm not letting you do it without me," Charlotte said.

"It's dangerous," he argued.

"Exactly. I want to be zooming out of here when it happens. Steal the car, snag the evidence, totally deprive Snømann of his ill-gotten gains."

"Quietly then," said Jack and led the way, walking in a

waddling crouch from their hiding position by the shelves, keeping the nearest SUV between him and the Svens. Charlotte followed close behind.

They moved silently while the Svens yelled orders and encouragement back and forth. Jack levered the door a little wider. He gestured to Charlotte.

"You first?" he mouthed.

"Me?" she mouthed back.

"I'm driving," he mouthed with a bonus mime.

She gave him a glowering stare but crept forward, snaked up to the high seats, and scooched across to the passenger's side.

"New car smell," she noted in a whisper.

"Feels classy," whispered Jack, following her.

She slid down low and glanced as much as she dared out the window.

There was movement from outside the warehouse. Several men were striding in. And as the central one flapped his coat about him irritably, Charlotte saw it was Snømann.

"He's here," she hissed to Jack.

"Okay, okay," Jack whispered. "Just working this out. It's keyless and automatic. Not quite what I'm used to."

Outside, moving round to the back of the SUVs, Snømann was shouting at his men. First there was a gabble of something foreign, then a yell of "All of it! All of it!" He barked out a name which wasn't Sven. "Give me the detonator," he said. "We've waited long enough."

"Detonator?" said Charlotte, worried. "Is he blowing shit up now?"

. . .

ABOVE THE HEDGEROWS at the edge of the paddock were the flashing lights of racing police cars.

Behind her in the sleigh, Santa Luka was rolling around and trying to land punches on the Sven who had fallen into their sleigh. Meanwhile the one SUV still in the paddock was trying to ram the tractor to a halt, but only succeeding in ripping up its own sides against the tractor's giant wheels.

While all of this was thoroughly engaging, Anika was more concerned about the gas cylinder and bomb package that had fallen from her hands and into the footwell. As she bent to get it, a booted foot lashed out and nearly broke her nose.

She swore and ducked, trying to pick up the bomb. They were sufficiently far from the marquee now (where people still huddled at the entrances to watch the noisy sleigh vs SUV battle). Getting the bomb away from the sleigh was kind of necessary now.

She grabbed the gas cylinder and, as she stood, yet another collision between SUV and tractor jolted her.

"Fuck's sake, Gallagher!" she tried to yell over the wailing sirens. "Drive straight!"

"You wanna drive?" Gallagher yelled back at her.

In the back, the Sven stood on the rear seat. He'd found a mock Christmas present and raised it to smash over Luka's head. With the kind of speed she'd never seen him employ in his working day, Luka rammed a gloved fist into the Sven's gut. The man doubled over and, as he did, Santa Luka delivered a powerful right uppercut to his jaw. The Sven's feet lifted off the ground. He reeled back, hit the scrolled backboard, and tumbled over off the sleigh.

Luka turned to Anika, panting, his nose bloodied. He blinked at the bomb package she held. "You still have that thing?!"

He grabbed it from her, swung like a shot putter and heaved it away. It was a good throw, and might have cleared the paddock entirely, if not for the towering Yule Goat. The package impacted on the side of the Goat's head, nearly snagged on one of the horns, then toppled down. Halfway to the ground it exploded.

Anika ducked instinctively. When she came to reflect on the day later, she might concede that her initial instinct was to hide behind Luka's bulk. In turn, he wrapped his arms over her and bent low against the sleigh seat.

"Fuck me!" squealed Gallagher from the tractor cab.

When Anika was able to get from under Luka, she looked up and saw, through the haze of smoke and straw, that the Yule Goat, sturdy thing that it was, hadn't been toppled by the explosion. But its chest was on fire and it was swaying. One of the legs gave way.

As a child, Anika's Uncle Riz had tried to make her sit through the Star Wars films. She'd found them slow, weird and nonsensical, although she had liked the creatures on the Teddy Bear planet. Now she suddenly remembered the bit where Luke and his friends fought the giant robot walking things on the snow planet using their speedy snow-glider vehicles. She was reminded of this because the Yule Goat fell in much the same way as the big walking robots: slow, like a toppling tree, and collapsing in a heap as it came.

It was unfortunate that it did so just as the first police car turned into the paddock. The Goat came down, its huge head rolled free and landed on the cop car, denting its bonnet and cracking the windscreen.

The driver of the Sven SUV, probably seeing the cavalry was here, attempted a direct escape through the other side of the paddock. The SUV rammed a hedgerow and fence, ploughed through, nearly came entirely unstuck in the low ditch on the other side, and headed off across a field.

"Oh! Fleeing now!" said Gallagher and wheeled the lumbering tractor round in pursuit.

Luka, holding Anika with one arm and the side of the sleigh with the other, screamed at his friend. "What are you doing?"

"Hot pursuit!" yelled Gallagher.

"In this thing?"

"We've got weapons, haven't we?"

The tractor rumbled through the hole in the hedge the SUV had left behind.

Luka looked to Anika. "How are you with automatic weapons?" he asked.

59

CHARLOTTE

Charlotte couldn't say she heard any explosion, not above the noises in the echoing warehouse, but Snømann tossed the detonator aside as though the job had been done. His expression almost looked sad. He shouted to his minions to get the drugs loaded into the vehicles.

There was the sound of a door, and Cameron forced himself into the small gap in the back seats between the front headrests and the huge stash of cocaine.

"Room for a tiddler?"

"Shush! Quietly!" said Charlotte. "Honestly, Cameron. Why *are* you bringing that fork with you?"

"Defence," he said, clanging it on the door as he pulled himself in.

Charlotte peered out to see if anyone had heard the noise. They had. Oh, they had. A dozen heads were looking their way.

"Fuck fuck fuck," she squealed. "Drive, Jack! Drive!"

"Think I've got it," said Jack.

He depressed the ignition, stamped on the accelerator, and the SUV shot backwards. It collided with the tall vat of molten wax with a crunch.

"That's reverse!" said Charlotte, somewhat needlessly.

A Sven reached for her door. She stabbed the central locking button. The Sven pulled ineffectually at the handle.

"Get out of the car!" yelled Snømann and pulled out his pistol.

"Drive!" Charlotte screamed.

"I'm trying!" Jack screamed back.

He shifted the gear stick and pulled away. The apparatus behind the car groaned and crunched, and suddenly the bubbling vat was tipping. A tide of liquid wax poured down onto the ground and over the rear of the SUV.

There were screams. The SUV lurched, turned, and failed to clear a shelf. Jack stopped and reversed to try to take the corner again. As he did, Charlotte looked out. Svens slipped and slid in the spreading pool of red wax on the floor. In the centre of the steaming, cooling wax, a figure was straining to get up. Snømann was coated head to toe in dribbling red wax. His teeth gritted, maybe in anger, almost certainly in pain. That wax looked *hot*.

His yell of rage was incoherent yet perfectly clear.

He raised his pistol and fired at Charlotte. It didn't go off, but a spray of hot wax splurged out from where spent shells were ejected. She gulped.

"My whole life just flashed before my eyes," she panted.

"Yeah?" said Jack, reversing.

"There was a lot of swearing."

Jack put the vehicle in drive, turned past the shelving and straight down the aisle to the exit.

"Woo-hoo!" hollered Cameron. He had a rear passenger window open. "Can't catch us!"

"Don't encourage them!" said Charlotte.

Jack looked at his wing mirror. "Don't think they need encouragement."

Charlotte looked back. They had a decent head start, but the two remaining SUVs were now coming after them.

They shot out of the warehouse into grey daylight. Ahead were the closed gates between the warehouse area and the public car park. Jack floored the accelerator.

"Hold onto your potatoes!"

Charlotte fumbled with her seatbelt and at least had a hold of it when they hit the gates. She was rocked in her seat, but at least she didn't brain herself against the windscreen. Jack fought to control the rocking vehicle, managing to avoid parked cars and pedestrians on his way out of the car park.

"Still following us?" asked Jack.

Charlotte looked back. "Still following us."

"You did steal all their nose candy," said Cameron.

Charlotte winced. "It seemed like such a good idea at the time."

There was the rattle of gunfire, the crack of glass, and a spatter of muted thuds.

"At least the drugs are shielding us," said Jack.

"Cocaine," said Cameron. "Is there nothing it cannot do?"

There was a queue of traffic by the big double roundabout.

"Side road," said Charlotte, pointing.

Jack took the turning, the SUV wobbling on the road.

"Clopton Howes that way, or the back route into town that way," she said, as the road split ahead.

"Yeah, I don't know if I want to—" Jack went quiet. He was staring out of Charlotte's window.

She looked. On the other side of the hedge she could see what could only be accurately described as a Volvo SUV being chased by a tractor being chased by Santa's sleigh. And in the back of Santa's sleigh was Santa Claus and an elf. Santa was firing a stuttering machine gun at the SUV and the elf was handing him ammo.

"That's Luka," said Charlotte.

"Is it?"

Charlotte shook her head. "You know what's the hardest part of this scene to process?"

"No idea," said Jack. "Your plantsmen have stolen a sleigh and are engaged in a moderately low speed pursuit with armed gangsters?"

"Luka in a Santa suit. The number of times I've tried to get him to dress up as Santa. Seriously, the man's impossible."

Jack raised his eyebrows. "It surely is the end times."

Firing continued from behind. The vehicles on the other side of the hedge closed in. Just as they reached the junction, the SUV in the field ploughed through the hedge and nearly side-swiped Jack's vehicle off the road. He managed to squeeze ahead, forced to take the right hand turn towards the town centre.

Charlotte looked in her wing mirror. The tractor and

sleigh had careened through after them and was now between the two SUVs.

"What's happening?" said Jack.

"There's us," she said. "There's an SUV with half a hedge stuck in its grille. Then another one. Then the tractor – that's Gallagher driving. Then the sleigh. Then another SUV. Oh, and the police are joining us."

"*And a partridge in a pear tree!*" sang Cameron.

"Is he still drunk or just a nutter?" said Jack.

"Fifty-fifty," said Charlotte. "He's never been any use."

"Never been any use?" said Cameron. "The bloody cheek!" He ripped open one of the boxes that were pretty much pinning him against the front seats and pulled out a cellophane-wrapped package of cocaine.

"This is no time for testing the goods!" said Charlotte.

Cameron squeezed across to open a rear window, leaned out as best he could, and hurled the coke package. It exploded on the roof of the pursing Volvo, spraying a cloud of cocaine into the air. It made a surprisingly festive effect.

"Missed." Cameron grabbed another and hurled it. He managed to throw this one with better accuracy. It struck the SUV square on and exploded its contents across the windscreen. The blinded vehicle braked sharply and was rear-ended by the SUV behind. It fishtailed across the road, overbalanced and, on two wheels, ran straight off into a drainage dyke.

The car behind it bashed it aside and continued the pursuit. There was a red and furious creature at the wheel.

"Mr Snømann doesn't look very happy," said Charlotte.

"Yeah?" shouted Cameron. "Well, he's fired!"

"He bought out your company, Cameron," Jack pointed out.

"Yeah? Well, he's whatever fired is when you do it to bosses," said Cameron and tossed further cocaine packages at their pursuers.

GALLAGHER, driving the tractor at its top speed of forty miles an hour, was already mentally composing his defence to the court.

You see, your honour, we didn't have a choice, he told the hypothetical judge. *We were holed up in a warehouse and these bad dudes were after us. Yes, we were working with them at first, your honour, but we didn't realise it was bad stuff. We just thought it was having fun with guns and hanging around the woods at night. Yes, your honour, we did starting shooting off some guns when we being chased by them. No, we didn't shoot any innocent passers-by. My mate, Luka, is dead careful. I think...*

Above the sputter of gunfire, Gallagher could hear Luka's cackling belly laughs. He swivelled in his seat for a second to look back.

In the sleigh, Anika the elf was crouched, her hands over her ears, while Luka fired a Heckler and Koch at the SUV behind them. Holes peppered the bonnet. Steam vented through the fractured front grille. A tyre exploded and the SUV swerved and rolled onto its side, blocking the road.

The small queue of police cars behind the wrecked vehicle came to a halt and officers leapt from their vehicles.

Gallagher turned away, in case any of them might later recognise him.

Mostly dead careful, your honour, he amended his imaginary testimony. *To be honest, I just had my eyes on the road...*

Behind him, Luka shouted, "Ho, ho, motherfucking ho, you bastards!"

The two vehicles ahead were racing onward. In the first one it looked like Cameron Clasp was leaning out of the window and tossing snowballs at their pursuer. No, not snowballs...

Gallagher couldn't make the tractor go any faster. They were losing them as they came into town.

60

CHARLOTTE

In the town, Jack took a turn into Welland Street.

"We're not shaking them!" he said, glancing at his mirrors.

"Well, you're hardly driving at speed," said Charlotte.

"The posted speed limit is thirty," he said.

"It's a high speed chase!"

"In a built up area. There's a compromise to be had!"

There was a bang and the SUV wobbled violently.

"And they've shot out our rear tyres!" shouted Cameron. He leaned out to throw another cocaine bag.

"Great," Charlotte muttered.

"We need to abandon this vehicle," said Jack.

Nearer the town centre, people were about, doing their last business in town before everything closed for Christmas. Festive lights hung across the streets and in the windows of all the shops still open.

As they rounded the swooping bend in front of St

Stephen's Church, Charlotte saw the lights on the pedestrian crossing change and a woman with two children stepping out.

"Brake!" she yelled.

Jack stamped on the brakes. The Volvo slid to a halt, front tyres mounting the pavement. Charlotte, startled, forgot how to either breathe or swallow and tried to do both at once. In the headlights' glare the pedestrian, equally startled, began to fling her arms and shout abuse.

"Out! Out!" Jack urged.

Charlotte fought to get her door open. "You too, Cameron!" she shouted.

Stumbling, they moved across the pavement.

"We need somewhere to hide," said Jack.

Charlotte looked up at the church. The door was open. Light streamed from within. "Sanctuary," she said.

"Absolutely top hole that! Haven't had so much fun in yonks!" said Cameron.

Charlotte looked at him. He still carried the garden fork he'd brought with him. And he was dusted from head to toe with cocaine. His eyes were wide and staring.

"Yes, yes," she said. "It's been a very exciting day for you."

There was the squeak of rubber and the other SUV braked to a stop behind their abandoned vehicle.

One of the Svens jumped out of the driver's seat, pistol in hand. From the passenger side emerged a thing of nightmares. Snømann was still covered in molten wax. Where it clung to him, it had hardened into sheets of red. Where it had fallen away from his face and hands, it had left raw pink skin, like bad sunburn. His silver hair and once immaculate beard had become stiff, spikey things. There was madness in his eyes.

The Sven holstered his pistol and ran to check the abandoned SUV. But Snømann only had eyes for the three people on the church steps. He gritted his teeth and growled wordlessly.

"Boss! Boss! The gear is here!" called the Sven, opening the SUV's driver door. "Come! Let's go!"

Snømann seemed entirely uninterested in the millions of pounds worth of cocaine he'd been chasing.

"He seems really angry," said Jack, gulping.

"I think I have this effect on people," said Charlotte.

"Don't worry," said Cameron. "I've got this."

Charlotte had no idea what he'd got.

Cameron stepped forward with the garden fork, held it like a javelin, and with a cry of "King Neptune!" hurled it at Snømann.

There was such confidence in that throw. It was a shame it didn't translate into actual results. The fork clattered to the pavement at Snømann's feet. He picked it up in both hands, wringing it, like he was throttling someone.

"Great. Now you've armed him!" said Charlotte.

Jack grabbed her hand and pulled her towards the church door. She in turned grabbed Cameron to haul him along too.

She stumbled into the warm, candle-lit glow of the church. Many of the pews were full and, up front, before the altar, a group of children were gathered, mostly wearing dressing gowns, many with tea towels on their heads.

"*And in the manger, the baby Jesus was born!*" the one doing the narration spoke into a microphone. *"Soon, the wise men arrived!"*

Jack slammed the door behind them and tried to make the uncooperative bolt lock. In the audience a hundred faces turned to look at them.

"Sorry," Charlotte mouthed with an apologetic wave.

"They had come from afar and were very tired!" continued the narrator.

Charlotte led the others down the aisle, looking for a decent cubbyhole in which they could hide. While the children tried to continue with their play, most of the congregation's attention was still on the three new arrivals.

"Really sorry," Jack whispered.

"Just passing through," added Charlotte.

Across the other side of the church, Charlotte saw the figure of Reverend Ralph Robertson. His furious hawk-like gaze was firmly on Charlotte. His vestments fluttered about him as though he was about to take off with outrage and fly at her, vampire-style.

On stage, three kids in tinfoil crowns shuffled towards the dolly in the manger.

"The wise men knocked on the stable door!" said the narrator.

There was a crash against the church door. It shook on its hinges. The sound echoed through the high building.

"Who is it?" said the girl playing the Virgin Mary.

Before the on-stage wise men could answer, the church door boomed again.

"Really!" said Reverend Ralph indignantly. "We won't

have these interruptions!" He flung a finger at Charlotte. "And you're barred!"

"We need help!" she said.

"I'm calling the police!" said Ralph, fighting his flowing white surplice to get his phone.

"Do! Please!" said Jack.

"You always spoil things, Charlotte Mitchell," called out a woman from the audience.

Charlotte put her hand to her eyes to see better against the stage lights.

"Barbara! Is that you?"

"You're not wanted here!"

"Can we not get a bit of Christian forgiveness? At Christmas? For fuck's sake, Barbara!"

The door boomed a third time and there was the sharp metal snap of the door bolt shearing apart. The doors were flung wide and, roaring, Snømann stepped in, red from head to toe and brandishing his gardening fork.

"It's Satan!" howled a member of the congregation.

There were many gasps.

Charlotte heard an older man saying to his neighbour, "I don't recall this version of the Nativity."

"Oh, they just keep changing it, don't they?" said his neighbour irritably.

Snømann advanced menacingly down the aisle towards Charlotte, Jack and Cameron. Reverend Ralph rushed forward to remonstrate. Snømann swiped his arm, giving the vicar a vicious back-handed punch to the nose. Flakes of red wax went flying, and Reverend Ralph stumbled to the ground, stunned.

"Ooh," said the elderly nativity critic. "Now the vicar's involved!"

"It's all gone flipping post-modern, hasn't it?" muttered his neighbour.

"You!" Snømann snarled at Charlotte. (He might have been talking to any of them, but Charlotte really felt his glare was fixed on her). "You ruined everything! I had a plan! I was going to make changes!"

Jack held out warning hands as they retreated. "Get back!" he warned, tremulously.

"Yeah, get back, Satan!" yelled a congregation member.

And, as one, the audience and the children started booing. Oh good, thought Charlotte, quite deliriously. They think it's a pantomime!

"It's over!" shouted Jack. "You've lost! The authorities are coming!"

Snømann spat. "Lost? This is a set back! I'll kill you, kill all of you, and start over." He repositioned his hands on his fork, ready to attack.

Cameron stumbled on the edge of the low stage, recovered, and patted himself down, sending out puffs of cocaine. There was almost nowhere left for them to retreat to. There was the stage, a gathering of a dozen children – and no way was Charlotte putting them between her and the wild-eyed Snømann.

She planted her feet firmly. "No more, Mr Snømann! This has to end!"

The wax on his face cracked as he broke into a maniacal grin. "And who is going to stop me?"

The door banged as it was once again thrown back on its

hinges. Everyone turned to look as Luka, Gallagher and Anika stepped into the church.

"It's Santa!" yelled a little girl.

There was sudden cheer.

"Oh, now Santa's in on the act, is he?" muttered the critic.

"And an elf!" muttered his friend.

"And some sort of chavvy goblin man?" the first asked. "It's diversity gone mad."

Luka stepped forward and pumped the shotgun he was holding in both hands. "Step away from the kiddywinks, Snømann," he commanded.

Snømann twirled his fork and faced Luka. "You want to take me, Santa Claus?"

Among the boos, Charlotte could hear the two critics grumbling.

"So, it's Satan versus Santa is it?"

"Well, I'm not sure who I want to win, if I'm honest with you. Very conflicted."

Luka advanced down the aisle. Snømann leapt forward, ready to lunge with his fork. Luka obviously thought twice about firing a shotgun in a crowded church, reversed it instead and used it as a club to parry Snømann's thrust. The shotgun strap tangled with the fork tines and both men twirled together, grunting and shoving.

Anika ran forward to tend to the woozy Reverend Ralph. Gallagher stood in the sidelines and shouted advice at Luka.

"Gut punch! Gut punch! Get in there!"

And the amassed people of St Stephen's Church hollered with cheers for Santa and boos for Satan.

"This has got to stop," muttered Jack.

"Fifty quid on the fat man," said Cameron.

Charlotte looked round for a weapon. There were none to hand. Bibles and kneelers were hardly offensive weapons. Her eyes latched onto the manger on stage. It was actually a wooden chest of some sort. Maybe oak or mahogany. It looked heavy.

Snømann abandoned his fork and, with his free hand, landed several solid punches on Luka, two in the chest, then one on the side of his head. Luka stumbled and bellowed. The crowd roared.

"Fucking kill all of you!" Snømann hissed.

Charlotte grabbed the manger, darted forward and with all the enraged force she could muster (which was actually quite a lot) brought manger and dolly Jesus down on Snømann's head. It was a stunning blow. Literally. Snømann went down, hard and fast, flat on his face, and made no movement to get up again.

And suddenly there was silence in the church, apart from Luka's exhausted panting. The children stared. Parents and worshippers stood silently to get a better look.

Charlotte bent and picked up the little dolly. One of its eyelids was stuck shut.

"Jesus defeated Satan?" said one of the elderly critics.

"I think so… Yes! Baby Jesus defeated Satan!"

And the cheer that erupted was louder and longer than any that had come before.

Charlotte held the Baby Jesus aloft, Lion-King style, over Snømann's prone form. It seemed the right thing to do. At the back of the church, Anika was helping a dazed Ralph Robertson to his feet.

"Jesus! Jesus! Jesus!" chanted Gallagher and at least half the congregation joined in.

At that point, the doors burst open on their hinges one last time and a bunch of police officers charged in.

The lead officer – Charlotte recognised Sergeant Akhtar from when she was arrested – pushed his cap back on his head and looked around in amazement.

"Can someone tell me what's going on here?"

Jack Hartigan laughed and Charlotte felt his arm slip around her waist.

61

ANIKA

By the time the police were done with Anika, night had well and truly fallen over the town.

A policeman had spent the best part of the last four hours questioning her and re-questioning her about the events of the day, while it seemed every available room in the station and every police officer for thirty miles around interviewed a hundred other people about the same events. He had been patient, if somewhat confused, as she told her story, and now she wished him a pleasant evening and a very Merry Christmas as he held open the security door for her to go out through reception.

Reception was full of people yet to be interviewed. Daffyd and Tom seemed to be competing to tell their version of the events in the marquee to a pair of disinterested parishioners of St Stephen's Church. Across from them, a rather teary-eyed Sophie and a bloody-nosed Reverend Ralph Robertson were going through a cathartic bit of mutual therapy, and it wasn't clear who was offering the most consolation to whom.

The doors to the station opened and police led in a filthy and bedraggled pair who, on second glance, appeared to be Marcus and Maremba, the owners – maybe former owners, maybe no longer former owners – of Bloomers Garden Centre. Anika had no idea what the story was there. She'd get the details off their ex-daughter-in-law Karen before New Year.

The maybe-current maybe-former owner of Hedgelord, Cameron, sat in a corner with a silver sheet bundled around his shoulders. A paramedic and a police officer were crouched before him, talking to him in tones which suggested they'd been at it for several hours.

"But apart from the cocaine, is there anything you've taken?" asked the paramedic.

"I didn't so much take it as sort of become one with it," he said, twitching.

"Because your resting heart rate is still over a hundred and twenty," said the paramedic.

"And I apologise for asking again," said the police officer, "but can I check that you're unhurt in the—" she waved a hand vaguely over his crotch "—trouser area?"

"For the last time, I'm fine!" snapped Cameron.

"Because we had credible intel that the terrorists had chopped off *bits*."

"What is everyone's fascination with my todger?" he said. "Do you need me to show you? Do you? Do you?" Wobbling, he stood upright and flung aside his silver blanket.

Anika decided to make a swift exit before she saw his

penis again. The silver-plated version had been quite sufficient. She didn't need to see it in the flesh.

Outside, the night air was pleasingly chilly and, apart from distant sounds of traffic, it was silent. Anika allowed exhaustion to creep over her. It was probably time for bed.

She and her parents were meant to be watching the fourth *Die Hard* film together that night, a fresh addition to their Christmas tradition. They'd been up, wondering where she was, when the policeman had allowed her to call and ask them to pick her up. She'd probably have a lot of explaining to do before being allowed to go to bed. If she could somehow rephrase the whole thing to make it sound like a superb CV-building exercise, rather than a chaotic farce, that would be good.

A short distance away, by the roadside, stood Gallagher. He was smoking a fag. His shoulders were hunched against the cold and he hadn't spotted her.

"Hey," she said, approaching.

He turned, cupping his hands around his roll-up.

She sniffed. "Smoking weed outside a police station," she smiled. "Ballsy, to say the least."

"Man, I need it," he said. "Gonna take a shitload of weed to come down off this buzz."

He offered the joint to her. She automatically declined, then immediately changed her mind. She took a long draw and tried not to cough too much as she held it.

"It has been a weird day," he said, taking his roll-up back.

She laughed, releasing the smoke. "Weird week. Weeks, plural."

He nodded in sure and certain agreement.

"Is Christmas at Hedgelord always like this?" she asked.

Gallagher laughed. "We used to have normal Christmasses before you turned up."

"Ah. Maybe I'll find out next year."

He pulled a face and shook his head. "C'mon. You're not coming back. You're better than this place. Better than us."

She drew back to give him a sceptical look. "Better than you? You're kidding. You and Luka are like role models to me." She looked about. "Where is he, by the way?"

He tilted his head back. "Still in there. Since he went all Chunk Norris with the weaponry, the police have decided they have a *lot* more questions for him."

"But he's gonna be all right, yeah?"

He shrugged. "You know what? He seems to wriggle himself out of any trouble. And anyway, they can't keep him."

"No?"

"He's promised to make me Christmas dinner tomorrow."

"A traditional Christmas dinner. Nice."

"From the old country, mind. It's, er, fried dumpling, cabbage rolls, caramelised nuts and, er, herring under fur coat."

"Herring what?"

"Under fur coat. Apparently, it's a thing."

She gave it some thought. "Well, the caramelised nuts sound lovely."

"And we're going to watch *The Professionals* TV show all day."

"Wow. Amazing."

Along the street, a car pulled up and tooted its horn. Anika peered at it. "That's my parents, I think."

"Cool."

As she looked down the street, she saw two people come out of the police station doors and walk up the pavement away from her. In the silhouette created by the orange street lights and the Christmas illuminations which covered the pub across the road, she saw it was Charlotte Mitchell and Jack Hartigan. They walked hand in hand and, as they moved away, leaned closer together, putting their arms around one another.

"So they're a thing now," said Anika. "Again."

"I don't know if they're worse together or worse apart," said Gallagher, taking a final drag on his roll-up before dropping and grinding it underfoot.

Anika knew exactly what he meant but said, "I think we're all better together, aren't we?"

He smiled. "What a terrible thought."

Her parents flashed their lights and tooted their horn again. She took Gallagher's hand and shook it, much to his surprise.

"Merry Christmas, Gallagher," she said. "I hope it's a good one."

"No promises," he said.

She headed towards the car.

"And a Merry Christmas to you too!" Gallagher shouted after her. "And a Happy New Year!"

"Oh, let's not push our luck!" she said, waving back at him, and hurried to join her family.

ABOUT THE AUTHOR

Heide Goody lives in North Warwickshire with her family and pets.

Iain Grant lives in South Birmingham with his family and pets. They are both married but not to each other.

ALSO BY HEIDE GOODY AND IAIN GRANT

Top of the Tree

A BRAND NEW comedy story from the best-selling authors of the 'Festive & Furious' books.

Anika Chowdhry has only been at Hedgelord Garden Centre for a month, but somehow she's in charge. She's dealt with outrageous Santas, grumpy elves, and even Scandinavian gangsters, so how hard can it be to tidy up the post-Christmas chaos?

Very hard, as it turns out, especially when her laziest colleagues would rather fry bacon on the barbecue than lift a finger, and her boss is busy rewriting history on local radio.

So when a mysterious protestor called Geeta shows up demanding a giant fibreglass "bauble coach," Anika finds herself dragged into a woodland adventure involving collapsing ladders, exploding prosecco, and a treetop-village fantasy gone badly wrong.

It's New Year's Eve, she's supposed to be at her cousin's legendary party, and instead Anika's stuck in the woods with anarchists, drunks, and an army of killer badgers.

Can Anika keep control, keep her cool, and still make it to midnight? Or will she discover that the wildest party of all is happening up a tree?

Top of the Tree

Clovenhoof

Getting fired can ruin a day...

...especially when you were the Prince of Hell.

Will Satan survive in English suburbia?

Corporate life can be a soul draining experience, especially when the industry is Hell, and you're Lucifer. It isn't all torture and brimstone, though, for the Prince of Darkness, he's got an unhappy Board of Directors.

The numbers look bad.

They want him out.

Then came the corporate coup.

Banished to mortal earth as Jeremy Clovenhoof, Lucifer is going through a mid-immortality crisis of biblical proportion. Maybe if he just tries to blend in, it won't be so bad.

He's wrong.

If it isn't the murder, cannibalism, and armed robbery of everyday life in Birmingham, it's the fact that his heavy metal band isn't getting the respect it deserves, that's dampening his mood.

And the archangel Michael constantly snooping on him, doesn't help.

If you enjoy clever writing, then you'll adore this satirical tour de force, because a good laugh can make you have sympathy for the devil.

Get it now.

Clovenhoof

Sealfinger

Meet Sam Applewhite, security consultant for DefCon4's east coast office. .

She's clever, inventive and adaptable. In her job she has to be.

Now, she's facing an impossible mystery.

A client has gone missing and no one else seems to care.

Who would want to kill an old and lonely woman whose only sins are having a sharp tongue and a belief in ghosts? Could her death be linked to the new building project out on the dunes?

Can Sam find out the truth, even if it puts her friends' and family's lives at risk?

Sealfinger

Printed in Dunstable, United Kingdom

74370110R00214